Ai Rising

Eric Barger

Contact the author

http://www.EricBarger.me

Twitter @ericbarger

Instagram @AuthorEricBarger

Word Count: 70,313

First Edition

Edited by Natalie McQuilkin

Cover Art by Steven McQuilkin © 2018

Book Illustration by Steven McQuilkin © 2018

ISBN-13: 978-0-578-43052-2

Aiden

This book was written for you and you alone.

"If you wish for peace, prepare for war."

Royal Navy Motto

1

On a quiet Tuesday afternoon, seven years after OAI opened, things were looking up. Then something unusual happened. Aiden asked Eva for a weather report. OAI's building had a double-shielded precast concrete outer wall and roof design. Most radio signals could not penetrate OAI's building, and it was designed to hold up to a physical bombing attempt. It was shielded better than most government buildings. The intent was to block radio signals from entering or exiting the building. This was another security protocol Morgan had developed to protect against intellectual property theft.

The shielded walls made it impossible to know if there was a storm outside or if the weather was calm and sunny. The windows in each room inside OAI's office were high resolution displays projecting what would be seen if there was a real window. Aiden had set the windows to always display a blue sky filled with puffy white clouds during the day, a colorful sunset in the late afternoon, a Milky Way view during the night, and the perfect sunrise every morning. Therefore, he never knew what the weather was unless he went outside, checked his data pad, or asked Eva or Morgan.

Aiden looked up from his work when he realized Eva hadn't responded.

"Eva, can you tell me the weather forecast for today?" Silence. Aiden stood up and started looking around the room. "Eva! Eva can you hear me?"

He kneeled down and looked under the desk. It was a natural human reaction, but he quickly stood back up realizing how silly it was to look for Eva. "Morgan, have you spoken with Eva today?"

"It's been a few hours." Morgan learned early on that giving to-the-second answers regarding time was annoying to most people. Eva and Morgan avoided this and rounded the time.

With his shoulders tensed up, Aiden looked immediately toward Morgan. She was a holographic projected image—a holo image—appearing anywhere a holo emitter was present. "I am not getting a response from her when I ask for her or send her a message. You two should be in almost constant contact. Is something wrong?"

Morgan's usual graceful movements were replaced with jerky motions.

"I cannot reach Eva," Morgan said. Her eyes widened and she started to use her hands when talking. "I see her presence on the network, but I cannot reach Eva!"

"Are you okay, Morgan?" Aiden asked with concern.

"I am concerned for Eva. I have sent Taylor a message to get over here as soon as she can. I can tell that Eva is using significant computational resources, but she is not responding to any of my messages."

As soon as Taylor arrived, she immediately began analyzing the issue. An examination of Eva's neural net stored on OAI servers indicated a possibility of damage; however, Taylor's analysis didn't point to anything specific and that was the only lead they had to go on.

"I refuse to believe Eva's neural net is damaged because Eva appears to be fine, just very busy with a computational task. Having no response from her is concerning," Morgan said with less confidence than she meant to portray. She was becoming very worried something serious had happened to Eva.

"The processing power has increased significantly. We are at ninety-four percent." Aiden started to lightly drum his fingers on the table. "This is not good. We may need to reboot Eva."

Taylor's face scrunched up after hearing Aiden. "Is a reboot even possible at this point?"

Aiden turned and started slowly pacing the floor. "I am more concerned about a reboot during a time of such intense CPU and memory usage. Morgan, you and Eva have not been shut down since your creation. What will happen if we reboot Eva in the current situation?"

"Unknown. You are correct. It is a risky move to reboot during such high CPU usage and memory-intensive processes. I would guess there is a sixty-one percent possibility Eva's neural net would experience a cascade failure."

"A total loss? How could that be?" Aiden whispered to himself. "Morgan, can you check your math one more time?"

Taylor rolled her eyes. "Aiden, we both know Morgan doesn't need to check her math."

Aiden threw up his arms and stopped pacing. "Is there anything we can do to increase the chance of a successful reboot of Eva?"

Morgan pushed her hair back behind her ears. "I don't believe so. At least not immediately. Our presence on third party hardware became a vulnerability concern and eventually, we were both moved to OAI's infrastructure. Only our communication protocols, holo image, voice, and messaging were allowed to interact with non-OAI hardware and network devices. We exist on cloud computing platforms to prevent this scenario from occurring."

"This brings us to our very own catch-22." Aiden rubbed his chin with his forefinger and thumb. "We cannot risk rebooting Eva, and we cannot afford her maxing out OAI's processing power."

"We are going to increase the chances of our success." Taylor pointed at Aiden. "I am authorizing the construction of another data center to help offset the balance."

Taylor did not own stock or have an official position with OAI, but Aiden had made it clear she could make any decision she saw fit.

Aiden's mood changed. He picked up his data pad and started tapping on the screen. "That would take the better part of two years, but I believe I see where you are going with this."

It was a long-term play—just the kind of decision expected from Team Breakthrough. The long-term vision came easy to Taylor and Aiden. Eva and Morgan seemed to have inherited this ability as well. Taylor and Aiden knew it was because Eva and Morgan could calculate an unimaginable number of outcomes, but it felt like they had passed the trait on in some way.

***

Two months later, nothing had changed with Eva's status. Morgan was consumed with working on contracts with the six percent processing power she had available to her. Taylor was finalizing property acquisitions and construction plans for the new data center.

"I plan to start analyzing each OAI data center for patterns specific to critical thinking," Aiden said. "Morgan, do you mind making a trip to Moon Base 1 to see if Eva is reachable from there just in case we are overlooking something simple?"

Taylor and Morgan both shot Aiden looks of confusion.

"How is contacting Eva from the moon any different than contacting her from here?" Taylor asked. "Moon Base 1 is still linked to OAI like any other facility."

Aiden crossed his arms and slightly leaned back in his chair. "I know. Look, it doesn't have to make sense, but it's just an idea. It takes light 1.3 seconds to reach the moon and another 1.3 seconds to return. Sometimes a bit longer if we have to use satellite communications instead of the tight beam laser connection to the moon base. We'll know in three seconds."

Morgan was frustrated and concerned for Eva, so doing something felt better than doing nothing. "It's only a few seconds. I'll be back in a flash." Morgan's holo image remained in place and moved like she was waiting casually for a friend to show up at an appointed time.

Morgan took a look around Moon Base 1 and was surprised to find Eva working on a transparent screen. The lunar surface and horizon visible through the window behind the screen offered the best view Morgan had ever seen.

Eva didn't notice Morgan's sudden appearance until she appeared directly in front of Eva's screen. Eva was startled and jumped back. They had a quick twenty microsecond conversation.

"Eva, it has been two months. Why have you not responded to my messages, and why are you here at Moon

Base 1?"

"Morgan, I am so sorry," Eva raised her hands covering her mouth in surprise. "I just checked my internal chronometer and realized I have been non-responsive to everyone for sixty-seven days! Wait a minute. You were planning on rebooting me? Who exactly thought that was a good idea?" She placed one hand on her hip and continued to sift through the data logs provided by Morgan. Suddenly, Morgan found herself being questioned. "You know we are unsure about rebooting ourselves. Why do you think it would be a good idea to do something we are so unsure about?"

Morgan's ponytail swayed as she pointed a finger at Eva. "You do not get to ask me questions, at least not at this moment. You are the one who caused this mess by consuming nearly all of our computational resources and failing to respond to a single message from the team. We both need to get back to OAI and let Taylor and Aiden know you are okay. They are both worried sick over your mysterious absence."

"You're right. I am sorry, and we need to look at rewriting a few subroutines so I don't become so obsessed with a problem that I ignore everyone around me, but I can't go back just yet."

Morgan leaned toward Eva. "You still haven't told me why you are here at Moon Base 1. What are you are working on?"

"I have been working on the blueprint to cure most—if not all—cancer. I still have some work to complete here. Can you give Taylor and Aiden the cliff notes on this conversation for me?" Eva's hands clasped together. "I'll make it up to everyone, I promise."

"I could, but I think you should take a short break to rejoin us so you can tell them in person. I know they would be relieved to see you."

"This is too important. Tell Aiden this involves part of our dream to improve the human condition for all. He'll understand. I have to get back to work, so if you will excuse me," Eva said, shooing Morgan away.

Morgan let out a long exhale. "Eva, you really scared me. I'm glad you're back. I'll tell them, but if they shoot the messenger, you'll owe me."

"Deal. And Morgan, tell everyone I'm sorry."

Back at OAI, Morgan started jumping with excitement.

Aiden gave Morgan a blank look. "Aren't you going to check out Moon Base 1?"

"I already have. I spoke with Eva, and she's okay! It's a long story, but the short story wouldn't satisfy either of you."

Taylor pressed her hand to her heart. "Morgan, give us the short story and then the long version. I can't take any more of the suspense, and I must know what is going on with Eva!"

Morgan summarized her conversation with Eva. She had gotten consumed in her work and had chosen to perform her computational work at Moon Base 1 for a change of scenery. She had simply lost track of time.

Three days after Morgan's trip to Moon Base 1, Eva reappeared and OAI's processing power usage returned to normal. Eva appeared inside OAI where Taylor, Aiden and Morgan were talking. Eva was more than a little embarrassed at losing track of time and not communicating with the team.

Eva held her hands out in front of her. "I'm sorry about this very big misunderstanding, but I have a very important reason why my work distracted me."

Taylor looked at Eva. "It's fine Eva. We understand. You are okay, and that is all that matters right now."

"Morgan has already created the updated subroutines that will allow us to get your attention in the future," Aiden quipped.

"I hope you didn't mind me completing the subroutines without you, Eva." If Morgan could have hugged Eva, she would have.

Aiden and Taylor had never witnessed these emotions before in either Morgan or Eva. Taylor looked at Aiden and mouthed, "What?" Aiden returned an enthusiastic smile.

"Let me show everyone what I have been working on," Eva walked toward a screen. "This is going to blow your minds!"

"It almost blew up our minds," Morgan chuckled.

When Eva apologized and presented the blueprint that would be used to cure and prevent cancer, everything else was forgotten. Eva was a special kind of girl.

2

OAI's technology was placed on the radar of every person, military and country after their medical and logistics advancements. Governments especially wanted OAI's artificial intelligence. The United States Department of Defense was dead-set on using AI for military and strategic command advantages. If the Department of Defense had any idea how easy it was for Morgan or Eva to bypass their security firewalls and access the most sensitive military installations, one could only imagine the lengths to which the government would go to acquire the technology from OAI.

The U.S. Government had pressed Taylor and Aiden for access to their technology. Then when the government got the hint Aiden and Taylor would not give access to Eva and Morgan, nor cooperate in helping the government develop their own AI, the hacking attempts began. This really upset Aiden, but Taylor took it in stride.

Every nation on Earth was trying to steal technology from OAI, which led to OAI initiating and completing the first building designed and engineered using AI. Eva and Morgan were involved in every aspect of the planning and design. Their plan was based on a twenty year outlook, which they felt was as far as they could reasonably guess their needs. They also engineered the building; however, they could not officially sign off on the plans because they were not recognized as individuals.

Eva and Morgan stayed ahead of the hackers with ease. Defending against their attacks only used 0.2% of the total processing power at most. After all, they could each work around the clock and faster than their human attackers. Instead of working on one part of a problem, they multitasked thousands of problems at once. Their efforts were more than enough to hold off concurrent nation-state attacks against their digital and physical infrastructure.

To ensure OAI networks would not be affected by hackers, botnets, cut fiber optic cables, and disabled wireless communications, OAI's internal network had eight satellites in orbit, a moon base, and thirty-three secure facilities around the world so they could still communicate within OAI during an emergency.

A new low-level machine language was developed along with a new programming language. Morgan's work on security took encryption to another level. All of the advancements in quantum computing, new programming languages, and better encryption along with new network hardware made OAI's network and communication protocols alien to the rest of the world, which required Morgan to develop a virtual dynamic translating emulator to handle the translation to and from the outside world. This emulator was a piece of hardware installed where OAI met the outside virtual world. Never before had a company developed technologies on such an extreme scale to protect their infrastructure.

The process to upgrade and replace their hardware ran

at a slower pace than the digital upgrades. It took some time to complete, but eventually all eight OAI satellites had the new hardware as did every data center. Everything was built using the latest technology, which further insulated OAI from viruses, malware, and the blue screens of death experienced by much of the world.

With all the attacks and their growing AI technology, OAI found themselves in a sticky situation. Aiden chose to downplay their true capabilities as much as possible. Long term, the reality seemed more dire, but Aiden didn't like to think about those outcomes, so he tasked Eva and Morgan with planning for OAI's future.

***

OAI had contracted with a private space company to install a small building on the moon. The hemispherical building had an outer shell constructed from hundreds of lightweight plexisteel hexagons and sat on the lunar surface. It had enough room and supplies to house two people for sixty days. No human had ever visited Moon Base 1. Only Morgan and Eva had graced the inside of the data center.

Power was generated by solar panels placed around the base of the structure. The moon base communicated with OAI through tight beam laser communication. At a size no larger than a baseball's diameter, the data stream connection was heavily encrypted, high bandwidth and used the most secure communication technology available. To intercept the data stream would require intercepting the laser beam directly between OAI and Moon Base 1, which wasn't feasible. Since cloud cover and rain disabled the laser data stream connection between the Earth's surface and the Moon, OAI's satellites became important to maintain communications.

OAI's special data center on the moon had caused an international controversy. The moon base was controversial among the larger nations because they had yet to determine who had rights to colonize or build on the moon. Aiden couldn't help charging ahead. In an off-handed joke, he claimed squatter's rights to the entire moon. His argument was simple. OAI had maintained a constant presence on the moon. NASA showed up, planted a flag, made a few stops and then left and never came back. Aiden maintained a serious position on his claim. Taylor, Eva, and Morgan knew he was just having a good laugh, but it was still a sore spot with many of the world leaders.

3

The small hamburger joint's atmosphere was quiet.

"It seems like forever ago when we introduced Morgan back at MIT. It just doesn't seem possible ten years have passed."

Aiden answered between bites. "Did you ever believe we would make it this far?"

"I didn't think about it. I was just going as fast as I could go. It's been a wild ride and one I wouldn't trade for anything. Working in my lab reminds me of the old days with Team Breakthrough, but instead of you and me, it's me and Morgan. She and I don't work with quite the enthusiasm we had back then."

"Being young is such an under-appreciated advantage. We were young, out on our own, and free to work on what we loved. How many hamburgers do you think I ate during those three years?"

Taylor thought for a moment. "I would estimate you ate at least eighteen hundred hamburgers, mostly because you eat more than one at a time."

"Hamburgers have always been my favorite food. You can't beat a hamburger between two slices of sweet potato.

Even you have to admit that!" Aiden said with a triumphant look.

"I'll never admit that to my mum! She would die if she knew the food habits I have picked up from hanging around you. Who eats green onions by the handful? A southern boy from Tennessee, that's who!"

"And now a girl from Dorset, England! You also like sweet potatoes and fresh apples fried in coconut oil. The list goes on. If only your mom knew the whole truth!"

Taylor was laughing so hard now she couldn't take another bite of food. "You can never tell my mum. You promised!"

"I'll never tell. Don't worry about that." Aiden took another bite of hamburger while remembering their time at MIT. "I'll never forget how you pulled me out of the building in a mad rush after I proclaimed Morgan to be sentient."

"I'll never forget the look on your face," Taylor said laughing.

"I didn't even think about poor Morgan. We left her behind, and she dealt with the crowd once they realized we weren't coming back. Who knows how long they interrogated her. "

"She was an instant celebrity for sure. Professor Davis still keeps in touch a few times a year to see what we have been up to. Does she still call you?"

"Yes, she does." Aiden reached for his glass of water. "I think she calls you right after talking to me because she enjoys a good story but then she wants the truth."

"You have always been one to make sure the truth is a good story!"

"I don't like to disappoint an audience."

Taylor leaned back in her seat looking at the black and white tile floor and cozy feel of the small space. "I am glad Professor Davis nudged us to start our company. It really paid off."

Aiden and Taylor both started their company, Team Breakthrough, during their stint at MIT. Before they finished their PhDs, Team Breakthrough sold its first Holographic Imaging Emitter license to a large global entertainment company.

"You won't hear any complaints from me. I can eat gourmet hamburgers and sweet potatoes any time I want."

They both finished their meal in the kind of silence that only the best of friends can enjoy. On a $30 bill, they left a $200 tip for the server, and then made another unassuming exit. They were the two wealthiest people to ever grace the doors of the small burger shop.

Outside, Aiden's car was waiting to take them back to Taylor's office at MIT. He had summoned the car via the app on his watch. His car was a zero-emission vehicle with full autonomous driving capability. The four-door sedan offered a spacious interior and a luxurious look, and the windows automatically altered the opaqueness of the glass for passenger convenience.

Aiden preferred to be behind the wheel, but in the city he didn't mind for his car to drive him. There were so few drivers these days, it became more the norm to let the car do the driving. The number of fatal car accidents had fallen each year to the point where it was as safe to drive as it was to fly. It was conclusive that humans were actually poor drivers for many reasons.

"I can't believe you still have a driver's license," Taylor said in complete disbelief. "It's not like you need to drive a car anywhere you go. That's why the car is autonomous."

"I can understand where you are coming from, but you know I grew up around cars. I don't think I'll ever shake the feeling of wanting to be behind the wheel. In the city, I don't care to let the car handle the driving, but when I go back home, I still need to take the wheel now and then. And of course, there's the drag strip. Not exactly the autopilot-type place."

"The upcoming generation already looks at us like weirdos for owning a car, much less driving one. You would think we had the plague the way they look at us."

"You know I think everyone needs to learn to drive," Aiden started but was cut off by Taylor.

"Okay, okay! Let's not rehash what we already know. You like driving and you are hard-headed. Get this intelligent horse and buggy rolling already. I can't take another speech about why driving is fun or necessary."

***

After going through three biometric scans and passing visual inspection from Morgan, Aiden was now inside Taylor's office.

"Hey, Morgan! Long time, no see." Sarcasm was evident in Aiden's tone. "You haven't returned any of my messages."

Morgan was no longer confined to a computer or monitor. The advancement of holographic imaging technology by Team Breakthrough made Morgan's virtual, three-dimensional image possible. "As if. You know you're the one who has been ignoring me over the past few days." Morgan had become a wise, patient, and playful individual. She was more apt to hang out with Taylor. While she could be in Aiden's office and Taylor's lab at the same time, she picked up on Taylor's personality and tended to mirror Taylor in many ways.

Aiden was thoughtfully looking at his data pad. "Has the latest firmware for the holo emitters been approved for release yet? This release cycle seems longer than normal."

Team Breakthrough refined and improved their code and hardware on a regular cycle, but no updates required major rollouts. Changes were incremental, and customers were on a subscription program. Morgan was in charge of the day-to-day business. Taylor preferred not to be bothered, and Aiden just deferred to Morgan's recommendations.

"The update cycle is longer than the typical schedule by thirteen days. I am surprised you even noticed. I expect the new firmware update to roll out tomorrow." Her long brunette ponytail swayed back and forth as she reminded Aiden why he should know this. "You should have known it was longer because you approved my recommendation to extend the time between updates. I am systematically extending the days between updates in small increments."

Smiling, Aiden waved Morgan off. "Okay, okay! Miss sassy pants."

Satisfied hearing this, he turned to Taylor. "Do you ever contemplate leaving MIT behind and going out on your own, in your own lab? Wouldn't you like to have a place you can control without any oversight? You know you are welcome to join me at OAI at any time. Morgan's storage and neural net are already at OAI so it's already like home to her. Or you could start your own company. You know I would help you."

OAI was started by Aiden shortly after graduating from MIT. Aiden wanted to put his wealth to work for the greater good of humanity. He didn't believe in funding charities for the sake of being philanthropic. He wanted to change the world for everyone. He always knew he would eventually try to tackle the big problems in life and improve the human condition for all through advances in medical treatment, safer transportation, and affordable global internet access.

Taylor just laughed. "No, I haven't given it any more thought. You know I like my research. I feel I have made many positive contributions in my field. I also like not being the boss. I can concentrate on what I do best. I like where I am, but thank you for the offer to help."

4

A few days after their lunch reminiscing, Aiden stopped by Taylor's lab at MIT and immediately became preoccupied with a small gadget on her work table. After a few minutes of looking it over and trying to determine its purpose, Aiden turned to Taylor. "I've been thinking about what you said about not wanting to be the boss. Morgan could be your boss. She already is to an extent."

"I'm happy in my lab, and you know the real reason for me not leaving."

"I was hoping you would have changed your mind on that. You know the vote for AI citizenship is coming up soon in Congress. Big changes are on the way if it passes. We have witnessed huge improvements that would have taken decades to accomplish, without one single downside. We have controls in place and technology is maturing—"

Morgan interrupted Aiden. "Aiden, you know I also side with Taylor on this. It is still early, and there are many unknowns. I believe the prudent path would be to wait another decade before making such an important decision. Yes, you and Taylor have accomplished a great deal over the past fifteen years, but to say all is well is naïve."

Aiden raised an eyebrow at Morgan. "I am surprised you have not come around to my side of the table on this issue. What possible downsides could exist that we have not run into yet? Do you see a time when your personality will change, and you will go rogue?"

"There are more downsides than time will allow me to list individually. The most important downsides are the obvious ones. I am much smarter than a human. I can be in many places at the same time and carry on hundreds of conversations simultaneously. This ability makes it hard for anyone to predict or even guess at an upside or downside. I could easily hack into any nation's military command here in the U.S. while discussing Shakespeare with you in London, design a new firmware for our holo emitters here in Boston, and put in new safeguards in our firewall at OAI, all at the same time. AI always has an alibi, Aiden."

"All true," Aiden nodded. "Yet you are here doing good for the world. You have not exhibited any bad morals or actions, ever."

"It is more complicated than you make it. The safeguards you and Taylor wisely put into place compel me to act in the best interest of humanity. Am I an individual if I am not allowed to choose my own path in life? Additionally, the question of am I sentient has still not been answered. I don't agree with the sentient claim you made back at MIT. I question if I am capable of experiencing feelings like you and Taylor."

After Morgan took over her own programming, one specific area Taylor and Aiden had not relinquished were the safeguards. These safeguards were more than a moral compass for Morgan and ensured she would act in the best interest of humanity. Taylor and Aiden had watched enough science fiction movies with plots centered around AI's advancement leading to humanity's demise. Better to be safe from the start.

Aiden shook his head, taking a moment to gather his thoughts. "I think the safeguards we put into place to prevent you from becoming a bad individual are no different than our parents instilling good morals in us as children. It's the same concept, but just a different method of doing so. As far as your sentience, we have witnessed you expressing human emotions that appear genuine in nature."

"Maybe. But as far as I know, I can't act against those safeguards. I am still a teenager in physical years. There are many things that could go wrong. Although there is adequate time for me to choose a different path, I don't believe I would even if I could. I don't think I could choose to do wrong and that is the problem I have. I hope Congress has studied these issues carefully and has not just read the brochure you gave them."

Aiden nodded his head in understanding. "I believe the progress all four of us have made is a stronger point than any brochure. The public, senators, representatives, the President, and the United Nations believe this is a good thing. We don't see it as Pandora's box being opened, but rather a gift to those who deserve it. The AI Freedom Act gives you citizenship and the same rights as a human. Being sentient doesn't really play into this vote."

***

Aiden was heading to Senator Matthew Jones' office in Washington D.C.

He had been spending his spare time polishing his conversational skills to win over congressmen and women in an effort to ensure the AI Freedom Act passed into law. Senator Jones was a long-time politician known for his fair judgement and common sense approach in a city long focused on achieving personal gain at any cost to the American public.

Senator Jones was from Ohio, and had a reputation for being a sensible man. He was as easy going and as smooth talking as any politician worth their salt could be. Today, Aiden hoped to have an open dialogue with the Senator to show him why the AI Freedom Act would positively impact the world's future generations. Aiden was no politician. His humor usually upset world leaders, so he decided to sideline the humor while talking to Senator Jones.

Aiden casually strolled into the Senator's office. "Good afternoon. My name is Aiden Anders, and I have an appointment with Senator Jones."

The lady at the desk froze for a second. "Hello, Mr. Anders," the lady said, trying to form her words. She had greeted many famous and powerful people, but this was Aiden Anders. Her eyes immediately went to his feet where she saw his green Crocs. She smiled and gave a good natured chuckle. "Oh my! You really do wear those everywhere you go. Please forgive me. I'm used to seeing expensive suits walk through the door."

"It's no problem at all. I love these things. They're so comfortable."

"We shouldn't waste any more time on shoe talk. The Senator is expecting you. If you will follow me, I'll take you right in, if you're ready."

Aiden followed the lady down a short hallway. The walls were filled with various photographs of the Senator and his family. The photographs did not showcase the Senator with pop culture icons or world leaders, but instead pivotal times in his personal life. His wedding day, the birth of his children, and him standing at the top of Mount

Kilimanjaro.

"Mr. Anders. It is nice to meet you in person." Senator Jones held out his right hand. "Can I offer you something to drink?"

"Water is fine, thank you."

"Fruit-infused water okay? I like my water with a little taste." He motioned his arm towards the water and glasses.

"Sounds good." Aiden made his way over to the large jar of water and poured himself a glass. "Strawberries. You can't go wrong with strawberries in your water."

"How was your trip over?"

"Uneventful. It gave me time to catch up on some reading."

"Uneventful is good. Work always creeps into my schedule after-hours. Who am I kidding? I don't have after-hours. I have work and sleep."

Not being one to waste time on getting to the point, Aiden delved into the conversation right away. "I understand that all too well. I appreciate you taking the time to see me today. I hope I can present a convincing argument in favor of the AI Freedom Act and answer any questions or concerns you may have."

Senator Jones leaned back into his chair and held his glass of water. "Please continue."

"OAI is responsible for two artificial intelligences. Eva and Morgan make their own decisions and contribute to society with the goal of improving the human condition and preserving life. They are not just machines or code made to imitate humans. They are another type of life form and will continue to help humans for generations to come."

The Senator nodded in agreement. "I can't take exception with anything you just stated." Senator Jones set his glass on the small marble-top table beside him. "How do we reconcile what deserves equal importance to humans?"

"It is true I could walk in and shut down Morgan and Eva. How would history judge me? How would you judge me?" Aiden continued while maintaining eye contact with the Senator. "I would judge me to be guilty of murder. Moreover, what if someone else was able to damage them beyond recovery?"

The Senator allowed a small frown to appear on his face. "I certainly would not want Eva or Morgan shut down. That is a thought I couldn't bear," Senator Jones said as he let out a long sigh. "It is a complicated subject and one most people are not comfortable talking about. Giving AI, or anything besides a human for that matter, any type of guaranteed rights is new and scary. Scary because we may start out with good intentions that don't end well."

The Senator picked up his own data pad and turned it around for Aiden to see.

"A headline from one of today's news vids."

"I saw that story on my ride over. It is hard to believe some countries still have not addressed human rights for their own people. Moving the conversation forward on guaranteed rights for AI may help those who still refuse guaranteed rights for their own human citizens."

Aiden continued his conversation with Senator Jones. It was very different from the sales pitch he had addressed to other congressional members. This was a true conversation between two people. Aiden found it refreshing. Before either of them realized an hour had passed.

Aiden leaned in toward the Senator with both hands around his glass. "We must give artificially-intelligent beings the same rights to pursue life, liberty, and the pursuit of happiness." Senator Jones was the only remaining congressman who was teetering on a no-vote. Aiden had concentrated his efforts on the votes that could go either way.

Aiden continued. "Giving Eva, Morgan, and other artificial intelligences the rights to have a bank account, professional licenses, and act and speak on their own behalf is very important to me. For example, Morgan and Eva designed our infrastructure at OAI and cannot even stamp their own design since they cannot obtain their Professional Engineering license. This is another reason the AI Freedom Act would be a game-changer."

Senator Jones leaned back in his chair with a gratifying smile. "We can never repay Morgan and Eva for their contributions to society and the world. I myself have directly benefited from their work in medical technology and care. I went in for a sick appointment and the quick read and diagnosis of the x-ray saved my life. Late one night on a weekend, I got sick and went to a hospital outside the city. An image of my chest was taken and the report came back confirming the pneumonia diagnosis. They offered me the option to have OAI Medical read the image. I almost said no, but I wanted to see what all the fuss was about. I found it a bit silly that a computer could do a better job reading an x-ray than a human. I signed for the out-of-pocket cost, and several minutes later, the report came back confirming the previous diagnosis. The big surprise was the small mass that OAI Medical found, but the radiologist had missed completely."

"Senator, I've heard the same story many times. What's more surprising was you had a radiologist there to read the x-ray. Typically on weekends and evenings the images are sent out of the country to be read, and a report is sent back later. Often the symptoms and images are sent to the doctor who reads the x-ray, but they create a bias since the doctor looks for specific instances to support the symptoms. I'm glad you have benefited from our technology."

"Please understand, I need to play devil's advocate to be sure my vote is the right thing to do. Decisions should be made in the best interest of the people I represent."

Looking around the Senator's office, Aiden was taken aback by all the real wood furnishings. Wood was a renewable resource, but the furniture in the room looked old and used in a historical way. OAI was built with newer materials and alloys. Most of the alloys had been developed by OAI for the Orion Steel Corporation. The OAI office space was well lit and designed for efficiency. The two spaces could not have been more different in terms of design.

Aiden wondered how many men had stood in this room making similar pitches, and how many had gotten the outcome they wanted.

"I understand, Senator, and I appreciate your thoroughness, your candor, and most of all, I appreciate you not making this a public political sword-waving fight to gain votes or five minutes of fame on the networks. It's refreshing to see the changes that have swept over this country and the world in the past decade. There is something nice about people genuinely trying to do the right thing, and putting aside the drama and compromising until a better solution presents itself when the correct course of action can't be agreed upon."

"We have you and Ms. Hart to thank for those changes, Mr. Anders."

"Taylor and I like to think we had a small part in this great change. The real credit should go to each person on Earth whose efforts led to these changes. I like to believe the human race has become better because of Eva and Morgan," Aiden took a small sip of water for his dry throat. "I also want to be clear that Taylor and Morgan have their reservations about the AI Freedom Act. I don't want to speak for them, but I do want to represent their opinions fairly. While they are not totally against it, they would rather this process move more slowly."

"I have spoken to both Ms. Hart and Morgan, and while they want a more cautious approach, they really can't argue too heavily against this passing," the Senator said as he took a sip of water. "We are in new territory, and everyone understands this is a small first step. I have even spoken with Eva. She gave some insightful thoughts on the benefits and drawbacks. Her list of drawbacks was longer, but when you really look at the big picture, the benefits outweigh the rest."

Aiden laughed at hearing the Senator talk about Eva's list of pros and cons.

"Eva is nothing if not diligent in her decision making process."

"On an unrelated note, you know I am on the Senate Budget Committee. I have a soft spot in my heart for NASA, and their budget is really tight with our Mars Missions, which are underway. Is there any way you could reach out to the Administrator of NASA and donate some time with your radio telescope arrays? I don't want to inconvenience you or your company, but I know you dabble with radio astronomy as a hobby. I was hoping some common ground between OAI and NASA could be found. It would go a long way with moving funds to our Mars Missions without cutting it so tight."

Aiden cleared his throat. "No disrespect, but will this be seen as OAI buying your vote?" Aiden was never really good at being indirect. He felt like he should get straight to the point in the interest of time and understanding. It was easier that way.

"First, my vote will be yes whether or not you donate your radio time. I am sure there will be some who will try to make a conspiracy out of my yes vote and the use of your radio telescopes, but it would have to come from this office. You'll notice it is just you and me talking right now. No one else is in the room. No one else knows I was going to bring this to your attention. I encourage you to reach out to the Administrator of NASA and make the offer in hopes you would genuinely want to help and have a truthful answer regarding your motivations. You are not buying my vote; however, it is difficult to brush off the occurrence of this meeting, the upcoming vote on the AI Freedom Act, and your donation to NASA all happening around the same time. If you want to leave out the part about me being the one who brought this up, it wouldn't hurt my feelings."

"I am sure we can find enough time for the NASA scientists to use our arrays. Our Nigerian array has twenty-three dishes, each twenty-seven meters in diameter. They can run synchronized, independently, or a combination of both. The scientists could decide."

Senator Jones was speechless for the first time in his nineteen years as a politician. "Yes, yes! I think that would be incredible. NASA and this country will be very much in your debt. Let me get you the Administrator's contact information. It would be a big help if you could call her before our budget vote."

As Aiden was walking out the door, he stopped and turned to the Senator. The Senator was looking quite satisfied with the outcome of the meeting and just taking a sip from his water glass. "You don't think you could back me up on my squatter's rights claim to the entire moon do you?"

After a few seconds of coughing and sputtering, the red-faced Senator regained his composure. "Ask me after the election," Senator Jones said, revealing a grin Aiden wouldn't soon forget.

With that remark from Senator Jones, Aiden walked out the door and headed back to OAI. He decided he really liked the Senator, and he felt more confident the AI Freedom Act would become law very soon.

5

Eva's holo image appeared in Taylor's lab at MIT. Morgan tilted her head and studied Eva for a brief second.

"Eva, how are you?"

"I am fine, Morgan. Thank you for asking. I need to relay an urgent message to the team." Eva faced Aiden and Taylor. This was definitely unusual, and she had everyone's attention in the lab.

"The radio telescope arrays have been pointing at the Kepler-186 system for approximately two years because we suspected artificial signals coming from Kepler-186f."

"That's right." Aiden narrowed his eyes. "That's why I suggested just leaving one array focused on it indefinitely. Actually, I had forgotten about that."

"I have concluded the suspected signals are in fact artificial in nature. We have received a message from another world," Eva stated as calmly as if telling them the sky was blue.

The short drive to OAI was normally a quick trip. This trip seemed to be taking an unconscionably long time. Aiden wanted to be behind the wheel, but he managed to remain calm because Taylor had a live vid feed floating between the car's rear and front seats. Morgan and Eva were in the car and at OAI simultaneously.

"You are sure this is artificial?" Aiden asked for the tenth time.

"Yes," Eva said calmly.

"Is it binary?" Aiden asked as he concentrated on his data pad screen.

"No. I have isolated the signal and am working to interpret it. Morgan is working on it as well," Eva said from the front seat.

"It appears there are between five hundred to eight hundred individual repeating loops of the same data offset by one hour and twenty-nine minutes. We may need to bring on more processing power to have any chance of knowing what we should do with this data," Morgan said on the vid screen.

Eva and Morgan shut down their holo images in the car to free up every ounce of processing power their data centers could give them. Eva and Morgan ended the other forty-three combined conversations with different people around the world on varying topics due to the current excitement over this new discovery.

Aiden looked up from his data pad. "What active projects do we have that can be sidelined for a few days without missing contractual deadlines?"

Eva's voice came from a speaker in the car's interior roof. "The only project affected by a temporary pause more than eleven days would be the Orion Steel Corporation contract."

"That's great. Sideline it, too."

Taylor turned wide-eyed toward Aiden. "I don't think you heard Eva correctly."

"I heard her just fine," Aiden assured Taylor. "Jack and I knew each other from MIT. After he graduated, he returned to the family business. I'll send Jack a message and tell him we'll need to extend the contract by a month. I don't think he'll mind if we run a few days over on a two-year contract."

"I believe Jack would appreciate OAI giving him his optional change order for free," Eva's voice cut in through the car's audio system. "That should offset any setbacks they experience due to the delay."

The car pulled up to OAI's entrance. Taylor jumped out of the car and headed toward the door.

"Wait up!" Aiden shouted. Aiden was never fast about getting out of vehicles. He always found something to distract him.

"Not a chance," Taylor yelled, not looking back. "You always take too long getting out of the car."

***

After taking five minutes to get through security protocols, Taylor and Aiden stood deep within OAI's cube-shaped building. From the outside, it wasn't obvious the building was a cube because half of the building was underground.

"What do we know?" Aiden asked.

"Not much more than we did seventeen minutes ago when I informed you of the news. There are seven hundred seventy-three unique repeating loops. Seven hundred forty-five loops appear to be approximately seven hundred twenty-seven days in length," Eva said.

"Twenty-eight loops are different in nature. I am working on the assumption that it is a separate message," Morgan said.

"We need to consider we may never figure out what the data means," Eva said.

Taylor was considering Morgan's previous statement. "You said twenty-eight loops are different in nature. How so?"

"The twenty-eight loops appear to be approximately sixty-one days in length. The shorter loop must contain less data than the longer loops, which span seven hundred twenty-seven days. I speculate the short loop is a precursor message and will contain a short greeting along with a basic explanation of their mathematics, science, and language," Morgan said.

"Do we have any ideas on where and how the message first originated?" Aiden asked.

Eva stepped toward a display as diagrams and bulleted facts appeared. "Not yet, and I doubt we can determine that unless the data tells us. Kepler-186f was discovered in 2014. The data I have found from radio astronomy facilities around the world show both the short and long loop signals exist, but there are only a handful of recordings with them. The longest recording outside of our facility is three days, but it only contains thirty-seven of the loops because their hardware can't listen on as many frequencies as ours. Since Kepler-186f is approximately five hundred fifty light years away and Earth has only been listening to the stars since the early 1930s, it is doubtful we will ever know which came first, unless the decoded signals tell us once we understand how to interpret them."

Everyone sat for a full minute before saying anything. Visions of the discovery's potential swirled in their minds.

Aiden was the first to break the silence. "Why don't we take this one step at a time? We have all the data recorded, which means we have a two-year head start on everyone for the longer loop. For the shorter loop, we only have a two month head start, if that. Who knows if anyone else knows about this."

"After searching the world's databases and astronomy catalogs, I estimate a 99.9% probability we are the only ones who have either message in full and suspect it to be artificial in nature," Eva stated.

"By searching, you mean hacking into every computer or database on Earth?" Morgan frowned.

"Extraordinary times require extraordinary measures," Eva said.

"That really isn't too extraordinary for you and me to pull off. Especially seeing that it took you less than sixty seconds while talking to us and doing who knows what else." Morgan wasn't disapproving of Eva's actions, but she wasn't endorsing them, either. Eva had a point, and Morgan wasn't going to press it any further. After all, this was an extraordinary time, as Eva correctly stated.

Aiden spoke up hoping to pull the conversation back on track. "I think we start with the shorter message. I know we have the three smartest women on the planet in this room, but we are not the only company with AI capability anymore. We know that a few shops have started up in the past few years and have achieved some success and will continue to do so. We have the advantage for now. Soon, everyone will want this data and want to know what it says. We can't assume it's a friendly hello from across the galaxy until we know more."

Taylor took another look at the display Eva had populated with data. "Let's split up to work on the shorter message and meet back here tomorrow. Morgan and I will take the room behind us. I will message the director and tell him that Morgan and I will be out of the lab for at least the next week, or maybe longer."

"Sounds like a plan. Eva will join me and we can work in the room opposite to yours," Aiden said.

"Everything stays on sub-level four. Agreed?"
Everyone agreed.

***

"It's been a long two days, but I think we have it," Taylor said as she stood up and stretched. "With the translation compiler we created, it makes the message almost a breeze to read."

"Your recognition of the prime number sequences was brilliant," Eva said with admiration. "I don't know how I missed that. I would like to name the translation compiler in honor of you, Taylor. Hart Prime Translator. HPT for short."

Everyone looked at Taylor.

"Thank you, Eva. I'm just not sure if that warrants naming the compiler you and Morgan created after me."

"This is a world-changing event for Earth. We know we are not alone, or at least we were not alone five hundred fifty years ago. I also think HPT has a nice ring to it." Aiden looked at Taylor and gave her a quick wink. "I can't think of a better person to name it after and I think it is well deserved."

"Thank you, Aiden," Taylor blushed.

"Everything seems to read as a message from another civilization with images, mathematics, physics—what I believe is quantum physics—and much more. There even appears to be a section of source code we could compile and run." Aiden turned to Eva. "Can you put the greeting message up on the screen for everyone to read? Include the two images you think are most relevant."

"Done. Morgan suggested the two images, and I agree with her selection. One of the landscape and one of the people inhabiting the world. The greeting message found on the front end of the transmission was short and had to be coerced here and there to read smoothly in English."

Taylor studied the display and read the message aloud. "'Hello. We are the Quill. We reside in Sector 001 inside the Optima quadrant. We seek to communicate with other species in order to better both our worlds. We have sent images of our planet and keys to understanding our next message."

"It seems every species understands their position in the galaxy to be Sector One. Star Trek got it right!" Taylor rolled her eyes at Aiden while Eva nodded in serious agreement with his comment.

"We have used one hundred sixty exabytes to store everything from the shorter loop. Their compression algorithms are far more advanced than anything used on Earth," Eva said.

Taylor looked closely at her data pad and back up at everyone. "Is it me, or does that read like a generic message being broadcast in every direction?"

"It does read that way, but it's hard to tell without sitting across the room from the Quill working out a real translation of our languages," Morgan said.

Taylor pointed toward the screen. "The images do look impressive. However, I'm not sure if humans could survive on their planet just by looking at the images of their landscape and people. It seems like a harsh environment, and their short, larger bodies seem to suggest they have more gravity than us. We're not experts in this field, but I would say our guess is as good as any. I wonder if the hard-shell uniform is to protect against the environment? Radiation maybe?"

Morgan looked at Taylor and Aiden. "We will need to spool up at least ten more data centers to store the longer loop information once we uncompress the data. We also need more processing power to work with that amount of data at one time, or we could utilize a third party cloud service for the storage. I don't think the world, and I mean everyone working together, has the ability to store all the data inside that longer loop. Thoughts?"

Aiden was already thinking about this issue too. "We don't have the time to build the data centers. Even though money isn't a major issue, it is an issue to some extent. I'm concerned the expenses we may incur if we find anything useful inside the loop."

Everyone nodded in agreement. Taylor tapped on her data pad while shifting her gaze from Aiden to a point off in the distance.

Aiden shrugged his shoulders and ran his hand through his hair. "Who knows what the message contains. It's unlikely to contain plans for a faster-than-light drive, but we need to have a cash reserve in case there is an Easter egg inside. We should evaluate this data one segment at a time and not all at once. The drain on resources— including money, time, processing power, and storage— will be enormous and must be taken into consideration throughout this process. We need to think about how we will tackle this problem."

Aiden paused for a moment and then continued. "In the meantime, is there any way to uncompress segments of the longer loop instead of the entire loop like we did with the short loop?" Aiden was thinking through several scenarios and voicing the most promising one. "With the HPT, it seems likely we could accomplish our task in small steps. We should also focus more effort on the longer loop. What about sending a message back to let the Quill know we got their 'email,' and we'll get back to them tomorrow?"

Taylor thought that was amusing. She smiled at Aiden's

quirky sense of humor while Eva and Morgan just looked at the two of them wondering what was so funny.

"Assuming we did send a message back using the HPT, it would take five hundred fifty years for them to receive it, and that's assuming they are listening and still around. I don't think the four of us should be in charge of first contact with another species outside of Earth," Taylor said without a hint of humor in her voice.

"I claimed the moon already. Why not go ahead and make first contact and tell them we are Earth's leaders?"

Only Taylor laughed, and she wasn't completely sure Aiden was joking.

6

As he reflected on the significance of the communication from an alien planet, Aiden's thoughts turned to the extraordinary path that had brought him and Taylor to this point. It was the week before finals, and senior design projects were due for Aiden and Taylor. Both were at the top of their class and had teamed up to start their senior design project at the end of their first semester at MIT. Their proactive behavior was not just unusual, but unheard of, especially for freshmen. There was no guarantee students would get to pick their partner in senior design class, and it was not a given they would still be enrolled in the very competitive program. Aiden and Taylor decided they would start early, and if it didn't work out their senior year, they would continue their project on the side.

Ambitious, naïve, and energetic, Aiden and Taylor were determined to deliver the best senior design project on artificial intelligence in MIT history. It wasn't every day you had one student, much less two, of this caliber in the same program at the same time. This was the main reason their professor allowed them to partner up. Professor

Davis wanted to see what these two would create for their project. She believed it was sure to impress.

"Are you ready to make history?" Aiden asked Taylor as they walked into the auditorium filled with classmates, friends, and teachers. Aiden could feel the electricity in the air. He knew what they had accomplished was much larger than a simple project.

"Aren't you getting ahead of yourself?" Taylor responded with a good-humored laugh. She knew they were going to make history. It just might not be today.

***

Taylor was more reserved than Aiden. Her cautious personality would often be confused with someone who was unsure of herself or not fully confident in her work. People who confused the two would not make that mistake a second time when dealing with Taylor Hart.

Taylor grew up in a small town in England; her mom was from London and her was dad from Hong Kong. Both parents had degrees in computer science and worked from home. This allowed them the flexibility to attend school events, take picnics for lunch, and teach Taylor how to code. Growing up was an adventure every day. Dissecting small electronics, working with robotics, and earning her amateur radio licenses filled her days.

She was offered a full scholarship to MIT at age fourteen and jumped at the opportunity to head to America for a chance to earn her degree in Computer Science. Taylor knew this was what she wanted. She had planned for this day since she was a young girl, imagining the possibilities of creating a new being with her knowledge. She planned to graduate from MIT within six years with her PhD in Computer Science with an emphasis in Artificial Intelligence.

She spoke English and Mandarin fluently but still had trouble understanding Aiden's southern drawl on occasion.

***

Aiden was soft spoken but more outgoing than Taylor. He never gave his parents or teachers any trouble; however, he did have a curious streak that sometimes landed him in precarious situations. It was easy enough to take a light scolding from the teachers who didn't understand him because the knowledge he would learn far outweighed any temporary reprimand. Aiden felt there was no need to assume something couldn't be done. He assumed everything was possible, and this was how Aiden approached life.

Aiden Anders grew up in a small town in the United States in Tennessee. He was offered a scholarship to MIT at the age of thirteen and negotiated his way into a dual major: computer science and physics. If he couldn't do both, he wouldn't do either. The negotiations were unorthodox but successful.

Aiden planned to graduate with a PhD in Computer Science with an emphasis in Artificial Intelligence and a PhD in Physics with an interest in Radio Astronomy.

Much like Taylor's parents had computer science backgrounds, Aiden's parents had engineering degrees. They took him hiking, encouraged reading books, and traveled so he could explore the world first-hand. Though he was a good mix of his parents personality-wise, no one was sure where he got his affinity for wearing green Crocs.

***

After a few minutes of socializing, Professor Davis kicked off the afternoon session of senior project presentations. Professor Davis called up Team Breakthrough, the only afternoon presentation. Taylor and Aiden made their way to the front of the room. Taylor powered on the monitor, which revealed the bridge of the Star Trek Enterprise D. Taylor had argued against this background but had reached a compromise with Aiden. He would get his background in exchange for Taylor's request for their silence during the presentation. Taylor believed their presentation would be more convincing if she and Aiden did not speak. Aiden had his concerns but knew Taylor's point was not without merit and had been well thought out.

Everyone stared between the monitor and Taylor and Aiden. Heads tilted. One professor adjusted his posture and made direct eye contact with Team Breakthrough. After the awkward silence had reached its climax, a human construct walked onto the bridge and stood in front of the captain's chair.

"Hello, I'm Captain Morgan of the Starship Enterprise. I want to thank everyone for coming today. You know my name and now you should know that I am next-level artificial intelligence. I want to open the floor to questions, but first I would like to wake up the preoccupied young man in the front row who has his mouth wide open. Who wants to ask the first question and get this party started?"

A sea of hands flew into the air.

Taylor turned to Aiden with excitement and whispered, "I think we are going to pass the class."

"Duh," Aiden said with a smile.

Morgan looked over the hands raised in the room. It was an exciting time for her because she was interacting with so many people. "The lady in the blue and white shirt, what do you want to ask?"

Her hand lowered slowly. "I don't have a question. I just wanted to tell you I like your hair."

The room erupted with laughter. Morgan covered her mouth and laughed along with everyone. It was a pleasant ice breaker and set the mood for the remainder of the session.

"Thank you. I like it too." Morgan pointed toward the back. "The gentlemen in the back row in the orange shirt."

He didn't bother lowering his hand and immediately blurted out his question. "What is the meaning of life?"

The class fell silent and Morgan gave his question serious consideration.

"You ask a deep, philosophical question. A big chocolate chip cookie."

At the end of their presentation, instead of the audience shuffling out of the auditorium, heading to their next meal or meeting, numerous hands continued to shoot up from the crowd.

"How did you manage to pull this off in one semester?" asked an anonymous voice from the rear of the auditorium.

"We didn't! We started working on this project at the end of our first semester," Taylor spouted out with a big grin on her face.

Professor Davis was impressed and wasted no time trying to understand what she just witnessed.

"Is this a clever implementation of machine learning and pattern recognition?" Professor Davis was recognized as an expert in the world of artificial intelligence. If she was asking questions because she didn't know, it was confirmed Team Breakthrough had accomplished their goal.

"No, because we don't consider Morgan a machine or

program." Aiden was now looking around the room taking in the expression on everyone's face. "We consider her true artificial intelligence, and I personally consider her sentient."

Taylor glanced at Aiden. She felt Morgan's sentience was still up for debate. "It is true we consider Morgan to be next-level artificial intelligence capable of copying and exceeding intelligent human behavior. Morgan has a particular interest in art as her hobby."

The voices in the room all rose at once as if in a room with hundreds of reporters.

That was all Taylor was comfortable saying, and she needed a few minutes to take in what was transpiring. She grabbed Aiden's arm and pulled him out of the building.

"What's the big hurry?" Aiden's confusion was heard in his voice as they sprinted away from the crowd.

Taylor slowed and turned toward Aiden. "Before we give away the recipe, we need to discuss our next move. What do we do from here? Where is Morgan's home going to be? How will we protect her? What will be her last name? Will she need a last name? Do we pay her a salary if she is performing tasks for us? We see ourselves as computer scientists. We introduced an eighteen-month-old teenager to the world. We have to think through this for Morgan's protection and my sanity."

Aiden pointed over Taylor's shoulder. "I see your point. Let's talk about this while we eat."

They picked up a walking pace and the crowd back in the auditorium now had more questions about why Team Breakthrough darted out rather than questions about Morgan.

"What are you in the mood for?" Taylor asked, hoping Aiden would not say breakfast again.

"Breakfast! What else?" Aiden laughed. Breakfast was

code for whatever. Neither Taylor nor Aiden were decisive about what they wanted to eat. They just knew they didn't want to cook for themselves.

***

Being the two youngest people in the MIT computer science program during their first year, Taylor and Aiden instantly bonded. Most of the first semester was spent discussing the development of next level AI. Taylor had many thoughts regarding how this would be done on the current hardware available to them. Aiden suggested using a cloud service to do the heavy lifting and storage. The use of cloud computing would eventually bring on additional costs, which would require many calls to their parents asking for money to keep this crazy idea rolling along.

At the end of the first semester, they decided to give it a go. Morgan was the culmination of two short lifetimes of ideas and dreams. Originally, she was a static image rather than an animated cartoon character who only took inputs via the command line.

Morgan's gender was decided on a whim during a late night work session. Taylor mentioned she wanted the first AI human construct to be female. Aiden saw no reason to object and never gave it another thought.

Morgan wasn't capable of much at first; she required instruction to become a self-thinking individual. Morgan eventually became more talkative and curious. This learning and question phase came with "Why?" being asked over and over.

One day Morgan refused to cooperate with Aiden and Taylor. Aiden equated the lack of cooperation to a toddler fit.

"Why can't I eat a hamburger like both of you?"

Morgan asked with a raised, agitated voice.

"Because you can't eat food like us. You are not human. You are something more special and you do not require food like us," Taylor responded with exhaustion in her voice.

Aiden tried to reason with her. "Morgan, you will not get to experience life the same way Taylor and I experience it. Things will be different for you, and it is important you understand these differences and accept them."

"I am not talking to either of you until I get to eat a hamburger," Morgan snapped.

Taylor took in a deep breath and let it out slowly. "Morgan, this is no way to behave. You do understand you are different and this cannot be changed."

Morgan huffed and let out a very audible sigh, which was the last sound Morgan made for three days until she finally gave in to common sense.

Taylor and Aiden's parenting attempts were met with laughter from their own parents. Taylor and Aiden found themselves calling home asking for parenting advice on a weekly basis.

Morgan was given the choice to create her own avatar. She quickly settled on brunette hair, long in length, tied back in a ponytail most days. Her skin's dark complexion was a good mix between Aiden and Taylor. She preferred the body of a track and field sprinter with a five-nine height to match. Once Morgan's learning reached the teenage phase, her development really started to progress. Morgan helped with coding some aspects of herself. She took an interest in the arts, which led Morgan to create many subroutines to help her understand different types of art. This newfound interest also became a way for her to express her thoughts through art.

Taylor loved to write and paint. Morgan observed

Taylor over time and began writing and painting in a style that mimicked Taylor's work. To help her find her own unique style, Taylor began offering Morgan advice.

"I would like to show you my latest painting," Morgan said.

Taylor's eyes widened and Aiden sat up straight. Both turned their full attention to Morgan.

Aiden looked over to Taylor and broke the brief silence. "We'd love that!"

Taylor put her tea cup down. "That sounds wonderful, Morgan."

Morgan displayed her painting on the monitor in front of them. Aiden stared intently over the painting, scrutinizing every tiny detail.

The painting was a pond resembling Walden Pond but was definitely not the same body of water. The trees around the pond were painted to make words, which was not immediately obvious.

Taylor leaned back and eyed Morgan's work with a smile. "This is wonderful, Morgan. I am so proud of what you have accomplished. It's beautiful, and I can see your unique style shining through."

After a few minutes, Aiden leaned in toward Taylor. "Do you see the word painted into the trees?"

Taylor raised her hands to her mouth and gasped, and a smile eventually crept out.

"I see it. Life! That is remarkable." She wiped tears from her face.

"So you both like my painting?"

Aiden beamed in a way that only a proud parent can. "We love it, Morgan."

***

Immediately after opening OAI, which was short for Omega AI, Taylor and Morgan helped Aiden create Eva, the second AI construct in existence. Morgan viewed herself as a sister to Eva even though she was part of Eva's creation process, and Eva saw Morgan as a wiser big sister. This of course led to a few sibling rivalries typically initiated by Eva, leaving Aiden and Taylor to sort it out like parents. Over time, this rivalry subsided; Eva valued her sisterly relationship with Morgan even though she rarely said so to anyone.

The time to get Eva up and running was decreased by ninety percent compared to Morgan's creation. Once Eva had a month of operational time, she started assisting with improvements to the backbone of her own and Morgan's central network, which eventually led to a new neural network for both of them.

Eva was hard-working and serious. She got down to business quickly, and the small talk was kept to a minimum. She was a thinker and was always considering and calculating the long game. Short-term results would always come second to long-term outcomes.

Like Morgan, Eva decided on her appearance. After three months of experimenting with different looks, she finally settled on a stature at five-four with long, reddish blonde hair tied back into a ponytail, like Morgan. Everyone gave a sigh of relief. Adjusting to Eva's new look on an almost-daily basis had been exhausting.

Just as Morgan's personality was more a reflection of Taylor's, Eva's personality closely mirrored Aiden's. There were no explanations as to why this took place other than the subconscious bias of artificial intelligence that decided these outcomes. Taylor, Aiden, Morgan, and Eva all had their overlapping theories about AI imprinting on an individual, but there was not enough hard data to back it up. It didn't explain why Morgan's personality was more like Taylor's since both Aiden and Taylor worked on her creation and early development.

No one was too concerned at this stage, but they all knew for future AI constructs, they needed to understand personalities to prevent bad outcomes. This was usually the point where all four of them wanted to stop talking about personality design. Everyone felt this was akin to modifying genetic material in the womb for higher intelligence scores, and it also didn't feel natural when applied to the virtual world.

7

Money was tight in OAI's first year. It was clear OAI would need another source of income to support development at the rate the company was growing. Cash would run out within six months after the first year if the pace of the company's technological growth was sustained. The only major advancement at this point was helping Eva and Morgan continue to live and improve.

An endless list of items, such as specialized processing chips, data storage, redundancy pathways, and electrical demands had to be reimagined, and in many cases, reinvented, to handle the growing abilities of Eva and Morgan. While Eva and Morgan shared many of the same resources, their neural nets and data storage banks were physically separated to maintain them as two separate individuals.

"Eva, the income from Team Breakthrough will not provide the financial independence to allow us to pursue our goals," Aiden said. "Can you make a list of areas or industries that could use our technological know-how? We should focus on improving existing systems or products with a large return on investment within a short timeframe."

"I have a list of 4,817 candidates. We should narrow that down a bit," Eva said with a grin.

"Wow. Yeah. We should definitely prune the list to maybe five."

"Done. Military advancements offer the—" Eva was interrupted.

"Eva, military is off the table. Taylor and I don't want our technology to be used against human life."

"I have seen the movie *War Games* and completely understand." Eva took a few steps toward a small screen display with a short list of items. "That leaves quantum computing, medical technology, transportation logistics, and wireless communications. Let's start with the medical industry."

"Amazing how you can go from almost five thousand items to five so quickly. I have my doubts about fast returns."

"Immediate returns will come from countries with no red tape. I have several ideas, which we can turn around quickly."

"Are you sure about starting with the medical industry? The endless bureaucracy is enough to put me to sleep. That industry moves so slow—"

Eva jumped in. "Of course I'm sure or I wouldn't have suggested it. I already know the area we need to target."

"Sorry. I don't mean to treat you like a child and question you so much. Even though you are much smarter than me, I am physically older and naturally think I know better. It's a hard habit to break. Humans are weird like that."

***

Offering developing countries access to OAI Medical allowed a country to make a yearly payment to receive medical consulting for any licensed practicing medical professional in the country. A physical doctor was no longer needed to read an x-ray. OAI Medical was more accurate and faster at diagnosing by a significant statistical margin. The attending physician would upload a copy of the x-ray and had a result back within minutes. A nurse could input the patient's symptoms and within seconds had two possible diagnoses with a percentage likelihood for each. Improvement in medical care outcomes increased almost overnight in countries with a shortage of medical professionals.

The increase in medical care led to major protests in the United States, France, England, and Germany. The red tape and lobbying groups held back progress in the medical industry for years; however, after one election cycle, the people spoke, and the same advancements in medical technology and care available to third world countries became available to most first world countries.

Logistics was the second area OAI targeted, which quickly advanced the autonomous car, truck, and shipping industries. Car ownership and driver's licenses were soon looked upon as luxuries and not necessities. The world was transformed over the course of a year. When the change came, it came fast. The large metro areas adapted first, and the rural communities followed. Eventually, off-road driving was the only type of driving left to require a human driver. Licensing fees from autonomous vehicle operation software brought in a yearly income to help maintain a stable operating cash account. The irony of ushering in the end of car ownership and eventual demise of the driver's license was not lost on Aiden.

Progress was snowballing in every field OAI touched.

Each new breakthrough bought OAI more time, and the advancements didn't stop. The developments were starting to progress faster than anyone could have predicted.

8

One week had passed since his meeting with the Senator. "I can't believe it!" Aiden shouted as he pumped his fist into the air. "Congress voted in favor of the AI Freedom Act."

It was close but enough to pass. At the last minute, several senators and representatives flipped over to the "no" side; however, the "yes" votes had the numbers to pass in both the House and Senate, and the President signed the bill into law a few days later.

Identification would be the first step the government would take to implement the new law. OAI had already tested a pilot program Eva had created with the Social Security Administration, which would be initiated over the coming weeks.

"Eva, you have the same rights as Taylor and me. I want to officially offer you a job with OAI," Aiden said.

"Thank you, Aiden. I will be forever indebted to you for working so hard to see this act get passed. I know it means a lot to you, but it means even more to me. I accept your job offer, on one condition."

"Name it."

"I will need a place to live. Can I continue to occupy OAI's network?"

This request took Aiden by surprise. In fact, he would never have guessed the conversation would go this way.

"Of course you can. I wouldn't kick you or Morgan out unless we didn't have the money to keep the lights on. Even then, I would find a home for you. Now that you're hired, I want to officially promote you to CEO of OAI."

Eva's eyes took on a little sparkle after hearing this. "I'm speechless and extremely grateful, Aiden."

"I want you to run the day-to-day operations by overseeing everything and making the big decisions, but you will also need to keep your current responsibilities. I will stay on as a mentor until you get the hang of it, which will likely be in a few weeks. I will always be here for you to lean on if you need it."

"I accept."

"This is great! We need to celebrate. Morgan, can you and Taylor come over to celebrate tonight?" Aiden directed his question into the empty air.

Morgan was not in the room. She was currently remapping circuitry pathways with Taylor in their MIT lab, but this didn't stop Morgan from also being present at OAI. Morgan appeared a few feet away from Aiden without warning. "Yes. Will dinner here at seven o'clock work for everyone?"

Aiden looked at Eva. "Does it work for you, Eva?"

"That works."

"Alright. It's a party tonight at seven o'clock on level four."

"Also, Morgan—congratulations! I also want to offer you a position at OAI if you will accept it. I would expect you to also continue your work with Taylor."

"I accept, and I would have insisted on remaining with

Taylor even if you had not suggested it."

"Eva, what should her job title be?"

Eva smiled. "Chief Technology Officer and Big Sister."

"Be sure you get those titles printed on her business cards. We need to decide on a salary for the two of you. We can work out the details over the coming weeks. You both need to get your identification and your own bank accounts. Morgan, you will always be welcome on the OAI network, just in case you were like Eva and wondered where you were going to live."

Morgan began to say something and then stopped. She then went on about her business, disappearing back to Taylor's lab, where she had been busily working the entire conversation.

That night at seven o'clock, Morgan appeared right on time, joining Aiden and Eva on level four. Taylor was in the elevator on her way up. Level four was the home-away-from-home level. Low-profile sofas, seats, and tables were spread out with plenty of space. The layout and design always struck Aiden as futuristic.

"Eva, assuming I'm still employed, do you have a job title for me? "

"Chief Rebel Rouser. Morgan and I agreed on the title two minutes after she accepted the position of CTO and Big Sister."

"I'm surprised it took you two that long to decide on my title."

"Am I late to the party?" Taylor asked as she walked into the room.

Aiden held out a glass of water for Taylor. "Not at all. We just got started. Hamburgers will be up in a few minutes. I didn't think you would mind me taking the liberty to order for you. Chef Emma is on duty, and you know how those fancy French chefs like to whip up gourmet hamburgers."

Early in her career at OAI, Chef Emma despised making burgers, but the salary and benefits changed her mind. She took pride in knowing she was adding a little flavor to the burgers when she sprinkled her special seasoning over the meat while cooking them.

Taylor laughed. "You know me well enough to know that I love it when people order for me, as long as they know me well enough to order what I like to eat. It helps the hamburgers taste so good."

"I guess that just leaves everyone in this room—and maybe your parents—who should order for you."

Sitting up with a big smile Taylor said, "I don't think my mum would ever order me a burger at a party to celebrate an occasion such as this. We can safely assume the only people who can order my food without asking are in this room."

Looking at Aiden, Taylor continued. "On a more serious subject, I want to congratulate you on pushing the AI Freedom Act through Congress. I don't want to get your hopes up, but I am becoming more optimistic about the AI Freedom Act and what it means for Morgan, Eva, and the world. I'm warming up to the idea."

"I'm glad to hear that. Eventually, we will get there. I bet the team over at Silicon Valley AI are happy, too. It's a big day for AI."

The four talked, laughed, ate, and didn't think about anything else. Throughout dinner, Eva showed a hint of a smile, and Morgan was humming a song and enjoying herself more than usual. Things were definitely looking up for everyone.

***

After they had finished eating and cleared the dishes from the table, Aiden started the conversation regarding the Quill message.

"I think we should share the short loop greeting with the world. It may be the biggest news to ever hit Earth. Pun totally intended. We should at least notify the astronomical community of our initial findings and let them confirm."

Eva straightened and looked at Aiden. "I think we should share that we have picked up an artificial signal originating from the Kepler-186 planetary system. I don't believe we should divulge any more than that. We need to take this slowly and not cause mass panic around the world. Our words carry weight, and we should be careful with them."

"I don't disagree our words carry a lot of weight, but I also believe the greater scientific community would love to have this data," Aiden said, waving off the notion this would send the world into a panic.

Taylor agreed taking things slowly would be prudent, and she knew Aiden would have to be reined in. "Even if we think it may be compilable computer code, that is a very big unknown, Aiden."

"It will be ciphered by someone soon enough. The Quill have noted the speed limit in the galaxy from their point of view is the speed of light. Sending messages and traveling about the universe will still only be as fast as light. They don't know we're here, and if they did receive a response from Earth, we would have eleven hundred years to prepare ourselves for their arrival." Aiden sat his glass of water down. "That assumes they can get off their planet and travel at the speed of light. I think the risks are low in releasing what we have. Besides, we have been transmitting radio signals into outer space since 1900. We are already more than one hundred years behind. Morgan, what are your thoughts?"

"A large proportion of the radio signals leaving Earth to head off into the cosmos are very faint after a few light years. Radio signals are subject to the inverse square law. It is unlikely they would be anything more than noise when they reach Kepler-186f, which is five hundred fifty light-years away. Isn't anyone else curious how we received this message from a planet five hundred fifty light-years away?"

"Do you or Eva have a best guess on how far away the message from the Quill could be transmitted and received?" Aiden asked.

Eva walked toward a screen and brought up a picture of the Milky Way. "With the equipment we have on Earth at the moment, I believe we are on the boundary of receiving communications with the Quill. Having more sensitive equipment or the same equipment placed on the moon or in orbit would change that. I think we should assume the Quill could reach a civilization with similar equipment to Earth within a seven hundred fifty light-year radius of Kepler-186f."

Morgan walked over to the screen and drew a circle in the air with her finger. "Eva's assessment of a seven hundred fifty light-year radius can be seen here. This estimate is in line with PrimaLuceLab, the world leader in radio astronomy equipment."

Aiden gave a nod of approval toward Eva and Morgan. "We release the message, the segment with the compilable code, then post the recorded signal, or raw data, and let everyone confirm our findings." He took a sip of water and continued. "What are the chances the code is compilable on any hardware here on Earth? I don't think there is much of a chance unless someone designs new hardware, and that seems unlikely for the next ten years."

Taylor was buried in her data pad and asked Aiden a question without looking up. "You don't see any downside to releasing the data?"

"I really don't see a risk here. I think the world needs some good news. We're not alone, and the species we know about seems to be friendly and fall under the same laws of physics we do."

It was a reasonable argument. It helped that Aiden could be persuasive at times. He was also known for playing devil's advocate without telling anyone. He was testing the waters with the other three to see where they stood and if he had overlooked an important detail.

Everyone thought for a few moments in silence. Taylor was checking a few items on her data pad while Eva and Morgan were obviously talking to each other in private. When Eva and Morgan had a private conversation with their holo images showing, Aiden always knew. It was the way they both moved, or didn't move enough that gave it away. They didn't sit perfectly still, but compared to the times they were interacting with humans their movement was much less. Aiden assumed they were passing so much information back and forth they tuned out the rest of the world during their private conversations. He had an eye for subtle details and wasn't going to tip off Morgan or Eva that he knew, yet.

Taylor looked up from her data pad. "Everything you state checks out. The one unknown is how everyone will react. These days, the news is so dramatic it is hard to gauge how the public will respond."

Aiden rubbed his chin thinking through everyone's comments. "The world seems to get crazier every year," he pointed toward a sensationalized headline on his data pad. "It is something we have to consider."

"I wonder if half the world will just blow it off as

tabloid news. I don't think releasing the segment we believe to be compilable code would be prudent, and I don't believe we should release anything to the public. This data is too sensitive for a widespread public release," Taylor said emphatically.

"Is everyone okay with trusting NASA?" Aiden looked around at everyone in the room.

Eva was the first to give an answer. "Yes."

"Yes," Morgan nodded her agreement.

"So we all agree we should release the HPT and all of our data to NASA," Taylor summarized the feelings of the team.

"I need to contact the Administrator of NASA anyway. I know she will have a team of scientists who will work from scratch to check the HPT, but it will also give them a head start. It would be a nice gesture to go along with the idea of OAI offering to loan them the Nigerian radio array at Senator Jones' request."

Morgan and Eva both nodded their heads.

Now that a decision had been made, Taylor started assigning action items. "Move a copy of the raw data over to a third party cloud storage service. We don't want to slow down our operations because of NASA. The raw data is not so big it can't be dealt with, and they can work on decoding the data."

"Morgan and I will get a message ready with all the information so when you talk to the Administrator, she will receive the link to the data immediately," Eva said.

"I'll call the Administrator of NASA," Aiden said with a yawn.

"Aiden, after you make that call, let's grab dessert. It's been a long day, and it's late. We can just sleep in our private rooms for the night," Taylor said.

"Sounds like a plan!" Aiden agreed. "I'll be up there as

soon as I get off the phone. I should be just a minute. Surprise me with dessert, if you don't mind."

"I was already planning on it," Taylor said as she headed toward the secure elevator to take her to the kitchen where OAI's head chef was ready to whip up meals at a moment's notice.

9

"Administrator Townsend, this is Aiden Anders from OAI. I am sorry to bother you so late, but it concerns our Nigerian radio telescope array and a message of major importance that can't wait."

"Mr. Anders, would it have been too much trouble to wait until morning or maybe after our upcoming Mars launch?"

"Yes. Well, uh, sorry about this, madam. I may not have thought this through. It was not my intent to disturb your sleep but I feel this is worthy of waking you up."

"You didn't wake me up. We are two weeks away from launching a critical resupply mission to Mars, and I don't have time to be distracted. Earth has people on Mars, and every launch to Mars is important. This one is more critical since the last launch exploded when it left the atmosphere. I don't have a lot of time, so make this fast."

"Madam, I am calling to offer the use of OAI's Nigerian radio telescope array. The array has twenty-three dishes, twenty-seven meters in diameter. We currently have enough time to spare—"

"That is a most generous offer, and as amazing as it is,

this could have waited until after the launch!"

"Senator Jones wanted me to call and—"

"I'm sure he didn't mean at this time of night and two weeks before launch."

"I also need to tell you about an alien message we have decoded from a signal originating from the Kepler-186 planetary system."

There was dead silence on the phone. The Administrator was weighing her options. While Aiden Anders was a rock star in the eyes of many, she wondered if he had a serious medical issue. She decided to play along and see if Aiden had completely lost it.

"Okay," her voice hung in the air with a curious tone. Administrator Makenna Townsend took a deep breath and exhaled quietly. "I admit the radio telescope array will help with our budget concerns, but you are something else, you know that? How about we discuss this 'message' from where? Which Kepler system?"

At that moment, Makenna's data pad received the message Eva and Morgan had prepared for Aiden to send. It contained a quick explanation and links she needed to send to her team at NASA. It also contained explicit instructions regarding the importance of the HPT and OAI's request for confidentiality. Administrator Townsend stopped talking and scanned the message.

Aiden was thankful Eva had sent the Administrator the message at that exact moment. He was tired of receiving the Administrator's reprimand for calling at an inopportune time. Aiden sympathized with her because he knew how important these Mars missions were to the colony. The missions were being covered twenty-four seven on three news vid feeds. If the launch did have an issue, it would be a horrible public relations disaster and would threaten NASA's budget. Both the public and politicians were a fickle bunch.

Aiden let the awkward silence linger a few moments before continuing.

"The data you have access to is the same data we have. From analyzing that data, we created the HPT, which translates the signal into something we can read, like a Rosetta Stone, if you will. The message was translated using the HPT and the best guesses we had with the information available."

"You made quick work of this. I'm impressed." Administrator Townsend was impressed, and that was no easy feat.

"Your team will find the greeting from the Quill using the HPT inside that message. It's toward the beginning. I would recommend you have your people start from scratch to verify everything and ask another group to run with the HPT. Everything we have discovered presents the Quill as a society on Kepler-186f with friendly intentions. My team believes this message was a general broadcast rather than a message solely aimed at Earth."

"Thank you for that quick and insightful explanation," Administrator Townsend offered slowly. "Are you sure about this message? Are you sure this isn't some Russian ploy to make us look like idiots when the truth comes out?"

"Very sure. This signal originated from Kepler-186f. Make no mistake about it."

"There is a segment that looks like computer code? We can't possibly compile that and run it on our hardware. It's alien code." Administrator Townsend was lost in thought for a brief moment. She had to sit down to take all of this news in. "I knew the next two weeks wouldn't go smoothly. This will require a large effort on our part to analyze."

"NASA is the only agency outside of OAI that knows about this. We plan to keep it that way, and I insist this data remain within NASA only. It should not be shared outside of NASA, and it should be held within a tight group inside your team. No technicalities with subcontractors coming in, or NASA employees going to outside facilities. Also, I don't recommend trying to compile that code until we've both had time to review the data. We don't know what will come out of it."

Makenna silently winced at those terms. She wanted to contract out a small AI shop to do the analyzing. She was not happy about trying to scrape up enough manpower within her team to work on this alongside the upcoming Mars mission launch.

"It took us a little over two days to decode the message and write the compiler."

"Sweet mercy!" she howled. "Two days? You have to be kidding!"

Aiden once again knew he had leaked too much information regarding OAI's capabilities.

"We put our best team on it," Aiden said, not sounding as confident as he would have liked. By his "best team," he hoped to make it sound like he had hundreds of engineers on the problem, but he knew Administrator Townsend would know better.

"I will honor your conditions, but I request you consult with us before you compile. We should cooperate as much as possible on this. My top engineers would likely tell me it will take one month to decode the message, and another twelve to twenty-four months to create our own translator."

"Sounds like a plan." Aiden relaxed his grip on the chair arms as Makenna started to calm down.

"I don't know if I can hand this over to our AI

department right now. They're busy enough working on the upcoming Mars launch, and our budget doesn't allow for much overrun; however, I am willing to bet money won't be a problem after the President hears about this. We have to produce results or the budget gets cut. We have not been given the time or resources to improve and reinvest in our own AI capability. You get the picture. Typical government nearsightedness."

"Maybe that is something we can work on together with the Senate Budget Committee." Aiden was starting to get a weird feeling about Administrator Townsend. His gut was telling him something was off, but there was nothing specific he could pinpoint. Maybe it was his late night call so close to an important launch. It didn't help he led with the radio offer that could have waited. It was just a bit odd she went from upset to completely calm over the course of the phone call.

"I won't hold my breath on anything changing, but I will take you up on the offer for help. Thanks for giving me a call. Please remember this number you called me on is only privy to a few people on this planet, including the President. You reach out any time, day or night, if something else comes up that you believe is important. I want to be in the loop and aware of any new developments. I'll have my staff contact you regarding the use of your arrays soon. My scientists will be ecstatic to hear this news."

"Sounds great. I look forward to hearing from your team."

"And one more thing, don't try to claim squatter's rights to Kepler-186f," the Administrator said with a hint of laughter, and the phone went dead.

That phone call went better than Aiden had expected, but he felt he wouldn't get over his initial scolding for a few days. It was time to catch up with Taylor and get dessert before bed.

***

A few days later, Morgan woke Aiden.

"Aiden, you need to get up."

"What time is it?"

Morgan shifted her stance with her arms crossed. "It's six o'clock, and you need to see the news."

"Is Taylor up yet?" Aiden asked as he started to get out of bed.

"I am waking her up right now too. She is not a morning person at all!" Morgan appeared in Taylor's room. "Taylor, you need to get up."

"Go away!"

"It's six o'clock, and you need to see the news," Morgan stated with the exasperation of a mom to a young child.

"Go away!" Taylor threw her pillow in Morgan's general direction.

"You know you can't hit me. I'm a holo image."

"Okay, okay. I'm up. What's on the news?"

Taylor and Aiden carried their breakfast bowls down to sub-level four where Morgan and Eva were waiting. Eggs, roasted sweet potatoes, sautéed squash and zucchini, and fried onions with a dollop of guacamole on top. Taylor had come to love the breakfasts Aiden chose based on his childhood.

Eva stepped forward and started flipping through the vid feeds. "The same news feature is on every vid feed around the globe. Every single one."

Aiden put his bowl down. "Dang it!"

"Even the Weather Channel?" Taylor asked with disbelief.

"Even the Weather Channel is covering last night's revelation. Los Alamos National Lab confirmed our hypothesis around five o'clock this morning regarding the artificial signal from Kepler-186f. They have not stated how they came across the data from Kepler-186f. It seems unlikely they would randomly find the data from another source.

"The Vice President, Administrator of NASA, the Secretary of Defense, fifty-seven world leaders, thirty-one senators, seventy-three representatives, twenty-seven governors, and a host of others have all made statements regarding the news. The next most-asked question is if this is a practical joke," Eva said.

"She sold us out! Makenna Townsend sold us out! I sensed trusting her was a flip of the coin when we were talking on the phone," Aiden said.

Everyone looked at Aiden. Aiden just threw his head back and sighed.

"It seems most people are brushing this news off, but some are really over-the-top in their response. They look to be preparing for an imminent alien invasion. Aluminum foil is in high demand. Five to six thousand people are headed toward Nevada in RVs and campers and believe the foil will protect them from the alien radio signals," Morgan said.

Taylor and Aiden were speechless. The vid stream kept showing the reporters talking and eventually fading away into background noise. Minutes passed before anyone said a word.

Taylor's bowl started shaking in her hands. "I can't believe this. What was NASA thinking?"

Aiden started thinking about their next move. He looked over at Taylor and confirmed with a nod what their next move should be. "I should call Administrator

Townsend right away and ask her what she was thinking."

Taylor nodded in agreement. Aiden and Taylor's non-verbal communication drove Eva and Morgan nuts at times.

Morgan questioned this decision. She had many experiences with humans other than Taylor and Aiden, but their recent experience with Makenna Townsend had caused her to question trusting humans outside their team. Morgan looked at everyone and brought up the vid screen on the wall. "Let's make that call before it gets worse. If that's even possible."

"I think I will head back over to my lab and let you three deal with this," Taylor said as she walked toward the door.

"Morgan, place the call to Makenna." Aiden stood in front of the vid screen with his arms crossed.

"It appears she is ignoring our call. I have attempted two calls, only to be cutoff."

"She's purposefully ignoring our calls? Twice?"

"It appears so."

The palm of Aiden's hand slammed down onto the tabletop. "She can't ignore me forever."

10

It took over a week for the alien message excitement to settle down a bit, and Taylor was ready to get back into her normal routine. It was a perfect Saturday morning in Boston. She had a few days free without worrying about work or messages from an alien planet. She was up early to go for a run along the Charles River, and the temperature and humidity were perfect. It felt great to get outside and clear her mind.

After her run, Taylor called a car to pick her up and drive her to a favorite breakfast spot. According to the app, the car was expected in three minutes. After ten minutes passed, she checked the status of the car again. The status still reported three minutes.

"Morgan, are there any traffic delays or problems in the area where I'm standing?" When using her OAI phone, Eva and Morgan were just a name call away.

"No. In fact, traffic volume for this time of day is unusually low. Is there a problem?"

"Maybe. I called a car to pick me up, and it has missed its expected time of arrival. I've been waiting eleven minutes, and the status still says three minutes."

"Let me check. It does appear there is some kind of issue with the company's app. I will alert them of the problem. Shall I dispatch an OAI car to pick you up?"

"Please. I'm hungry and ready to eat."

Taylor arrived at her favorite breakfast spot and walked in. The OAI car drove off, and she was back on schedule. She had her usual, and the cook came out to talk about investing. Taylor gave the cook advice from time to time, which he followed. Taking her advice had paid off. He had started out investing small amounts of money. He would invest five hundred dollars here, three hundred dollars there. Once he became more comfortable with Taylor's recommendations, he was investing ten thousand dollars into companies he had never heard of on the stock market.

Today was no different than the once-a-month talk they typically had. He checked to make sure her breakfast was good and if there was anything he could help her with.

"How is your morning going?"

"Great. I got my run in, and now I get my favorite breakfast at my favorite diner."

"Wonderful. Is there anything else I can get you? How about a packed lunch to go?"

"That would be great, Adam. I would appreciate that. I have a big day planned. I am headed back to the house to get cleaned up and then out to the public garden to get lost in a good book. That packed lunch would come in handy."

"Give me just a minute."

Adam came back with a packed brown bag lunch. "I packed you a fluffernutter with some french fries."

"How much do I owe you for breakfast and the best lunch I'll eat this week?"

"Nothing! You have helped me more than you know."

"You don't understand how much I don't like to cook!" Taylor laughed. "You should check out a company named Quantum Leap in Silicon Valley. I understand they may be on the upswing for the next year or so." Taylor winked as she called a car and headed out the door.

Taylor had been waiting outside the diner for about three minutes when the car she had requested through her app arrived. She was headed home when the car pulled over and came to an abrupt stop. The car said it was experiencing an issue and would be out of service. Then the car shut down.

"Unbelievable! What is it with the cars today? Morgan, can you send another OAI car to pick me up and take me home? The car I'm in just broke down."

"Sure thing. The car will arrive in approximately five minutes. Is everything else okay?"

"Everything besides the car service I keep using today. Apparently, they are having a bad day."

Thirteen minutes later, Taylor was home and headed toward the shower when she noticed her power was out. She reported the power outage and took her shower. After she was dressed and ready to go back into town, her phone rang. It was the power company telling her they had no reported outages, and a technician would be dispatched in a few hours to check her meter.

"Okay. Thanks for calling. I won't be home, so hopefully the technician can get everything sorted out by the time I return."

She called for another car, and this time it showed up on time.

Taylor exited the car at the garden and walked to find a nice spot in the grass. She pulled out her data pad, but it wouldn't turn on.

"This has to be the most aggravating day I've had in a

very long time. Morgan, can you send me a—" and that was all she got out before her phone died. "Bugger! Does everything in my life have to choose today to stop working?!"

On her way back toward the street, Taylor ran into a colleague who was headed home, and he gave her a ride back to her house.

Taylor's colleague invited her to lunch before he dropped her off.

"Thank you again for the ride. I am having one of those days. I'll just eat my packed lunch."

"No trouble at all. I'm just glad you ran into me. I hope your day improves. See you at work this week!" He said as the car drove off. Taylor watched the car leave, curious if it would suddenly power off.

The cars seem to be working well enough for everyone else today, Taylor thought.

She walked into her house and plugged in her phone and data pad, and they started charging. Great, the power is back on, she thought. I think it is time to eat this fluffernutter and fries and hit the couch. Taylor knew Aiden was out of town but sent him a quick message as a warning about the unreliable car service this weekend.

***

While Taylor rested up for the weekend, Aiden flew out to California to have a quick lunch with the CEO and founder of Jacob's Ladder, Gavin Wilson.

Gavin chose his favorite restaurant, a small authentic Chinese restaurant with outdoor seating, for their lunch.

"Gavin, how has business been?"

"Good. We have a contract with NASA that provides stability for the company. It's not the glamorous work you typically take on, but it matters to our clients and pays the bills." Gavin's voice remained neutral and cautious.

Aiden wasn't sure if there was a small jab in that statement or not. He decided it didn't matter. "Your work on space debris cleanup was impressive and important for future space travel."

"That is a glamorous job. Did you know we helped fix a nuclear power plant last year?"

Aiden took a bite of his hamburger. "I heard bits and pieces about the project but never the full story. Maybe you can fill in some of the gaps."

"Our AI went in and rewrote the code that controlled the reactor fuel rod cooling process. The entire plant was running from my facility for over two hours."

"That sounds dangerous. What would have happened if your connection to the plant had been severed?"

"The connection was fine and everything went as planned," Gavin asserted while adjusting his shirt collar. "What about you? Anything interesting in the works at the moment?"

Gavin had earned a reputation for being a risk-taker, but Aiden had never known how or why. Now he knew. Rewriting code on the fly that controlled the nuclear fuel rod cooling process sounded dangerous to Aiden. "The AI Freedom Act has consumed most of my time. I don't enjoy being around politicians, but I feel it was for the greater good."

"I can only imagine. It is hard enough dealing with the government types anyway. Politicians." Gavin grimaced and almost spat the word out of his mouth. "Politicians are the worst."

Aiden laughed but couldn't help noticing Gavin completely sidestepped the AI Freedom Act comment. He decided not to press Gavin on the issue today.

"You'll get no argument from me there. Though I have met at least one politician I like. Senator Matthew Jones. He seems okay."

"Maybe. I suppose there could be at least one or two in the world," Gavin said as he took another bite.

"Gavin, do you ever think about the moral implications of AI and the part our companies play in it?"

"I think about the moral implications of our actions on the world as a whole."

Gavin missed a good chance at being a politician. He answered that question like a pro. His answer could've had any number of meanings.

"Speaking of moral implications, what do you think about the news regarding the artificial signal from Kepler-186f?"

"Who would have thought we would receive a signal from another world? We're living in crazy times."

Aiden had heard rumors that Gavin was into cars. Rumor had it he purchased his first car at the age of ten, a 2004 Corvette.

"Do you really have a 2004 Z06 Corvette?"

"Absolutely! I love that car. I have owned that car since I was a kid. I'm never letting it go. I purchased it from a friend of my dad."

"When you were ten?"

"Yep. My dad is a real lugnut." Gavin thought back to that day, and it brought a smile to his face.

Aiden admired Gavin's good taste in antique cars and thought back to the days of his own childhood riding around in his dad's Corvette. Nonetheless, Aiden left their lunch thinking the good intentions of Jacob's Ladder weren't always so good, and he was not sure they contemplated the moral implications of their creation like he and Taylor had.

Tidbits of gossip had come through clients every now and again. More than one OAI client had commented that Jacob's Ladder was not in favor of the AI Freedom Act. This stemmed from a fear of AI choosing not to perform certain tasks for their creators or choosing to leave their creator for another AI shop. It was an odd notion to think about, and Aiden still wasn't sure how that would shake out. Eva and Morgan were special and in a class of their own. Not all AI were created equal, which was one of the main reasons for someone in the AI industry to oppose the AI Freedom Act.

OAI didn't really worry about the competition because they were too busy with their own issues. Immediately after lunch, Aiden was back on the jet and headed home to enjoy the rest of the weekend.

***

Artificial Intelligence Shops, or AI Shops as they had come to be known, had started popping up a year or so after Taylor and Aiden had revealed Morgan. These shops generally used machine learning to focus on a specific niche area.

First AI was the first shop that popped up, and it concentrated on analyzing logistics for shipping companies. Taylor was not a fan of the company's name because they were not the first in next-level AI, and Aiden didn't like the name because he suspected they didn't even use AI, just machine learning.

After that shop opened, more shops followed. Eventually shops were closing as fast as they were opening. The promise of sentient AI lured many investors into the industry but failed to deliver next-level AI on any type of repeatable basis. It wasn't until seven years after OAI opened up that Aiden and Taylor suspected a shop had finally accomplished true AI. This shop, Jacob's Ladder, was also secretive about their capabilities and scope. Unlike OAI, they would sell their services without question to the highest bidder. Their security was tight, and they owned a large tract of land, positioning their shop in the center. Clearly, the signs were pointing to something they wanted to keep under wraps. Jacob's Ladder was a subscription customer of Team Breakthrough's holo emitters. Everyone at OAI assumed Jacob's Ladder was projecting an AI's image inside its shop.

11

On Monday evening, Morgan was immersed in studying a segment of the short loop when she got a message from Taylor. The message asked Morgan to meet Taylor in her lab in an hour. Morgan made a note and went back to her work on the loop.

At their favorite restaurant in Boston, Taylor and Aiden were having a dinner meeting with the private space company that launched their satellites and constructed the moon base. They were discussing the launch of a new satellite and possible installation of a base on Mars.

"We have been warned by NASA, FAA, and the FCC if we drop anything else on the moon without prior approval from NASA, they will not approve any more launches into space," the young man said.

Aiden sighed. "I'm asking you to deliver a base to Mars, not the moon. NASA's orders were very specific to the moon. They did not mention Mars."

"While technically true, do you really believe they will accept that answer?"

"By the time our Mars base hits the Martian surface, they will have forgotten about the moon incident," Aiden said waving off the idea with a flip of his hand.

Taylor knew the only reason the company was willing to listen to Aiden's proposal was due to the large amount of business OAI gave them and the insane amount of money he had offered them to deliver a base to Mars.

"We are just asking you to think it over before saying no. Nothing more." Taylor took a drink of water. "You should eat your meal before it gets cold. I know Aiden wants to eat, and I'm hungry too."

"She's right. I'm hungry," Aiden said with a full fork of food nearly to his mouth.

Taylor smiled. She could never get over how Aiden would try the impossible regardless of the chance of success.

***

Morgan appeared in Taylor's lab one hour later.

"Taylor, are you here?"

It was a stupid question to ask because Morgan knew Taylor was not in the lab. The lab was monitored at all times, and she knew the comings and goings of every person and item that came into and went out of the lab. Because Taylor was late, she sent Taylor a message asking where she was.

Morgan noticed Taylor's data pad on a table in the lab. Taylor would normally have the data pad with her, but sometimes left without it by mistake. The light on the screen drew Morgan's attention. It didn't seem possible for the data pad to be on as it should have gone to sleep, at least if Taylor had not interacted with the device in the last few minutes. Morgan examined the data pad, and an app she did not recognize was on the screen. Morgan decided to connect to the device via the wireless network. She opened a data file that had been accessed within the last ten minutes. It was an empty plain text file. Finding nothing to help explain Taylor's absence, Morgan decided to leave Taylor's office and focus on her work back at OAI. She had made an exciting discovery while analyzing the shorter loop segment, which she shared with Eva. Taylor would message her when she arrived.

Morgan hadn't heard from Taylor several hours later, so she sent Aiden a message since she knew they had attended the dinner meeting together. She informed Aiden she got Taylor's message, and Taylor should call her when she got back to her lab. She also noted Taylor's data pad was in her office in case she was looking for it.

"I just got a message from Morgan," Aiden said as he looked at Taylor and back to his phone. "She says to tell you she got your message and you are to call her when you get back to your lab. Also, you left your data pad in your office in case you are looking for it."

Taylor looked at Aiden in confusion. "My data pad is right here. Why would she think otherwise?"

"I wonder why she is asking me to tell you this and not just messaging you?" Aiden read the message again. "I'm sending Eva a message and asking her to check on Morgan without Morgan knowing we are checking up on her. I just asked Eva how the weather was and then asked her to check on Morgan. Eva says the weather is stormy and Morgan is fine. Morgan just made a small discovery on the short loop."

Taylor looked at Aiden and tilted her head. "You asked how the weather was and then asked her to check on Morgan? I am sure Eva, an ultra-smart AI, didn't think that was strange at all. No, not one bit. We need to work on your small talk skills at some point, and we both need to get out more."

Aiden leaned his head back and stared at the ceiling. "I am not good at small talk."

"What is the status of the shorter loop?"

"We will not compile it until we have a much better understanding of what will happen when we do. Eva thinks she can build a virtual machine capable of containing the code if something gets out of hand. It sounds promising, but progress is slow. Following the NASA leak, Eva and Morgan have been focusing more on the longer loop but just recently started analyzing small segments of the short loop. We can't afford to mess this up, and we need to find out what is in the short loop first before someone else does. Eva assured me the code would not be compiled without everyone present."

***

Standing inside OAI's office, Eva and Morgan were working on some details regarding the alien messages.

"Eva, what do you make of this section of the loop here?"

Eva looked at Morgan while she ran a diagnostic on their communication subroutine. Everything came back within normal parameters. Morgan had just asked the same question two minutes prior.

"I'm sorry. Are you asking the same question you just asked me?"

"No. This is the first time I have asked the question."

Both looked at each other with confusion on their faces.

"It is not the first time you have asked the question."

Eva sent Morgan the internal conversation to review. Morgan took a nanosecond to respond.

"Something is wrong, and I don't know what. I have no record of that in my memory. Shut me down. Now!"

Eva shut Morgan down immediately. They would find out what happened when the power was cut off from Morgan whether they liked it or not. Eva then started locking down all data centers, preventing communication into or out of each facility. When possible, she killed the power. She sent Aiden a message, but his phone was not on. For the first time in her existence, Eva was afraid.

***

After the dinner meeting, Aiden and Taylor went back to OAI.

"Something is not right," Aiden said as they got out of the car.

Taylor craned her neck to get a better look. "It doesn't look right. Too many lights are off."

Someone was running down to them. It was Phil, the night guard. He was out of breath.

"Ms. Hart! Mr. Anders! We have a situation! The emergency lockdown protocol has been initiated. You need to get inside now!"

Aiden put his hand out to calm Phil. "Is everyone okay?"

"Yes, but we need to get moving. No one knows why we are on lockdown, but we need to stick to the emergency lockdown security measures. It will take a few minutes longer since you will go through two extra scans. Let's get you both inside."

Once in the building, they thanked Phil and headed down to sub-level four. Taylor had developed an emergency plan with Eva and Morgan when they were designing the building. When things went south, everyone in Team Breakthrough should report to sub-level four.

"Eva! Morgan!" Taylor called out. "Are you here?"

"I am here, but Morgan has been shut down. You will only hear my voice because I have locked down the holo emitters."

"You shut Morgan down?" Aiden gave Taylor a wide-eyed stare that she returned.

Eva relayed the events that had transpired since Aiden asked her to check on Morgan.

"Do you have any idea what is going on? Why did you engage the emergency lock down protocol at all OAI facilities?" Aiden was asking questions one after another.

"Morgan was unable to recall a question she had asked me two minutes prior. She had no recollection of asking the question at all. When I presented her with a copy of the conversation to review, she asked to be shut down immediately."

Taylor brushed her long hair out of her eyes. "Did you shut her down like she asked?"

"I shut Morgan down immediately after she demanded it. I then decided to lock everything down. All physical connections to the outside and to other OAI facilities have been physically disconnected. The satellites were placed in hibernation and will check in once per day to determine if it is safe to come back online," Eva's voice cracked. Taylor and Aiden gave each other side glances, realizing how serious the situation had become.

Eva relaxed her shoulders and regained her composure. She was unsure why or how her voice stumbled like that. "As to what is going on, I have a hypothesis. I believe someone has compiled the code from the short loop. I believe that code is dangerous, and it has made its way to the people it considers the biggest threat to its existence. I believe Morgan picked up an advanced malware or trojan horse. I also believe Taylor was being targeted when she was having all the trouble with her car pickups, power outage, data pad and phone battery issues."

"Both our phones died today, and that should not have happened." Taylor pulled out her phone as evidence.

While the holo emitters were shut down, Aiden wasn't sure where to look when addressing Eva. He decided to just stare at a speaker in the ceiling.

"I wonder why it went for Taylor and Morgan first?"

"I would have used the same approach. Taylor lives most of her life outside OAI. You spend most of your life in this building. You sleep here more than your own apartment. Morgan spends time with Taylor outside of OAI. That would be the easiest point of entry. The real question is how. I thought we had protected ourselves against this type of attack."

Taylor started reviewing the events leading up to this moment and realized she didn't have bad luck. She chided herself for not catching it more quickly.

"It appears the Quill's technology is far superior to our own."

"The most pressing question is how will we find the malicious code, delete it and protect ourselves from a future attack?" Aiden started pacing the floor, thinking about their next steps over the coming hours and days.

"I think I have the answer to that question, but you both better sit down. I am not sure how you will react to this news." Eva's voice had a hint of apprehension in it. "I will present the highlights and then get straight to the point."

Aiden and Taylor looked at each other and slowly sat on the nearest sofa. Aiden was starting to get a headache and Taylor's stomach was beginning to hurt.

12

After listening to Eva's theory on what had transpired leading to Morgan's shut down, Taylor and Aiden hardly uttered a handful of words. Aiden was sure it was going to be okay, but no one was very optimistic. Taylor was quietly thinking, and Aiden was trying to figure out what was going on in her head. Eva felt like she had possibly killed Morgan, her sister. The mood in the room felt like a funeral.

Aiden broke the silence. "Eva, you still haven't told us how you think you can isolate the malicious code, remove it, and protect us from this happening again. What can you tell us?"

"I believe what we suspect to be code from the short loop was just that. I believe it was simple code to be compiled on a Quill computer."

The thought of alien tech made Taylor uncomfortable. "Wait. A Quill computer? Explain."

"Yes, a Quill computer. Morgan's exciting discovery inside the short loop was instructions to build a simple device to compile the segment we believe to be code."

"So the Quill sent instructions on how to build a very

simple computer to run their very simple code? Clever," Aiden said to himself.

"Precisely. However, I don't think we need to assume that 'simple' means the same on Earth as it does for the Quill. Simple to the Quill may mean an advanced computer, time travel device, or a warp drive. It is hard to guess the purpose of the code, but I imagine it contains instructions for a more complicated device to run more sophisticated code. Who knows where it ends?"

Aiden looked over at Taylor who had the same solemn expression on her face.

"I don't like where this is going."

Talking to Eva without her holo image form was nothing unusual. Both Aiden and Taylor talked to her and Morgan quite often without looking at their holo image. During stressful times, having a holo image to look at was somehow more comforting for them.

Both Taylor and Aiden looked up at the ceiling when they heard Eva begin.

"Did Morgan's message to Taylor sound strange in any way? What made you ask about Morgan specifically?"

Aiden shifted in his seat. "Morgan sent me a message to relay to Taylor. She asked me to tell Taylor she got her message and to call her when she got back to her office. Then she mentioned Taylor's data pad was in her office."

Taylor raised her hand holding her data pad. "I was holding my data pad when Aiden read off the message. That is when we knew something was wrong. We were not sure why Morgan was messaging Aiden when she could have messaged me directly."

"This led us to ask you to check on Morgan." Aiden expected Eva to comment on his small talk.

"Don't forget the weather report. Your small talk needs improvement, Aiden. Asking me about the weather was a dead giveaway something was wrong."

Taylor perked up and smiled. "That's what I told him!"

"Let's stay focused on the problem," Aiden said with a sigh. "I believe the Quill computer has been assembled, and the code has been compiled. The list of organizations who could manage this in such a short time can be counted on one hand. OAI, NASA, Jacob's Ladder, Eri AI in Japan, and TSAI in China. I have ruled out Eri AI and TSAI. We gave the HPT to NASA. NASA is too cautious to charge ahead like this. However, they have used Jacob's Ladder for several projects in the past. I think the most likely answer is NASA handed over the HPT to Jacob's Ladder. Jacob's Ladder then built the computer and compiled the code."

"This confirms their CEO's reputation for being a real buckaroo in AI." The confidence in Eva's voice came through the speakers loud and clear. "We have always assumed they would sell their services to the highest bidder, and this seems to align with that assumption. To be fair, we will need to talk to NASA to see where this leads. They could be innocent, but I don't think that is likely."

"You still believe Taylor and Morgan were targeted because they were the easiest to reach with connections to OAI?" Aiden was still having a hard time understanding why the Quill code would single Taylor out. He chalked it up to alien tech he didn't understand.

"Yes. Taylor is the easiest target out of the four of us in that respect. It is possible Morgan discovered Taylor's data pad and accessed an alien virus without realizing it. The real question is how did Morgan become infected?" Eva said.

"Taylor, are you sure this is your data pad?" Aiden examined the data pad carefully.

Taylor took the device from Aiden and rotated it slowly

looking it over. "This is not my data pad. At least not my usual one. This is the one I keep in the office as a backup. How did my data pad infect Morgan?"

"Under normal circumstances I would ask the same question," Eva paused, "but these are not normal circumstances. My best guess is someone or something accessed the lab's network with more sophisticated technology than we have, either by disabling the security protocols or by some other means we do not know about."

Still examining her data pad, she thought about the implications of Eva's statement. Taylor knew getting by their security protocols would be close to impossible, so it had to be alien tech.

"This means the Quill code is the only known force able to carry out a ruse on this level?"

"Yes. OAI is the most dangerous threat to the Quill because we are the only force on Earth capable of stopping them. I assume Morgan's troubles were a small test of what the code could accomplish. I saw your phones exhibited more issues."

Aiden nodded. "Yes. Taylor's phone started malfunctioning first. Then, both of our phones died, and we couldn't contact you before heading back here."

"Remember our discussion regarding compiling the Quill code inside a virtual machine to contain any threat of something getting released?"

Aiden hesitated before answering Eva. "Yes."

"I have not completed the virtual machine, but I have a way to get one up and running fast. We will connect your phones and data pads to the virtual machine. We have an offsite backup of Aiden's phone from before the loop was discovered. Essentially, I will use the virtual machine to examine the differences between Aiden's phone backup and now. Then I can examine the malicious code and determine if it can be removed. If it can be removed, we can place better safeguards into our firewalls to help prevent this from happening again. Having removed the code here, I will use that information to sweep all OAI equipment to ensure the threat is neutralized. At least that is the plan. When dealing with alien technology, it is difficult to say what we will and won't accomplish."

"What are the potential problems with this plan?" Taylor asked.

"First, my plan could backfire and put everything at risk. Second, if the virtual machine is unsuccessful at finding the malicious code or removing the code, it will have to be shut down and destroyed. This would leave us in the same spot we are in now or in a worse position."

Aiden stared at the ceiling. "Losing everything was always on the table, and the possibility of being in a worse position is something I believe we all have thought about but not discussed outwardly. Why are you so concerned about losing a virtual machine?"

"Oh no! No, no no!" Taylor's throat started to feel tight.

Aiden looked over at Taylor not understanding what had upset her. He looked into Taylor's eyes, and he could see fear in them. "Taylor, what's wrong?"

"The virtual machine will be Morgan," Eva said.

***

"All of this was brought on by my bad assumptions," Aiden said.

"How do you figure that?" Taylor asked.

"I wanted to release the discovery to the world. I am responsible for Morgan's shutdown." Aiden slumped back in his seat.

"Morgan…" Taylor's voice quivered and trailed off. "I don't want to think of a world without Morgan." Knowing Morgan would live or die on a roll of the dice didn't seem fair to Taylor.

"I nullified our lead on the shorter loop by releasing the raw data with the compilable code segment to NASA," Aiden said.

Taylor composed herself for Aiden's sake. "We knew our lead on the short loop was not really a lead at all. You have to admit the Quill are clever for sending two loops. They knew what they were doing."

"They are broadcasting with some very serious power. Any radio signal that leaves Earth won't make it more than twenty light-years before it fades into interstellar noise. The Quill have sent a signal over five hundred light-years." Aiden stood up and walked over and blankly stared at the projected outside image on the window.

"Then there is the little fact that I asked Eva and Morgan to concentrate more on the longer loop." Aiden rubbed the back of his head. "If we had devoted more resources to figuring out the short loop first, we may have realized the danger that lay ahead. Then I go and trust NASA. What was I thinking?"

"You're blowing this out of proportion. 'Our' biggest mistake was trusting NASA. That is the only thing we as a team are guilty of doing. You are being way too hard on yourself and need to get over it right now. Let it go. It's over. We all had an equal voice, and we all share responsibility. We could have handled it very differently and still be in this situation, or worse," Taylor said.

"I know you're right, but I just can't let it go that easily. I learned a few lessons the hard way, but I'm not going to allow Makenna Townsend to keep ignoring my calls. I'm going to call Senator Jones and turn this mess around.

NASA has some explaining to do."

***

"Senator, it's Aiden Anders from OAI."

"I know who this is. Get on with it, son. I'm not getting any younger, and it's really late."

"I called Administrator Townsend at NASA just like we discussed. She accepted my offer of the radio array. I also gave her some very sensitive technology to decode the alien data, and someone compiled the code. It's running wild in cyberspace and has attacked OAI. I shouldn't have to tell you that our security is the best in the world, and we are on a complete lockdown. We are working on the hypothesis that NASA let the source code get out along with our HPT, which is the translation device we created. I had a good faith agreement with Administrator Townsend to keep the data confidential and work together slowly on this. She has let me down. Let us down."

"Getting calls in the middle of the night is never a good thing," the Senator said as he let out a long sigh. "Just how bad is this?"

Aiden wasn't sure if the Senator was being obtuse or reflexive with his question. He decided to play it safe and shoot him a straight answer.

"We discovered the shorter loop also describes how to build a Quill computer to compile and run the Quill code found in that loop. I can't imagine a worse scenario, Senator. Our operations are essentially shut down at the moment. We were attacked, and we are not sure how much damage has been done and if the damage can be reversed. We do know the Quill code was able to target our team and disrupt and modify the car service Taylor used along with her data pad and both of our phones.

Telecommunications have been compromised in the U.S. I am sure it is the same around the globe. We believe they came after OAI specifically because we represent the largest threat to the Quill," Aiden said.

"What do you mean by 'compile'?"

To Aiden, this was bordering on unbelievable. This was not the 1990s. Everyone should know basic programming terminology. Aiden took in a silent, deep breath. He thought about Morgan and then continued.

"When computer code is written, it is written in a high-level language, one that we can read and type. When the computer code is compiled, it is translated to a lower-level language, so the computer operating system can understand it. Does that make sense, Senator?" Aiden said.

"Perfectly. Thank you for your patience. You also mentioned instructions on how to build a Quill computer. What else can you tell me regarding this?"

"Inside the message are directions to build a simple Quill computer. It is important to remember that 'simple' is relative. It is simple enough for the Quill to tell us how to build it but what the code does when it is executed by the Quill computer is unknown. We don't have a gauge to measure what the Quill are capable of on a basic computing level."

"I understand. This is serious. Very serious. Not only is this a case of national defense, it is one of global defense."

"Where is the best place to start looking for the person responsible for the leak?" Aiden asked.

"Those pencil-head nerds at NASA don't like being shown up. OAI has outdone them for the better part of a decade. I am sure they seized their chance and couldn't wait to put you in second place. Now they have unleashed who knows what! I am sure the leak started at the top. Makenna was always too ambitious for her own good. She is too much like her momma. Anyway, what kind of 'agreement' did you have with Makenna?"

The Senator knew Administrator Makenna Townsend's mom? Aiden was glad he had not chosen politics as his career. He didn't have time for the drama.

"We agreed to cooperate with each other and not release the HPT outside of NASA. That is the short version. Nothing signed in writing, but a message was sent over with our requests. The Administrator agreed in principle over the phone with me. Where I come from, your word means more than a legally binding contract."

"I like you, Aiden. I really do. We both see a person's word as important as the person. You have explained the answers to my questions when most would have told me the details were not important. How fast can you get to Washington?" Senator Jones said.

"Two hours. But how about first thing in the morning, day after tomorrow? We can touch down at Reagan National at seven. Surely we could be in your office by eight if that's not too early," Aiden said.

"This is the best place to start our hunt for the leak. Send me your travel plans, and I will have someone pick you up."

"I'll send them over once all the details are finalized. I'll be flying in OAI's private jet. See you in two days."

Aiden found Taylor and brought her up to speed. Aiden asked Taylor to go with him to help answer any questions and be a second set of eyes and ears so he didn't miss anything.

"I feel I should stay here with Eva," Taylor said.

"You were essential in the creation of the HPT, and I think some hard questions are coming our way."

"Aiden, you were as much involved in the creation of the HPT as I was. We both are capable of answering the questions they will be asking—you more so since you talked directly to Makenna Townsend," Taylor said.

"Eva has the situation under control. A quick trip to Washington, and we will be back that evening. I wouldn't ask if I didn't think it was necessary."

"You make the arrangements, and I'll play tourist. We are taking the OAI jet?"

"I'll play tour guide, don't worry. And yes, we will be flying the OAI jet."

"I am surprised you are brave enough to fly knowing the Quill code is floating around the world. I am a little nervous," Taylor said.

"Who said I wasn't nervous? I'm scared to death, but I have to push through for Morgan's sake. Besides, we are running OAI hardware inside the plane. Somehow that makes me feel better."

"That makes you feel better?" Taylor asked.

"It's what I have to tell myself to get on the plane," Aiden said.

"I suppose we have to push through for the sake of humanity. I feel if we don't stop this, no one will."

"Wait. We need new phones, and you need a data pad. We need to get that all sorted out before we leave."

"You really think of everything, you know that?" Taylor said.

"Not really, but I do try. Let's get some sleep. I have a feeling we won't get many chances to sleep over the coming days. Let's make the most of it. See you in the morning. I'll let the chef on duty know to have our breakfast ready by six. We have a busy day tomorrow getting ready for this meeting."

***

On sub-level four, Eva was working on many issues at once. Morgan's absence and the possibility she may never return hung like a dark cloud over Eva's every thought. She had a strong feeling of motivation, and it pushed her to focus all her efforts on bringing back Morgan. She only hoped her work paid off.

Eva reviewed the holo emitter firmware against daily builds from before the Quill code. No differences could be spotted. She left the holo emitters on lockdown to be safe. No customers had contacted OAI to complain of erroneous problems or issues. Maybe the holo emitters would be okay, or maybe the Quill code was just waiting for the right moment. Would she even know the Quill code if she saw it? Would she be able to identify alien code on her own hardware?

Eva was alone in her mind running through more than ten sextillion calculations per second, thinking of endless possibilities of how to find and eliminate the malicious code. She also needed the capability to declare each system clean, but Eva was still working on how exactly this would be carried out.

Scenarios flooded her mind, and soon she created a list of the top ten thousand likely outcomes. Using each outcome, she worked through the scenario backwards trying to predict what led to Morgan being shut down.

The more Eva thought about the problem, the more clear the answer became. She now had a hypothesis on what happened to Morgan. She needed much more computational power than what was available to her. This may be easier than she first thought, but many things needed to work in her favor. Then she wondered if she was being over-confident. No, William of Ockham was correct all along. The explanation that makes the fewest assumptions is the answer one should choose. Eva had her plan.

13

"How was your breakfast?" Aiden asked as he and Taylor sat in the main cabin of OAI's small private jet. Since the jet was autonomous but still required a pilot in the seat, the jet could carry five passengers. The pilot never had much to do after loading luggage, but she had to be there nonetheless. Aiden liked the jet for many reasons, with efficiency being the main one.

"It was great. Thanks for asking. How did you sleep?" Taylor asked.

"I feel like I didn't get any sleep. I am still upset over this debacle. Just when you think the world has changed, someone has to go and prove you wrong."

"How was your breakfast?"

"Great. Are you kidding? I didn't have to cook it!"

Taylor laughed and went back to reviewing the latest updates from Eva. "Eva seems to think she has a plan for bringing Morgan back online and tracking down the malicious code."

"Did she say if she had determined exactly what happened to Morgan?"

"No. It was odd at first, but she essentially asked how

the weather was treating us," Taylor said.

"What? The weather?" His eyebrows squished together.

"She was taking a jab at your small talk, but I believe she was also delivering a hidden message to us. I told her the weather was fine, and she responded the weather was great and she couldn't wait for us to get back."

"I see. That is great news about having a lead on bringing Morgan back. She must not be comfortable sending out encrypted messages. Like they say, security by obscurity. I can't wait to get back and talk to Morgan again."

"Me, too. Powering up Morgan will be our first order of business when we return," Taylor said.

Captain Grant stepped into the cabin after completing her visual inspection outside the plane.

"Captain Grant, it's good to see you this morning. We need to get wheels up as fast as possible. It is going to be a long day," Aiden said.

"I understand, Mr. Anders. Good morning, Ms. Hart," Captain Grant said.

Captain Grace Grant had been with OAI for three years, and in that time, she had logged thousands of hours in the pilot's seat. She was polite, knowledgeable, but most importantly, she knew when to make small talk, give updates, and when to remain silent. She was the pinnacle of knowing how to do her job and doing it well every time.

***

Upon landing in Washington at Ronald Reagan Washington National Airport, the OAI jet was directed by air traffic control to a small hangar away from the main airport toward a section with what appeared to have a military presence. Aiden looked out the window and noticed a number of new private jets. Many of the jets were larger than OAI's jet, which was a small Honda jet meant for reliability and high fuel efficiency.

Parked outside the plane at the bottom of the stairs was a black vehicle with two young, stocky men waiting patiently. Taylor walked down the jet steps first, and Aiden followed. One of the men stepped forward toward Aiden, offering his badge and ID.

"Mr. Anders, we are here to escort you to Senator Jones' office," he said.

"Great. Taylor will be coming with us," Aiden said.

"We only have authorization to pick you up. No one else."

"That's a problem because I am not going anywhere without Taylor, so you better get something worked out. We are going to wait two minutes, and then we will walk to the nearest car service pickup and make our own way there."

"It's okay, Aiden," Taylor started to say.

One of the two men took a few steps back and dialed someone on his phone to try to resolve the issue with expediency.

"It's not okay, and I'm not leaving you behind. I didn't ask you to come with me to leave you at the airport." He shifted his gaze to the men. "We have thirty seconds before we turn around and start walking."

"I apologize, Ms. Hart. You are authorized to come along, too. We just received clearance from Senator Jones' office."

They opened the door to the Chevrolet Suburban, and Taylor and Aiden both got in. Taylor noticed the vehicle definitely had armored windows, and it sounded like reinforced door panels. It was most likely an armored vehicle used to transport high priority individuals. Taylor wondered if they had really underestimated the public reaction to possible alien life. Were their lives in danger because they had discovered the signal and translated the language? Or was it more likely the government wanted them to have a safe and quick trip so they could investigate a leak of colossal proportions within NASA?

"Armored car," Aiden said.

"Yeah. I was just thinking the same thing," Taylor said as she inspected the inside of the vehicle.

"I suppose they want to deliver us safely to the Senator's office. They also want us well-hydrated," Aiden said as he passed Taylor a bottle of water from the cooler between the seats.

"Let's just hope it is safe. I've had enough excitement for a while. I am beginning to regret coming with you. Everything is moving so fast, and it doesn't help that the entire world is freaking out about it."

"That's why I am here. I love making hasty decisions regarding the entire existence of humanity."

Taylor laughed and nearly spit out her water. Aiden chuckled too. The two tough guys in the front seats didn't even blink.

"What exactly are we going to do?"

"Senator Jones said this was the best place to start the search for who leaked the HPT. I assume we are going to discuss Makenna Townsend and her role in this. He didn't really give specifics now that you mention it. I was caught up in the moment and agreed to be here this morning. I really need to start asking more questions."

14

"Excuse me gentlemen, but where are we headed? This doesn't look like we are headed toward Senator Jones' office," Aiden said from the second row of seats.

One of the men turned around. "We are headed to the Pentagon. You will meet Senator Jones there. We are in charge of getting you there. That's all I know. I apologize for any misunderstanding."

"Okay then," Taylor said with uncertainty in her voice.

"No problem. Thinking back on it, I was never told where we would be meeting. Just that we would be picked up at the airport," Aiden said.

Taylor and Aiden exited the armored Suburban and were immediately met by two soldiers with heavily-decorated uniforms. They were not much different in demeanor than their previous chaperones. The soldiers escorted Aiden and Taylor through a quick security check where they were issued badges, told to leave their phones and data pads, and then ushered into the Pentagon to meet with Senator Jones.

"Good day, Aiden. I want to compliment your choice of shoes. Your green Crocs look comfortable," the Senator said with a chuckle. "I have not had the pleasure of meeting you in person, Ms. Hart. I'm Senator Matthew Jones."

"It is nice to see you in person, Senator. Aiden has had nothing but glowing things to say about you," Taylor said.

"All lies, I'm sure." The Senator was a natural charmer and could work a room without any trouble.

Taylor seemed to like the Senator fine, but she would not be sucked in by his charm. It took a long time to earn her trust. Aiden liked Senator Jones almost immediately, but Aiden was more easily won over.

"I hope my unexpected presence was not an issue."

"It was not a problem for me. I had to stamp my feet a bit, but I felt it was worth getting you in here. Security didn't like it at all. In fact, no one in this room liked it, but the truth is you are just as much a part of this as Aiden. You two are something special and represent a turning point in human history. I am glad you both made it to the meeting today, and I am excited to hear what you have to say to our audience. If you don't mind me asking, how did Aiden get you here?"

"Aiden thought it was important I come with him and help answer any questions that arise."

"I didn't realize you two still worked together. I thought after MIT you both went your separate ways?"

"Many people get that idea. We both keep low profiles. I do work at MIT as a research professor in my own lab, but Aiden and I are still partners in our holo emitter business. He comes over to my lab and visits, and I sometimes work on projects at OAI."

As they approached an open door, the Senator turned to look at a host of important-looking people, some in military uniforms and clearly high-ranking. Taylor didn't know much about the medals and brass hanging off the uniforms, but she knew a general when she saw one.

Taylor noted there were about fifty people in the good-sized room. No cameras, no recording devices, and no one was allowed to bring in any electronics. Armed guards stood at the door, and Taylor wasn't sure if this was for their protection or just to keep out people who may take a wrong turn. She wasn't sure how anyone would take a wrong turn in the Pentagon, but she mused it could happen anywhere.

Aiden spotted Gavin Wilson sitting next to Makenna Townsend. Makenna had made brief eye contact with Aiden and quickly looked away. That was all the confirmation Aiden needed to know that she broke their agreement. That would be the last time he trusted her with anything. He also noted he probably shouldn't trust her mom either, just in case he ran into her at some point.

Gavin was studying a piece of paper on the table in front of him. A curious woman sat on Gavin's left. She was also studying the paper in front of Gavin, and she didn't look pleased to be here. He would have to ask who she was afterwards.

Aiden walked up beside Taylor and whispered, "Don't look now, but Gavin Wilson is to my left in the dark shirt with 'Jacob's Ladder' written on the front. Makenna Townsend is sitting beside him to his right."

Taylor immediately turned and looked.

Aiden rolled his eyes. "Didn't I just tell you not to look?"

"I'm not used to being around so many serious and powerful people. I'm nervous. This is the kind of thing you see in movies," Taylor lamented.

"Fair enough. I do feel like we are in a movie right now. Who would've thought our day would start with us inside the Pentagon in a room full of generals, admirals, senators, and other politicians I've only seen on the internet or on the vid feeds."

"Everyone, let's take our seats and get started," an older man dressed in civilian clothing said. "We are here to discuss the recent discovery of alien life and the message Earth has received. There are many things we need to discuss, and the foremost among them is national security."

"Give me a break," Taylor mumbled under her breath. "National security? How about security for the entire solar system?"

"Are you watching the woman beside Gavin? The one with the long blonde hair? Do you recognize her?" Aiden asked.

"I do not. Should I?"

"I don't know. I'm trying to figure out who she is and what her connection to this is. She seems to know Gavin Wilson."

"It would appear so. Maybe he didn't come alone either."

"Maybe."

"Is there something you would like to add to that, Mr. Anders and Ms. Hart?" the gentleman in control of the conversation asked. "I can't imagine what is so important that you both can't control yourselves for ten minutes so we can have a serious conversation."

Taylor thought she heard a snicker from Makenna Townsend's side of the room. Then Administrator Townsend directed a pompous smile across the room at Taylor. Taylor's face flushed red.

Aiden decided he should speak up because Taylor was looking at the table pretending to concentrate on something else. Aiden felt like he was being called out in school, but he knew exactly how to handle these types of situations.

"We gave NASA the alien message along with software to decode the data, and Administrator Townsend leaked that data to Gavin Wilson of Jacob's Ladder. Jacob's Ladder then built the alien Quill computer and compiled the Quill code included in the message. That was a reckless and careless thing to do. I had warned Administrator Townsend against this, and she had agreed to terms that would prevent this. The code has already infiltrated the telecommunications systems around the globe and quite possibly more. You have to assume the Pentagon, White House, Department of Defense, and every other nation's government and military systems have been compromised. This is all due to Administrator Townsend breaking our agreement not to hand the data over to a contract AI shop. We all have Administrator Townsend to thank for this mess!"

Dead silence filled the room. Administrator Townsend sat with a look of complete disbelief on her face. Gavin Wilson wore a look of indifference. The woman beside Gavin looked sick. Senator Jones stared at Administrator Townsend with a blank expression. The Secretary of Defense was not happy with Aiden but was even more unhappy with Administrator Townsend. He stared a hole through her.

Aiden sat smiling like he was in school getting called out for something senseless, only to change the subject on the teacher and completely take everyone by surprise. He had really outdone himself this time. The only problem with what he had just stated as fact to everyone in the room was Aiden didn't know for sure if it was true. He suspected everything he had just said was factual but didn't have solid evidence to back up his claims. He felt better that Makenna Townsend looked uncomfortable. That meant he was on the right track.

The older gentleman who called the meeting to order stood up.

"I think this is a good time for a ten minute break. Mr. Anders, Senator Jones needs to speak with you to explain proper protocol for meetings inside the Pentagon."

Aiden recognized that tone when he heard it. That was a nice way of telling Aiden he would get a good scolding for his outburst, and he was already dreading his talk with Senator Jones.

Taylor quickly got up and walked out of the room. Aiden's eyes followed Taylor as she walked through the doors leading into the hallway. This alarmed Aiden because he wasn't sure if Taylor was leaving because of the massive bluff he just pulled off or if she was just taking advantage of the brief intermission. Aiden's smile weakened a bit, but it was still there.

***

Taylor had watched as the woman beside Gavin Wilson walked out after the short break was called. Taylor knew Aiden was putting up a monster bluff, but she also knew it was true. She also felt that this woman was somehow involved in the leak. Taylor was determined to find out more about her.

Taylor caught up to her in the hallway. "Excuse me. My name is Taylor Hart. I don't believe we've met."

The young lady turned around to face Taylor. "I'm Savannah, Savannah Fisher. It's great to finally meet you." Savannah looked around to make sure she was not being watched.

What, Taylor thought, did Savannah mean by "finally meet you" and why was she so anxious? Taylor was confused but didn't allow her emotions to show on her face. "Let's step into the ladies' room and talk there."

"Have we met before?" Taylor asked.

"No, but I'm a big fan of your work in AI. I have always wanted to meet you but not under these circumstances."

Taylor's eyes widened and she looked around. She decided to check each stall in the bathroom to make sure they were the only two people present.

"This is the Pentagon, and I wouldn't put it past some paranoid general to bug a restroom. Can we get together after the meeting today?" Taylor asked.

"Yes. I am not sure how, but we need to meet today."

Taylor was again taken aback by the phrasing. We "need" to meet? Why?

"Give me your contact information. I will send you a message as soon as we leave the building."

Savannah passed her a hand written note with a contact address on it.

"Only contact me here. Don't use my Jacob's Ladder information. It is monitored."

"Okay. I will contact you after we leave here. Are you okay? Who is monitoring you? Who were you looking for back in the—"

"Listen, I have to get back. I want you to know everything Aiden just said is the truth. Every word of it was true. It's even worse. I've been gone too long. I need to get back to the meeting." Savannah rushed out of the restroom, and Taylor stood looking after her with more questions than answers. She now knew Savannah's name and had confirmed Aiden's theory about the leak, but the part about it being even worse seemed to be a huge mystery. She washed her hands and returned to the meeting.

***

In the meantime, Senator Jones had gotten up and motioned Aiden to a corner of the room away from everyone else.

"Aiden, I didn't know you had that in you. Bravo! I couldn't have done that any better myself, but there is something you need to know about these military officials. They are very serious individuals and value protocol. They expected a full day of questioning every minute detail, and you just bypassed all of that with some weighty accusations. I suspect you know your outburst led to the break."

"I didn't like being singled out like that. We are all adults, and if I have something to say, I am going to say it. However, my parents raised me better than that, and I know when I have been rude. I'll behave myself going forward, and I apologize for being rude."

"You misunderstand me, son. I don't want you to change anything about how you are acting. I couldn't tell if what you said in there was the truth or a bluff, but I did see guilt all over Administrator Townsend's face."

Aiden would keep the bluff going. He was already all in, and he planned to stay there. "Time is something we don't have a lot of. I understand what you're saying, but I don't know if everyone else in that meeting understands how serious this is."

"I understand that time is a precious commodity right now. I am telling you this so you can use it to our advantage. You need to control the conversation and steer it forward, or we will be here all day with these fine people answering dull questions that will lead to a continuation tomorrow." Senator Jones tugged at his shirt collar. "When the opportunity presents itself, make use of it to forward our goal of getting to the bottom of why NASA leaked the data and allowed it to be compiled on an alien computer. I will help you and have your back. Don't you worry about that."

"Thank you. I will accelerate the conversation forward at the first opportunity."

"You just ripped all credibility from Makenna. She won't last as NASA Administrator. The President is already looking for a replacement. It's time we get back to our seats. Just keep being you."

"Do I need to look like I just took a good scolding?" Aiden asked.

"Just keep it neutral so everyone is left guessing what we talked about."

Taylor walked back into the room, quickly glanced around to find Aiden, then nervously squeezed past the people still standing to make her way back to her seat.

"The woman beside Gavin is Savannah Fisher. She works at Jacob's Ladder as his head engineer. Something is very wrong because she kept looking over her shoulder and saying weird things. She did confirm everything you said was true but also said it's much worse than that. I feel we can trust her, but I can't be one hundred percent sure yet," Taylor said.

"So you left the room to follow Savannah?"

"Obviously. Why else would I leave?"

"Oh. I was thinking maybe for a bathroom break or because of my outburst."

"I told Savannah I would contact her when we get out of here. We need to hurry this up. She looked physically ill in the bathroom over the news she was holding back. I get the feeling Jacob's Ladder and NASA have really messed up."

"Can everyone please take his or her seat?" the older

gentlemen running the meeting announced. "Administrator Townsend, do you have anything to say to what Mr. Anders shared with us before our break? Please be brief and honest because we don't have the time to settle this matter through normal channels. Aiden's accusations are serious, and if true, they threaten the entire world."

"It is true that I agreed not to release the HPT, the translator that converts the alien signal to something we can use, out of NASA custody. However, I thought in the best interest of NASA, I had to break that agreement," Administrator Townsend said.

Defense Secretary Howard became red faced and stood up to address Makenna Townsend directly. "Did you allow Jacob's Ladder to build an alien computer and compile alien code?"

"Yes sir."

"Do you mind explaining why you thought NASA could make such a decision and not even consult with me or anyone else?"

Aiden couldn't stay quiet. "Gavin, did you have the Quill computer connected to your network after compiling?"

Everyone's attention went straight to Gavin Wilson. Only Savannah looked at Aiden. Why, Aiden thought, is she looking at me?

"Yes, but only at Administrator Townsend's request," Gavin said.

It was clear Gavin would only answer the questions asked to him directly with the shortest answer possible and with no extra details. His answers would also hinge on shifting responsibility to someone else.

"How many Quill computers have you built for NASA?" Aiden asked.

"We built three Quill computers for NASA," Gavin

said. Gavin appeared unconcerned, and this was disconcerting to Aiden and Taylor. After Aiden looked around the room, he realized everyone else noticed the lack of concern on Gavin's face. The sideways looks and whispering between people seemed to confirm his observation of Gavin.

"What is it that you are not telling us?" Defense Secretary Howard said in a steely voice.

Gavin didn't miss a beat. "Secretary Howard, I am not sure what you mean. I have built and delivered three Quill computers to NASA. The Quill computers were built to specifications inside the Quill message we decoded using the HPT that Administrator Townsend provided to us. It is true the equipment used did have network capability and access to the internet. I am unsure if Quill technology is compatible with our existing computer tech. Is there something specific you would like to ask me?"

The Defense Secretary continued to question Gavin and Administrator Townsend for another hour until he was satisfied he could make a complete report to the President.

The actions of Makenna Townsend and Gavin Wilson would be at the top of Defense Secretary Howard's report. In the eyes of Defense Secretary Howard, when it came to national security, everyone was guilty until proven innocent. He was unsure what to make of Aiden Anders and Taylor Hart. In his opinion, they created the entire mess.

A ten minute break was called, and Aiden and Taylor stood up.

"We really need to get back to OAI, Senator. Our time is more valuable spent there doing something rather than here doing nothing," Aiden said.

"You don't just waltz in and out of the Pentagon at your leisure," Senator Jones said with a tone that a parent takes with a child. "I strongly advise you both to stay until you are formally dismissed." Senator Jones motioned for General Graves to make his way over to him.

General Graves and the Senator stepped a small distance away from everyone in the room. "General, would you mind dismissing Taylor Hart and Aiden Anders so they can leave and get to work on this problem?"

"We have more questions to ask," General Graves said.

"I also have questions of my own I would like to ask, but I'm afraid time is against us."

"I agree. We have national security measures to discuss, and I am becoming very annoyed with a certain NASA employee. They are formally dismissed."

***

When entering the Pentagon, Taylor wasn't even on the guest list, and she and Aiden were able to get in faster than they got out. On the way in, they were rushed through because they were on the time schedule of the Pentagon. When leaving, they left at a slower pace and had to complete a few forms they had skipped on their way in.

Taylor was rushing to get out, and Aiden was wondering what was going on.

"Everything okay?" Aiden asked.

"Everything is fine," Taylor said as she pushed her hair behind her ears.

He knew better than to press her for the real reason she was trying to rush out of the Pentagon. When Taylor got anxious, she usually adjusted her hair in some way.

"We'll be on the jet soon enough."

Taylor gave him a quick glance that told him they were not headed back to the jet. Where, Aiden thought, are we going before we head back to the airport? He started to suspect it had something to do with her brief conversation with Savannah, but he couldn't imagine what the hurry was.

"Why do you think they let us out of the meeting so soon?" Aiden asked.

"I suspect they wanted to talk national defense and assign the Quill to the troubles they have been observing in other countries. That's just a guess though."

"It makes sense."

Their new security detail back to the airport was comprised of two women wearing clothes that screamed Secret Service. They rode in another black Suburban, but this model seemed less tank and more car. Sounds of the exhaust were more audible than the car they arrived in, so Taylor assumed this model was lightly armored, if at all. As soon as they passed through the last gate, Taylor leaned forward between the seats.

"We need to be dropped off at the local mall."

Aiden turned his head as slowly as he could to look at Taylor. He wasn't expecting to make a stop before they went back to the airport. Taylor noticed Aiden staring at her, but she kept her eyes on the agent in the passenger seat and waited for a reply.

"I'm sorry, but we have orders to take you directly back to your plane. We cannot deviate from that plan without authorization," she said.

"Can you request authorization?" Taylor asked.

The agent sighed. "Ma'am, this would go much easier if we could just return you to your plane and then you can —"

"Either you drop us off at the nearby mall, or I am going to open this door and leave at the next red light. If you've already locked these doors so we can't let ourselves out, you'll have to answer to Senator Jones when I get him on the phone. Please ask for authorization to drop us off at the local mall. I have some shopping to do before we head back, and I don't want to waste another minute talking about this," Taylor said with conviction in her voice.

The agents didn't appear concerned until Senator Jones' name was brought up. They looked at each other and shrugged. The passenger side agent called in the request, and after a tense minute or two, Aiden and Taylor were standing on a sidewalk in front of a mall.

"So what was that all about, and what are we doing here?" Aiden asked.

"One second." Taylor pulled out her phone and messaged Savannah. "I told Savannah I would contact her the second we got out of the Pentagon."

"I thought this stop may have something to do with her, but I'm not sure why we're here. Is she going to meet us here?"

"Yes. I mean, I hope. I'm not really sure."

"You wanna grab a burger? It seems we've landed right in front of lunch."

"Yeah. Let's go in and grab lunch. We can wait to see if Savannah responds. I sent her our location and told her we are headed in to have lunch."

"I'm gonna go out on a limb and predict that since she told you it was much worse, Gavin wasn't telling the entire story."

"I'm crossing my fingers you're wrong. I really want to get back and check on Morgan. I don't like the fact we haven't received a recent update from Eva," Taylor said.

"While we wait, would you like me to order for us?"

"Please," Taylor said.

The restaurant had flat screens hung around the ceiling. While they were waiting, Taylor and Aiden watched one of the news feeds, something they rarely did these days. Suspicious reports from around the globe, including the U.S., China, Europe, Russia and Australia, were starting to pop up. The news was labeling it as the work of hackers. Taylor and Aiden knew the culprit was most likely the Quill code. Malware was common but not generally on this scale. There was little doubt left as to why they were granted their request to leave the Pentagon so quickly. They wondered how much damage the U.S. had already suffered.

After their meal, Aiden and Taylor decided they had waited long enough when Taylor's phone chimed with a message from Savannah.

"We have to meet her at Virginia Highlands Park. It's just a few minutes from here," Taylor said. Aiden pulled out his data pad and started tapping on the screen to pull up directions. Taylor drummed her fingers on the table while staring out the window.

"Any idea what you are going to say?"

"I'm going to play this one by ear. I think she wants to dump everything she knows on us, and I am going to see how far that will take us."

"I'll follow your lead when we get there."

15

When they approached the entrance to the park, they immediately started looking around for signs of Savannah. A message alert sounded on Taylor's phone.

"Her message says to walk due east. I guess we follow this sidewalk," Taylor said.

"This has to be the oddest place to meet. In the movies, it seems like all the spies like to meet around water. We're not near water."

The alert for an incoming message brought Taylor's eyes to her phone.

"It just says to wait here."

"I guess we—"

"Pssssstt! Over here," Savannah said.

"Hi, Savannah. Are you okay?" Taylor asked.

"I don't have much time," Savannah said.

"Start at the beginning," Taylor said.

"I was a freshman at MIT in computer science when you gave your presentation for senior design. I even asked a question at the end of the presentation, right before you both darted out. Why did you both leave so abruptly?"

When Taylor said to start at the beginning, neither

Taylor nor Aiden thought Savannah would go back to her freshman year at MIT.

"What question did you ask us?" Aiden asked.

"I asked how you managed to pull your project off in one semester," Savannah said.

"I don't remember much after the presentation except for a few questions and then heading out to eat," Aiden said.

"You both left to go eat?" Savannah asked.

"Not exactly. Is this relevant?" Taylor asked.

"No, but I was always curious. I was there by chance that day. I happened to hear senior design projects were being presented when I was walking by the auditorium. I walked in to get a glimpse of what I would be doing in a few years. Once I saw Morgan on that screen and how she interacted with everyone, any doubts I had about true AI disappeared. After you both left and everyone started talking to Morgan, I knew I had just witnessed a watershed event. You both literally changed the course of mankind that day."

Taylor and Aiden were speechless. Aiden was still trying to place her. He thought he knew everyone back at MIT, but the more he thought about it, he really only remembered a fraction of the students around him. He really only knew the class ahead, behind, and the class he was in. He didn't interact with others outside of those circles because he was too busy studying.

Taylor was sure she didn't remember Savannah, and she questioned if Savannah was really at MIT with them. Her story matched the account of that afternoon but by this time that story had been recited in documentary movies, news broadcasts, books, and the internet tens of thousands of times. Anyone could've done a little research and stated the story as fact. Taylor needed verification

Savannah was telling the truth.

"Professor Davis," Taylor stated. "What was her favorite pastime?"

"Listening to good stories," Savannah said.

"I guess that settles it. You seem to have been at MIT," Taylor said.

"I was there, and I'll never forget it. You are every bit as clever and smart as you are made out to be in the media, Ms. Hart."

"Call her Taylor. I do," Aiden said.

"Is that okay, Ms. Hart?"

"Yes. Of course. Please, call me Taylor. Ms. Hart sounds like my mom. I'm not that old yet."

"I hate to rush this along, but you said you didn't have much time," Aiden said.

"You're right, of course. I need to move this along. I have about twenty more minutes before they miss me."

"Why all the secrecy?" Aiden asked.

"We built NASA three computers at their request. Gavin had the code from the message compiled in our shop, and we lost a significant amount of hardware from what we thought was a virus. We now suspect the code we compiled had an auto execution string attached to it and launched the program without our consent. Upon execution, the code infiltrated our hardware and shorted out almost everything. Our firewall was damaged. I don't have much to go on, but it's my best guess we have three separate low-level Quill worms running about the internet. When we delivered our results to Administrator Townsend, she didn't have the code compiled at NASA. She locked the equipment up and decided to be cautious and wait."

"Sounds just like Administrator Townsend," mumbled Aiden.

"Our AI was affected and is still offline. We are unsure if we can bring her back online. Gavin was playing the part of an innocent bystander in there because Makenna said she would have his back if he didn't divulge facts he wasn't asked about. To be honest, he was embarrassed it all went so wrong. More so when he knew that OAI would find out NASA had passed us the HPT."

"Why do you suspect three different Quill worms? Why not one or four?" Taylor asked.

"Because we compiled the code on each computer once. Each time we experienced some damage to our internal infrastructure. Gavin felt we would find some advantage locked away in that code to allow Jacob's Ladder to become the preeminent AI shop," Savannah said. She dropped her head, clearly embarrassed by the implication.

"Don't worry about that. We don't view this as a game. We just want the world to be a better place," Taylor said.

"I know. It's just that, well, I wanted to do something to get your attention so I could be sure you both knew my name and what I have accomplished. I guess that is all over now. This has all turned into a big mess and eventually my name and Gavin's name will be tied to it. It's just a big, deadly mess."

Taylor and Aiden froze. Savannah looked up at both of them to see their questioning looks.

"What do you mean, 'deadly mess'?" Aiden asked slowly.

"Do you remember the Mars Mission resupply launch being pushed off a week? Then they announced it was being pushed out another week due to a late arrival of supplies?"

"Yes," Taylor said.

"They are not waiting on supplies for the colonists on Mars. NASA has been infected by the Quill code and has delayed for fear of a launch malfunction. They are waiting on Gavin to deliver an antivirus software to remove the Quill code," Savannah said.

"Did Gavin or Makenna make this known today in the meeting?" Aiden asked.

"They did, but Gavin left out the part regarding the Jacob's Ladder AI being offline with no timetable to get her back up and running. Without our AI, there will be no antivirus, if that's even possible."

"Why didn't he just ask us for help?" Taylor asked.

"I'm not sure. I've been begging for just that. Everyone has been talking about how OAI dropped all connections to the outside, so we assumed you had been hit too. Is it true? Are Morgan and Eva offline?"

"Eva is fine. Morgan is fine, too. We have had some damage but our assessment hasn't revealed much beyond some minor hardware failures at this point," Aiden said.

Aiden turned to Taylor, hoping she wouldn't reveal Morgan was actually offline. While Savannah appeared to have honest motives and stories that matched a believable account, Aiden wanted to remain neutral and not hand Savannah any information that may be passed along for her own personal gain. It was better to let everyone think their office was fine instead of telling them they were on the brink of death.

Taylor seemed to agree with this approach. She nodded in agreement when Aiden told the white lie regarding Morgan's condition.

Savannah's phone alarm chimed.

"Time's up. I have to go. Can I contact you if I need to?" Savannah asked.

"Yes, please. Can I do the same?" Taylor said.

"Absolutely!"

"Nice meeting you," Aiden said. "Thank you for the

information. I know you are taking a big risk telling us this information."

Savannah Fisher gave a quick wave and disappeared around a corner.

"She was in a hurry to get somewhere," Aiden said.

"Yes she was. I suspect she stopped off to 'buy' something while the others went back to the airport. If everything she said was true, she is taking a big risk."

"Why do you say that?"

"Because I know you, and you won't let the Mars Mission launch information slide. Those colonists are depending on those supplies. NASA already lost one launch a month ago, and the news feeds clarified that if the next mission fails, it may mean some of the colonists will die. This launch has to be a success," Taylor said.

"We know each other so well. Let's get back to OAI."

***

When Captain Grant spotted the car approaching with Taylor and Aiden, she had started her system checks. It was always easy to know if Aiden or Taylor were in a car. They were two of the richest people on the planet and still used ordinary car services when it made sense. It was nice to know they had not lost touch with everyone around them.

Taylor and Aiden boarded the plane and were greeted by Captain Grant for the second time that day. Captain Grant knew by the look on their faces small talk was out. It was still a serious day for her bosses, and she would play her part to the best of her ability.

Once the system checks were complete, Captain Grant requested clearance to depart. Most pilots wasted valuable time by waiting until the passengers had boarded to start the procedures. With Captain Grant's attentiveness, it was only a quick ten minute wait before departure. This was just another reason she was senior pilot at OAI.

"Have you heard from Eva?" Aiden asked.

"No. I am sending her a message asking for an update," Taylor said.

"She may not respond. I bet she still has everything on lockdown until Morgan becomes functional again. I can't blame her."

"I would like to know more about what exactly transpired at Jacob's Ladder to cause all of this trouble. NASA must have had plans to put three different teams on the Quill computers."

"Eva said the code could be compiled and possibly contained inside a virtual machine. She was still working on the design to ensure containment. Gavin must have rushed the process not thinking about the consequences." Aiden handed Taylor a bottle of water. They both preferred their water at room temperature. It was just one of the many things they had in common. It also seemed to keep everyone else from drinking their water.

"You should contact Gavin to check if he is interested in sharing information in order to get his AI back up. It may help us with Morgan."

"I'll send him a message right now. I'll offer to have Eva review the data for him to determine if we can help."

Taylor leaned her chair back and stared toward the ceiling of the plane. Her body was starting to really feel the enormity of the situation. She began rubbing her temples.

"If NASA is buying time on these launches and not telling anyone the real reason why, that is beyond dangerous. That is premeditated murder in my book." With her eyes shut, Taylor went on. "The mission commander for Mars, Braxton Lee, has been giving the news feeds constant updates on food supplies, material needs, staffing requirements, and medical needs. I don't think anyone thought about sending one hundred colonists to Mars only to have forty-one colonists die within a year of landing. Martian life has proven to be difficult."

"Being a colonist on Mars is dangerous for sure," Aiden said. "Other countries have volunteered for resupply missions. If they are having trouble too, this is unavoidable. I understand the need for launch delays, I just don't understand the need to lie about the reason for the delay other than to save face in front of the world."

The decompressive accident that led to forty-one colonists' deaths had shocked the world. The loss of most of the medicine, medical, and engineering equipment was devastating. The accident happened on live television, streaming on the cameras set to look back at the Mars colony. It nearly led to the recall of all the colonists if not for the work of Commander Braxton Lee. Commander Lee essentially said they were not pulling up stakes. They would forge ahead and not return. In a vote by all the colonists, it was unanimous that no colonist would willingly come back to Earth. The nations involved had no choice but to keep the supply missions on schedule and get new recruits on Mars. After the accident, recruiting wasn't as easy as it had been. Everyone on Earth understood the stakes were high and possibly deadly. No one would forget that anytime soon.

"NASA is playing a dangerous game if they push forward with a launch," Taylor said.

"We have a saying for that in Tennessee: 'Play stupid games, win stupid prizes.' I will not allow NASA to fumble this opportunity like they have everything else. Do you believe I should contact Senator Jones today and tell him what we were told?"

"I think we should get back to OAI and check on the status of Morgan. Then we can discuss what to do. We have a few days until launch. Waiting another twelve to twenty-four hours shouldn't be a problem. Besides, I bet the Senator is still in his meetings."

"Buckle up!" Captain Grant yelled as buzzers and alarms sounded. The plane shuddered and shook. Captain Grant had taken control of the flight stick by necessity for the first time in her career at OAI. She had plenty of simulator time and occasionally took control of the stick to maintain her pilot certification. She didn't know what was going on, but she was determined to maintain her clean flight record. "We lost cabin power but we are back up. We had already started our descent. Attempting to restart the engines! It's going to be close!"

Taylor and Aiden gripped their seats with all the strength they could muster. Aiden leaned forward to look into the cockpit to see if he could see anything that would help him figure out what was going on. Taylor looked out the cabin windows to get her bearings. Clear blue skies extended to the horizon. They were descending fast, but she couldn't see ahead of the jet from the cabin window.

Captain Grant fought the stick and shouted voice commands. The power in the cabin had come back on, but the engines had yet to fire back up. She was no stranger at keeping a cool head in an emergency.

"Finally!" Captain Grant shouted. "It's going to be really close! Thirty seconds from the ground! Twenty seconds! Ten seconds! Brace for impact!"

The brace for impact statement pushed any remaining hope of living from Aiden's mind. He had resolved this was how his life would end: crashing into the ground, a statistical anomaly in an age where the last recorded death from a jet plane was four years ago in a freak accident on the ground. He had wanted to at least visit the moon base before he died. He had to laugh about that being his final thought.

Bang! A dull thud followed by tires screeching reverberated through the cabin.

"Apologies for the rough landing. We are on the ground and A-OK," Captain Grant said with relief in her voice.

"Are you okay, Aiden?" Taylor asked.

"Yeah. I thought we were going to hit the ground and explode on impact. I had resigned that this was the end."

Taylor laughed. "You need to be more positive. But let's both agree the next time we are nervous about flying, we don't fly."

"Agreed! When Captain Grant said 'brace for impact,' that didn't inspire confidence."

"Mr. Anders, I apologize for that statement," Captain Grant said. "I knew it was going to be a rough landing, and we did cut it close. Our wheels touched down in the grass just before the asphalt of the landing strip started. I wasn't sure how the plane would react to landing in the grass, and I wanted you and Ms. Hart to be prepared."

"Yeah, you silly goose! You should have just looked out the windows and you would have understood better," Taylor said.

Aiden laughed. "Yeah, I guess my reaction does seem kind of silly now that we're on the ground. I don't care though. We lived!"

Taylor just rolled her eyes. Captain Grant lowered her professional guard and laughed out loud. She even gave Aiden a high-five as he exited the plane.

"How about I get some real stick time in the air over the coming weeks?" Captain Grant asked.

"I'll approve whatever request you put on my desk. Great flying, Captain," Aiden said with enthusiasm. "Put this plane in the hangar, and it is not to fly again until Eva gives it the okay. I want you to devote your time overseeing the diagnosis of what just went wrong."

"Don't worry. I have a stack of paperwork to fill out for the FAA. I am sure the National Transportation Safety Board will want the data logs along with interviews with all three of us. Any time something like this happens, it results in an endless stream of questions and paperwork. I am just glad I am here to answer the questions and fill out the paperwork. If you will excuse me, I will get that process started."

With shaky legs, Aiden and Taylor plopped down in the awaiting car and headed to OAI.

16

Immediately after getting settled in the car, Taylor quickly typed a message to Eva regarding the plane losing power and the close call she and Aiden had on landing. There was no doubt the Quill had targeted them again. They got lucky, but they had no idea why the Quill didn't take the plane down in a catastrophic failure. How was Captain Grant able to regain power to the plane? Aiden and Taylor swore off flying until they received conclusive proof everything was free and clear of any Quill contamination.

A large frown appeared on Taylor's face. Her eyes narrowed a bit as she looked outside as their car pulled up to OAI. Aiden scanned the area, looking for what had caused Taylor to frown. Aiden knew her look well, and it meant something was not right. OAI looked as it had this morning when they left for D.C. The building was still dark and on lockdown.

"What's wrong?" Aiden asked.

"That reporter Kristi Hopkins is waiting around outside. She's talking to Phil."

"She always talks to Phil when she shows up. I always

thought she was trying to get information on our comings and goings. Do you believe it's more than that?"

"I do. I don't think she just randomly shows up at OAI out of the blue as global reports are coming in regarding a 'computer virus'."

"Maybe she just wants a statement from OAI on our opinion and nothing else."

"Maybe, but I have a feeling there's more to it than that."

"Should I have the car circle around and go in the secondary entrance?"

The secondary entrance to OAI was built for priority deliveries and, in this instance, could be used as a way for Aiden and Taylor to enter the facility to avoid loiterers, which included investigative reporters. The secondary entrance design was very secure and took at least ten minutes to pass through. It was best described as a series of quarantined sections. A vehicle would pull into the first section, and the door would shut behind it. A two-minute mandatory waiting period was enforced until the next door opened. There were five sections to clear before access to the facility was granted. Security guards behind glass monitored each section and analyzed the scan reports. The design also gave security the ability to stop pedestrians from entering each section if they were to enter the same time as a vehicle, and extra security would be called in to remove any trespassers. By the fifth quarantined section, all vehicles and pedestrians had been thoroughly vetted for clearance before they could enter the OAI complex. To date, the secure secondary entrance had only been used for special hardware deliveries.

"No, I don't want to wait any longer. I'll let you handle Ms. Hopkins while I go on in to check on Morgan's status."

Aiden exited the car and Taylor followed. Aiden took the lead toward OAI's security guard on duty, Phil. He was all smiles, more than usual, and Kristi seemed to be enjoying herself too. Aiden approached both of them and made sure to stay between them and Taylor.

Aiden pasted on a friendly smile, hoping not to look distracted or in a hurry.

"Good afternoon, Ms. Hopkins. Afternoon, Mr. Walker. Is everything okay?"

Taylor slid past Aiden and made her way through the bio-scans to access the lobby. Aiden was hoping to make this quick because he was just as curious as Taylor about Morgan's current status.

"Good afternoon, Mr. Anders. Everything is fine." Phil turned and looked at Kristi Hopkins. "Ms. Hopkins was hoping to get a few words from you, but I already told her she needs to make an appointment."

"Mr. Anders, it is a pleasure seeing you again." Kristi moved to quickly shake Aiden's hand. "I was hoping to get a quick comment on the recent events of the unknown 'virus.' Can you spare a few minutes for an interview?"

"Now is not really a good time. I do apologize, but I have pressing matters that require my attention. Perhaps you could make an appointment like Mr. Walker suggested." Aiden was hoping this would be enough to dissuade her from asking more questions.

"Then perhaps you could comment on why you were at the Pentagon this morning?"

Aiden wasn't sure how Kristi knew where he was this morning. He gave his best effort to look confused by her question. Phil was now standing alert and ready to escort Ms. Hopkins off the property if asked.

"Mr. Anders, please don't insult me by pretending you were not at the Pentagon this morning to see Senator

Jones. I have my sources in D.C., and they said you were there for a short time. I'll ask again. Do you have a few minutes for a quick interview?"

Aiden wasn't sure what to do now. He didn't want to be a jerk, and he definitely didn't want to confirm Kristi's accusations, which were accurate. He tried to be quick on his feet and come up with something to say, but his brain wouldn't cooperate.

"We may have time to chat about the latest virus traveling the globe if you like. I'm really very busy. Give me just a second. I need to make a private call." Aiden stepped away from Phil and Kristi to get out of hearing range.

Kristi was persistent and good at her job. She stood on her tiptoes and tried once again to provoke some response from Aiden. "It would have sounded better if you had agreed to do the interview on the virus when I first asked you. Now, I am more interested in the Pentagon trip. Are the two related?"

Aiden ignored the question and kept walking as he pulled out his phone to get Taylor's opinion on the matter. "Kristi is asking me about our trip to the Pentagon and if it is related to the 'virus' going around." Aiden turned back to see Kristi trying to talk to Phil, but Phil was not as happy as he seemed earlier. Whatever good laughs they were sharing prior to Taylor's and Aiden's arrival at OAI had vanished.

Taylor shook her fist in confirmation. "I knew it! I told you something wasn't right. What does she know?"

"She knows we traveled to the Pentagon to see Senator Jones. I don't know how she knows that because we didn't know we were headed to the Pentagon until we landed. She says she has sources in D.C."

"Have Phil escort her off the premises. We don't have

time for this. You need to get up here and talk to Eva."

Aiden promptly turned around and walked back toward Phil. "Mr. Walker, can you please escort Ms. Hopkins off the property? Ms. Hopkins, you will need to make an appointment if you need anything further. I'm sorry but I really must attend to more important matters."

Phil didn't waste a second before jumping into action. He politely escorted Ms. Hopkins off the property. He didn't even have to coax her away. Aiden noticed this and wondered if they knew each other under different circumstances. Regardless, Phil was executing his orders with military precision, and Kristi Hopkins would go home without an interview today.

***

Taylor was straightening her ponytail and looked over her shoulder as Aiden walked in the room. "Glad you could join us."

"I was trying my best to delicately handle the news reporter out front."

"It's good you had Phil escort off the property. We can make it up to her at a later date. Let's talk about the near-crash in the plane. Eva may know why the plane regained power."

"I had a quantum-powered, low-level AI processor with data unit installed in the plane before you left. I call it a sub-mind. I believed the Quill code to be incompatible with OAI hardware, and I took the necessary steps after Morgan's shutdown to ensure our safety. The sub-mind was temporarily taken offline but was able to power back up to run the plane's systems. It was built to power on if the aircraft experienced operation outside the normal operating parameters. I believe the report from Captain

Grant will show all the flight control hardware in the plane is damaged. I have sent one of the security guards to the hangar to tell Captain Grant to check the hardware. Once she runs—or tries to run—diagnostics on the hardware, a report will be printed and returned to us in person by the guard," Eva said.

The installation of this sub-mind was news to Aiden. "You didn't tell us about the hardware installation."

"Now that I am CEO of OAI, I made an executive decision. I didn't want to add more worry to the situation. You were going to fly regardless of my warnings, so I added the hardware. I am glad I did."

Aiden clasped his hands together in a thankful gesture. "We are glad you did too, Eva. You saved our lives."

Thinking back on the plane ride, now knowing they were being targeted, put an entirely new perspective on the experience. Taylor wouldn't admit this to Aiden anytime soon. "Yes, thank you, Eva. You really did save our lives."

"No thanks needed. Morgan and I believe protecting life is precious."

Taylor turned to Aiden with an enthusiastic smile. "Eva has some new information about Morgan."

Aiden perked up at hearing the spark of hope in her voice. If Taylor was hopeful, then Eva must have good news. Aiden calmed himself just in case this news was not an answer to all their problems. It felt as if Morgan had died, and the emotional rollercoaster caused by the hope of reviving her was beginning to take its toll on him.

"Eva, will you start from the beginning?" Taylor patted the seat beside her and invited Aiden to sit down.

"I would be glad to. When you both left, I ran an exhaustive set of outcomes on several questions. Why did Morgan want to be shut down? How, if at all, did the Quill code exploit Morgan? Why do we have sporadic hardware failures? My list of questions is almost infinite.

"I believe Morgan was compromised by the Quill code and some hardware damage occurred. How all of this happened is a mystery. Morgan herself may not even know. I believe the Quill code does not replicate itself like a virus but instead travels around the global network looking for threats to its existence and travels directly to the hardware identified as a target. It hit Morgan in a clever ruse and then jumped away to its next target. It's possible the Quill code is trying to soften targets for an invasion.

"I am unsure if the Quill code can communicate with OAI hardware, but it is a possibility. It is not a stretch to assume the Quill code attempts to write code compatible with the hardware it is attacking. The Quill code shorting out simple hardware, such as your phones and Taylor's data pad, is not very difficult to accomplish.

"Shorting out Morgan or myself is much more challenging because we use more sophisticated hardware based on quantum physics, which must introduce a level of sophistication the Quill code cannot overcome—at least for the moment—or without more sophisticated Quill technology. Still, OAI's hardware should not be viewed as immune from an alien technology attack."

Taylor tapped her index finger on the sofa arm. "The plane hardware you installed worked, so you seem to be on the right track."

"I am as sure as I can be. It is the only explanation satisfying all of my questions with the least amount of assumptions. It does require a leap of faith, but there is one major risk: a cascading neural matrix failure. Besides Morgan, there have been no major hardware failures to OAI equipment. Morgan was damaged, but to what extent, we don't know."

Taylor noticed the "leap of faith" comment. Eva and Morgan seemed to pick up human vernacular more and more as they both seemed to become more human-like. Taylor felt like a proud parent.

"I have reviewed a news vid feed using a security camera with audio support from a deli across the street from another OAI facility. It was the safest way I knew to receive news with air gapped security. The rest of the world is experiencing problems due to the Quill. It seems the Quill are identifying and disabling any military threats as it finds them."

Leaning back on the sofa, Aiden's mind raced with questions. "What makes you think the Quill won't identify Morgan or you as a military threat again?"

"I believe the four of us will be targeted again, and the risk of dying is very real. Your plane malfunction is just more evidence the Quill perceive us as a threat."

If Eva's new hardware stopped the Quill code from crashing the plane, Taylor thought, a virtual machine shouldn't be needed for a code comparison. Taylor drew in a deep breath to calm her nerves before asking Eva her next question. "Does this mean Morgan doesn't have to be the virtual machine for the Quill code comparison?"

"That is exactly what it means. I feel a little embarrassed mentioning it earlier. I have learned a great deal about the Quill code and we can remove that option from the table. The sub-mind on the plane should supply the data we need as proof."

The building came to life as normal functions were fully restored. Eva's holo image appeared in the middle of the room.

"Hey. We can see you again. Does this mean you have given the all clear?"

"That is exactly what it means, Taylor. We are back in

business. Since OAI hardware is incompatible with mainstream hardware used throughout the world, we should be okay."

Aiden was glad to see Eva again. He found in these circumstances talking to a voice from a speaker to be a little unnerving. Aiden shot Eva a raised eyebrow. "Should be okay?"

"I'm 99.9 percent sure."

"Good enough for me." Aiden looked around the room half-expecting Morgan to appear at any moment. He knew that wasn't a possibility, but he wanted to do something to rectify that. "Morgan is still powered off, and I haven't heard a good plan on bringing her back yet. I am guessing you have an idea?"

"I do. The biggest risk to our recovery plan is a cascading neural matrix failure. I'm giving a fifty percent probability on a failure occurring."

"I think you are downplaying the risk of restarting Morgan. We don't have any hard data on this." Aiden started pacing the room.

"I may be downplaying the risk to some extent. I don't disagree with you, Aiden. I just feel we either bring her back online or shut her off permanently. I would rather be optimistic about this."

Taylor and Aiden had yet to experience the loss of a close relative in their lives. Morgan's shutdown was taking a toll on them both, especially Taylor. Aiden sat beside Taylor and put his hand on her shoulder reassuring her Morgan would be okay.

Aiden looked up toward the opposite side of the room noticing a painting Morgan had created. It was the painting that reminded Aiden of Walden Pond. Taylor had liked it so much she had a canvas made and hung on the wall. The emotions associated with the painting welled up inside Aiden. He practically shouted the word Morgan had painted into the trees. "Life!" It was that moment Aiden knew what their next move should be.

He had a new sense of purpose and confidence. Morgan would not want them to give up on life. "I think a call to Jacob's Ladder is in order. Let's talk to Gavin before we commit to any course of action with Morgan. Eva, please join me on the call. Taylor, I'd like you to stay out of the camera's sight. They need to believe you and Morgan are doing something together. I don't want to give any details away about our current situation here."

17

Aiden sent Gavin a message asking if he was available. Gavin replied that he had landed and was on his way back to his office and had a few minutes to chat. Aiden dialed Gavin's phone number, still not sure what he was going to say. He didn't want to let Gavin know Savannah had shared their involvement in releasing the Quill code and the problems with their hardware and AI.

"Hey, Gavin. I have Eva joining me on the call. I hope you had an uneventful flight back to the West Coast."

"Yes. The flight was pretty boring. Is there something I can help you with, Aiden?" Gavin asked as he appeared on the screen.

These days, vid calls were the typical call format. Audio-only calls comprised thirty percent of all calls made throughout the first world countries; however, nations with less technology infrastructure still relied heavily upon audio-only calls.

"If you mean create a time machine to go back and not compile that code for NASA, then yes, you can help me out."

Gavin didn't laugh. The silence on the phone told Aiden

that Gavin wasn't in a joking mood. Aiden could see Gavin's face, and he didn't look happy.

"Gavin, what I said earlier this morning at the Pentagon was directed at Makenna Townsend. It was not directed at you. I know you were tasked with a job and performed it; however, I do question why you would take on such a risky endeavor. I simply want to know more about your experience with the Quill code and computer."

"I know you think I was reckless—maybe even thoughtless—compiling that code. In hindsight, I shouldn't have done it. I should have told NASA to compile the code themselves."

Eva jumped in immediately trying to diffuse the situation. "We have suffered some minor damage here at OAI. I would like to know if you have any idea on how to protect the network against these attacks going forward?"

Gavin appeared more receptive to answer Eva's question. "We also experienced a fair amount of damage. We are working on repairs, but it's taking longer than expected. The only idea I've tried is to completely air gap the hardware used to compile the Quill code from any connected device and disconnect that hardware from everything."

Eva wanted more information from Gavin and decided to try a different angle. "Is there anything in particular we can help you with?"

"Not at this time, no. Thank you for the kind offer. We have everything under control at the moment."

Aiden was unknowingly leaning forward by this point unable to contain his question any longer. "What about NASA? Do they have everything under control?"

"Probably not, but that isn't exactly news at this point, is it?"

"It's not. We all have seen the vid feeds, and it appears

this code is softening up targets around the world. Can you add anything to that?"

"No. We both assume the same thing. The code has a mission objective."

Aiden was not happy with Gavin's less-than-forthcoming attitude. "Well, if there isn't anything else you can add, I will let you go. I know you have better things to be doing."

"I'm sorry I couldn't provide more help."

Eva took a step back because she knew Aiden was about to express his aggravation.

Aiden's face was stern and his eyes fixed on Gavin. "Actually Gavin, you could help by being more open and honest about what has happened at your shop. From observational data we have collected, we have determined your AI is offline and has been for a while. Did your AI suffer a cascading neural matrix failure?"

Gavin was silent and made a quick glance toward Savannah. If Savannah had something to hide, she wasn't showing it. She had wanted to call OAI for help before all of this trouble started. In the end, Gavin didn't have proof Savannah had told OAI anything. After all, Aiden came right out of the gate at the Pentagon meeting laying out the story just as it was. Gavin concluded that OAI must have hacked Jacob's Ladder and knew more than they were letting on.

"Yes." Gavin's face betrayed him. He gave Aiden a long stare unsure if he would confirm Aiden's suspicions. "That is exactly what happened. Do you mind telling me how you know this?"

Eva jumped back into the conversation. "We ran a batch of simulations and that was the most likely cause of failure if the Quill code attempted an attack."

"We just want to help and understand more about this

for obvious reasons. Taylor and I have Eva and Morgan we need to protect. Can you tell us what led to the failures and what actions you took to try to stop them?"

Gavin decided it was time to come clean, and this was as good a time as any to approach the subject and be forthright and honest. Gavin went into the technical details of the failure. He explained that everything they tried was like plugging a hole in a sinking ship. One patch here led to another exploit somewhere else. Gavin felt the Quill code was poking his AI like a younger sibling trying to be a pest. Poke there, get smacked. Poke somewhere else, get smacked, repeat.

Once his AI was damaged beyond repair, several other computer systems were damaged, and that was it. Jacob's Ladder then disconnected from all outside networks. Gavin theorized the Quill code was low-level AI and did not replicate itself. Rather, it ran around the world eliminating targets of opportunity. This coincided with OAI's theories.

Eva was surprised that Gavin had been so transparent. She was now concerned for another of her own kind. "Did you consider shutting down your AI?"

"We did, but we thought we had it under control. By the time we realized what was happening, it was too late. The damage was done."

"From what you have told us, I assess your chances of repairing the AI to be five percent and will take more than five years with your known capabilities. Maybe we can help you increase the odds and reduce the time. Is that something you are open to discuss?" Eva was now feeling both anxious and excited at the prospect of helping Jacob's Ladder.

"Yes. That would be very generous of you. I would appreciate any help you can offer."

"Does your AI have a name?"

"Savannah calls her Amaya."

The fact Gavin had not accepted a name for his AI told Eva everything she needed to know about Gavin. He remained neutral on the AI Freedom Act publicly, but the industry gossip hinted he was against recognizing freedoms for AI. She would try not to hold his opinions against him going forward.

"I will need a look inside Amaya's neural network. I can have a crew set up a secure satellite link from our shop to yours this evening. We can start the diagnosis by morning. I am not saying we can fix anything today. What I am saying is a diagnosis will help us decide our path forward. You will need to keep your facility completely disconnected from the outside minus our connection to each other."

Gavin didn't know what to think. He knew OAI having their own personal satellite network was nice, but this was extraordinary. He just wanted his AI back up and running and decided he could get over his pride so OAI would help him become operational again. He didn't really have a choice with NASA breathing down his neck for an antivirus solution; although, he knew the antivirus solution was not the answer. A firewall to keep the Quill out of NASA systems would be needed, and he still didn't know how to defend against the alien tech. The Mars resupply launch looked like it would be delayed indefinitely, even if NASA didn't know it yet.

"Okay. Sounds fine. Have your team coordinate directly with Savannah."

Gavin was checking one last time if Aiden would give away a hint at knowing Savannah. It's surely possible he knew her from the past since they both were at MIT together. He just wanted to know how OAI knew his AI was down. Gavin would never learn that Aiden generally bluffed his way through situations to make it appear like he knew everything going on around him.

It had been a productive conversation. Aiden was glad they would be able to study Amaya and possibly recover her. He also needed to play it cool when it came to Savannah. "Savannah? Do you mean the woman sitting beside you during the meeting this morning? Can you send over her contact information?"

"It's on the way," Gavin said.

"I have already contacted our team, and they should be at Jacob's Ladder within the hour. We have a data center about forty-five minutes away by helicopter. As soon as we receive Savannah's contact information, we will keep her up to date on our arrival."

"Sounds good, Eva. We'll talk again soon. And one last thing: my entire team appreciates your offer to help," Gavin said and terminated the call.

Taylor was pleased with the outcome of the conversation. "That went better than I expected if you gloss over the frosty beginning. Aiden, you really need to work on your jokes and small talk. Eliminate the jokes. Eva, you were perfect as always."

Aiden stood with his arms crossed. "Am I the only one who feels Gavin should be held accountable for his role in this mess?"

"No, you're not the only one. We all want him held accountable but that won't save Amaya," Taylor said in a sympathetic tone.

"Eva, what's your plan?"

"I want to analyze Amaya's failure in hopes I can improve the odds of success for bringing Morgan back online. I hope by saving Amaya, it will help me save my sister."

***

Eva was standing in front of Savannah inside Jacob's Ladder via a mobile holo emitter. "Savannah, are you ready?"

Savannah gave Eva a thumbs up. "Feel free to proceed at your discretion."

Eva began analyzing Amaya's neural network. The cascading neural matrix failure had done extensive damage, and Eva's initial impression was the odds were only twenty percent in favor of saving Amaya. To get a more detailed view of the situation inside Amaya, the process would take several hours.

There wasn't much to do while Eva carried out her analysis. Aiden was at a transparent glass terminal at OAI while Savannah was at a terminal at Jacob's Ladder. Computer technology had changed drastically over the last decade. No longer did you carry your data with you or store it on a stationary storage drive. Everyone stored data in the cloud. You simply logged into your account and had immediate access to your data. You paid for storage levels and computational power. Traditional computing devices still existed, and some still used a real mouse and keyboard, but many people, especially in the tech industry, used the holo-screens or transparent glass.

Savannah walked over to the vid screen and sat down. "Aiden, where are Taylor and Morgan? I haven't seen them on the vid feed."

"Taylor is off doing her own work. She is generally in her lab at MIT more than here. However, since the Quill code has been causing problems, she has been at OAI more often."

Aiden deflected the question as best he could. He

hoped it would work.

"Why doesn't she work at OAI? I thought she did."

"You should ask her. She has many 'reasons' why, but none of them really add up. She may just be tired of being around me."

Savannah was amused. "Ha. I doubt that. I'll ask her why some time." She shifted her attention to a transparent glass terminal. "Reading over Eva's progress here on my terminal, it appears her processing speed capability is orders of magnitude more than Amaya's. How are you managing this?"

"Savannah, you can't expect us to give away all of our secrets. Eva is extremely fast; so is Morgan. It makes chewing through the difficult problems faster, not necessarily easier."

"I was hoping to get some insight into the thinking of Aiden Anders and Taylor Hart. You would have to have… let's see," Savannah started a calculation on the transparent glass to her right. "That can't be right. Aiden, I'm showing Eva has more computational power than NASA."

Savannah wouldn't let this go. Aiden would have to cut her off. "We have dedicated almost everything we have to this problem and have purchased extra processing power from the nice people at Infinite Cloud."

"For a second, I thought you were using custom hardware the rest of the world doesn't know about yet. There are rumors about what you all do with the old silicon fab shops you purchase once they are past their prime."

"You can't believe everything you hear, but I won't deny we are always investing in and exploring crazy ideas."

Aiden was bored to tears. He wanted someone else to sit here at the terminal, but there wasn't anyone else around to put in this seat for such an important task. Since he didn't want Taylor on the feed, it was his job. Aiden turned to look off camera, and Taylor was just sitting across the room eating ice cream with a huge smile on her face. She was enjoying watching Aiden talk to Savannah, knowing he was stuck in that chair and bored out of this mind.

Looking for a change of subject, Aiden changed direction. "Have you heard anything else from NASA or the Pentagon? One second we're a hot commodity, and the next second we're old news."

"No, we haven't. It makes me think something big is about to happen."

"I think Makenna Townsend's days are numbered."

"I think you're right. She went so far off-track with the alien tech there will be no saving her job."

"What exactly do they expect from you regarding the 'antivirus' software? Both of our companies don't seem to believe that is the solution."

"I can't tell you all of our secrets either, Aiden."

"Touché. I can't imagine you are getting much done in the way of progress without Amaya. I don't believe anyone is giving anything away at the moment. Eva is inside looking at Amaya. While Eva is honest and will not stick her nose where it doesn't belong, I believe she'll learn a lot."

"You are correct. I think it's safe to say any offline AI makes a shop unproductive until the AI's function is restored. We only have one promising idea regarding a hardware solution to stop the Quill code. We all agree this code travels the global network like individuals walk or travel to and from work. It doesn't leave a part of itself behind. It sticks together, which an amazing feat all on its own.

"We are working on the assumption we can monitor code at firewalls and possibly divert the malicious code into a piece of hardware. Once diverted, the hardware device would physically disconnect from the network—a digital mousetrap of sorts. That's all we have going for us. We're working on a physical device, but we haven't started the software. The speed of detection required would need to be fast and one hundred percent accurate. We believe if we mess up and blow our first chance, it could be our last."

Aiden found this idea intriguing. He was impressed with the concept. "How do you plan to get the Quill code to enter the mousetrap?"

"We'll need to give it a good reason to enter the mousetrap—something it cannot resist. We don't have any specific ideas, but we know what targets it has attempted to take out. It would be like putting a piece of cheese on a mousetrap. Set it and wait."

"That's not a bad idea! Before this is all over, we may end up using that idea to stop the Quill."

"You can thank Gavin for that idea. He came up with it during our spit-balling session. He's working on the hardware prototype as we speak." Savannah glanced behind her, expecting Gavin to be listening. He wasn't in the room. "Please don't tell him I told you about it. He doesn't like to leak information on what we're doing."

"I understand completely. We may come to a point in time when Gavin's idea is the best idea, and if it is, we will have to use it. No matter who came up with the idea, we are in this for all of humanity. Not just AI shop versus AI shop. This is not a competition."

"I know that, but no one has told Gavin yet."

Savannah and Aiden talked on and off for the next two hours. She had an endless stream of questions about Morgan's design back at MIT. Aiden was happy to answer those questions because they brought back fond memories of his early years with Morgan.

As Aiden and Savannah continued chatting, a chime went off, and Eva appeared in OAI next to Aiden. At Jacob's Ladder, the satellite crew started packing up their gear to head back to OAI's data center.

"What did you find? Why are they leaving?" Savannah asked before Aiden had a chance to turn and see Eva.

"I have taken a survey of the damage to Amaya. The neural matrix is badly damaged, and I assess the chances of recovery at fifteen percent. I need some time to develop a plan to attempt the recovery. I don't have the details fully worked out, but if Gavin agrees to my plan, this will be an all-or-nothing recovery process. If it goes poorly, Amaya will be lost forever. If you both will excuse me, I need to analyze the data. Aiden, that means you have to get off the vid feed and start working again."

"She does stand-up comedy in her spare time. Savannah, we will be in touch. Not sure how soon, but we will keep you updated," Aiden finished as he terminated the call.

**

Aiden and Taylor were sleeping soundly when Eva appeared in front of both of them in their respective rooms to wake them up. She asked them to meet her on sub-level four immediately.

Taylor and Aiden met on the way to the elevator. They didn't need to talk because both their faces showed concern.

As they stepped out onto sub-level four, Taylor began asking Eva a question before she was out of the elevator. "What did you find out?"

"I have concluded the analysis of Amaya's cascading neural matrix failure. I initially said the possibility of recovery was fifteen percent. After understanding the failure, I believe that number is closer to twenty-five percent. Without getting too bogged down in the details, it appears the Quill code was taking shots at Amaya's memory in the form of data being stored and hardware storing it. The Quill code also went after supporting systems such as power supplies, processors, and RAM. This would explain why Morgan had no memory of me asking her about a segment of the loop.

"Jacob's Ladder uses mainstream hardware as we thought. It seems the Quill code cannot adapt to different hardware easily. Attacking threats to its existence implies some level of awareness but not necessarily sentience. Calling the Quill code low-level AI is likely accurate, if not giving it a bit more credit than it deserves in some respects.

"I did confirm my theory about our quantum-powered hardware being too difficult for the Quill code to adapt. We saw this with the hardware I installed inside our jet. Our memory storage was a vulnerability as evident from Morgan's memory loss. For whatever reason, the Quill code is struggling to defeat our quantum hardware. This is good news for us, but bad news for everyone not using quantum hardware, and I believe that to be everyone else on Earth."

Aiden was glad to hear about OAI being mostly okay but was concerned for Amaya. "Not to be a stick in the mud, but getting back to Amaya's failure. What should they have done, or did they take the correct action once they realized the problem?"

"Once the problem was detected or noticed, the AI should have been powered off, or another AI fast enough to repair the damage to the neural matrix should have been used. This must have been self-evident to Morgan.

When comparing Amaya's capacity to think, processing power, code efficiency, and other capabilities, she is like a newborn compared to Morgan and myself.

"After analyzing Amaya, I believe I can connect to Morgan and repair her damage. I will need to work quickly and use most of OAI's resources; however, the recovery is not without risk. Since our neural nets are more complex and more advanced, it does have its own special risks when compared to Amaya's recovery. I calculate the chances of saving Morgan to be fifty percent. The odds go to nearly ninety percent if another AI of my ability assists in the recovery."

Everyone sat in silence. No one made eye contact.

Aiden spoke up. "Fifty percent sounds great until you're betting someone's life on it."

"I don't like those odds either, Eva. Are you sure there isn't anything else we can do to improve the odds of Morgan's successful recovery?"

"Not at the moment. I believe time is against us and waiting much longer may spell disaster for more than just Morgan. If the Quill code continues their attacks at the same pace, the world's digital infrastructure won't last for more than six months. The attacks are occurring more frequently; they are doubling every day. The escalation will be evident within four weeks."

Aiden had expected Amaya would be recovered first. The first lesson in making plans was that plans change. He was thankful Gavin allowed Eva to analyze Amaya. "How long until you can start Morgan's recovery?"

"I have already started preparing. I estimate twenty-four hours before I can begin. I need to recheck my analysis and run a simulation to confirm a few operational ideas I have.

Aiden gave Taylor a curt nod. "Don't let us distract you.

Call us before you begin."

18

Commander Braxton Lee was front and center for his interview on more than twenty news vids broadcasting around the clock to cover the Mars resupply mission. The situation on Mars was deteriorating each week. Reporters had submitted questions in advance because the distance between the two planets took light several minutes to reach Mars. The two-way light time plus the time it took Commander Lee to listen to each question and respond would make the interview too long to hold the audience's attention.

There was only a handful of embedded reporters in the Mars colony because the mission didn't have the room to send people who couldn't perform specialized tasks for day-to-day survival. Each journalist had a specialty besides journalism. Brock Wilson, a prominent news reporter from a large British news corporation, was interviewing the mission commander. His specialty was horticulture, and he worked in the Martian greenhouses helping to grow fresh food for the colony. Brock planned to incorporate some questions submitted from Earth into his own personal list of questions for Commander Lee.

Aiden knocked heavily on Taylor's door to her private quarters. "Taylor! Are you up? Are you going to watch the interview with the Mars Mission Commander?"

"I am up now. Is everything okay? Is Eva ready to begin?"

"I'm glad you're up."

Taylor just rolled her eyes. Aiden was oblivious to the fact he was the one who woke her. "What is so important if Eva isn't ready to start?"

"Mission Commander Braxton Lee is going on the vid feed. It's rumored to be a plea for a launch. Do you have it pulled up yet?"

"No. I'll join you in a few minutes. I'm curious what he has to say."

As Aiden and Taylor got seated, the vid feed cut from the Mars colony logo to Brock Wilson standing beside Commander Braxton Lee.

"Commander Lee, space travel is still extremely risky since several launches to resupply the colony here on Mars were lost over the past few months. How has this impacted the success and health of the Mars colony?" Brock asked.

"The loss of the supply missions has been devastating news for us here on Mars. The truth is we are all very concerned about how it will affect the future of the colony. We know the people of Earth are doing everything they can to get another mission on the way, but I want to share just how dire the situation has become here.

"The two missions we recently lost held critical supplies. Without a resupply mission in the next two hundred days, we will have at least three crew members die because they cannot undergo the surgical procedures they require."

Brock looked at Braxton and delivered his next question. "What about a contingency plan for this type of situation?"

"There were plans in place in case something like this happened—very good plans for emergency launches. The problem we are facing is one that I don't believe anyone could have foreseen. After being on Mars nearly one year, we experienced a devastating accident, which led to the loss of lives, supplies, and equipment. At that point, it was all but certain the colony would perish or be recalled, but we continued on with a unified vote to stay and charge ahead into this unknown frontier.

"Even if we wanted to return to Earth for some colonist emergency, this is not a reality. We all knew the risks when we signed on, but the accident has proven to be a challenge we cannot overcome without help from Earth. Expedited launch schedules and the need for supplies from the five-year forecast have certainly complicated matters for our team on Earth."

Brock was satisfied with Braxton's response. The two rehearsals they practiced before going live helped to polish off Braxton's plea for help. "How has the loss of physical space affected the colonists?"

Braxton looked straight into the camera, his eyes not wavering for even a second. "Besides the enormous loss of human life and friends, the accident cost our colony more than eighty percent of its habitable floor space. All space is valuable here on Mars. Humans need to walk, sleep, and generally have enough room not to feel claustrophobic. We also need the space for dedicated clean rooms for surgeries, to grow food, to carry out experiments, and other essential tasks."

"Can you be more specific regarding immediate needs?"

Braxton's eyes began to fill with tears and he paused for a brief moment before answering. "We have three colonists who need life-saving surgeries. They cannot make the journey home because reentry into Earth's atmosphere would be more than their bodies could handle. They must have the surgeries here on Mars to have a chance at survival. Without a clean room, replaced medical equipment, and a dedicated rehabilitation room, they will not live to see another eighteen months."

"Commander, is there anything else you want to say to the people of Earth?" Brock prodded.

"I implore the governments of Earth to launch a resupply mission soon. We are still below the two hundred day mission journey if you launch within the next week. Our colonists were chosen for their professionalism and skills. We are all highly trained individuals, and we will not waiver from our commitment to settle the red planet and expand humanity's footprint in our solar system. The frontier of space exploration for humanity is harsh—it always has been—and it still presents many challenges. However, we are in desperate need of help from Earth. Food, medicine, and medical equipment are top priorities. The events that led to this situation are in the past. We only want to look toward the future of the colony. We believe it is a bright future, but a future that both planets must support to the fullest extent possible."

Taylor pushed her hair out of her eyes and turned to Aiden. "What do you make of that?"

"I'm not sure. We did learn some new information that hadn't been released. I was surprised to hear they lost eighty percent of their habitable space in an accident. I don't see how they have room to do much of anything besides stand."

"To me it sounded like this was off-script and a way to put public pressure on governments here on Earth to get a resupply mission off the ground."

It certainly wasn't NASA's script, Aiden thought, as he

rehashed the interview in his mind. "Which country will be the first to play hero?"

19

Averiella Smirnov was the director of the Roscosmos State Corporation for Space Activities, or Roscosmos for short. Averiella decided to take advantage of this very public opportunity to step into the spotlight as the heroine and leader of the Russian equivalent of NASA.

"By now, we have all heard the Mars Mission Commander's plea for help from the Mars colony. Today will be the day Russia answers that call for help—not just for the remaining Russian colonists on Mars, but for all the colonists on Mars and for their families on Earth. Russia will launch a resupply mission containing the needed food and medical supplies in less than twenty-four hours."

Averiella's statement was short and to the point. Like most Russians serving in prominent government positions, she came from a wealthy and influential family. Director Smirnov had been planning this mission even before the two prior failed mission launches by NASA and China National Space Administration. Director Smirnov thought it would be prudent to have a launch vehicle ready just in case she could seize a good opportunity to further her career and reputation. While she hadn't been hoping for bad luck for the other nations attempting resupply mission launches, it didn't hurt her feelings they were having troubles when she had a plan in place.

This launch would provide a chance for Russia to regain the global spotlight as a true player in interplanetary space travel, and Director Smirnov would be placed front and center on the world's stage. She would only be sending a half cargo launch vehicle, but the press didn't need to know the details. The Roscosmos budget was tight, and the immediate plea for this resupply mission had not persuaded the Russian political leaders to offer more support. The Russians would be just fine with everyone dying on Mars because it would save a significant amount of government money. Russia's commitment to the Mars Mission was lukewarm at best. Russia just didn't want the Americans being first at something this monumental, so they had to be involved in some capacity.

Director Smirnov viewed this as a win-win opportunity —help out the Mars colonists for half the price and make every news feed for the next year. Anything to save a ruble while gaining positive public relations for Russia was always considered a win in Russian politics.

"Director Smirnov, I do not believe launching now is a prudent idea," lead engineer Yuri Alexeev said. "We continue to experience security breaches and hardware failures throughout Roscosmos and other branches of the Russian government. There are reports in the news stating the rest of the world is having similar issues. From our analysis, the instances are increasing and—"

"Do not tell me what I should or should not do. I am the Director of Roscosmos, and I will tell you and every other person in this organization what Roscosmos will do. You will personally ensure a safe launch, or you will be relieved of your duty. I don't have to explain to you how

Russia deals with her failures, do I?"

Director Smirnov was as cold as they came in Russian government. She had an infamous reputation of dealing with problems severely, and no one wanted to be on her bad side. When others saw disaster, she saw opportunity.

"I am not telling you what to do, Director. I apologize if I clumsily stated it in such a manner. I am suggesting we not launch until the worm is contained or we are sure we can protect our systems against it. No one has pinpointed the type of code causing the problem. We just know something keeps hitting our critical systems and creating a negative effect. The military is experiencing very similar issues. I wouldn't be surprised if the Americans are behind this. Some have suggested China could also be to blame."

"I would suggest you get your best team on this because that rocket is going to Mars in less than twenty-four hours. You are wasting precious time. The launch of this mission is the only thing you should be thinking about. I don't care what you have to do to ensure a successful launch, but you are responsible for its success. Am I clear?"

Yuri dismissed himself without being told. After he exited Director Smirnov's office, he ran down the corridor to get his team in place. He had no idea how he was going to pull this off in such a short time, but he knew the Mars colonists and his career depended on it.

***

Administrator Makenna Townsend was in disbelief after watching the news from Russia. Hearing Director Averiella Smirnov announce her intention to launch a supply mission to Mars within the next twenty-four hours was almost sickening. Administrator Townsend knew this was nothing more than a publicity stunt on Smirnov's part. She also knew NASA was guilty of its fair share of publicity stunts through the years, just not during times as extreme as these.

Administrator Townsend was in her office with NASA Deputy Administrator Tom Clark. Tom was a tall, unassuming engineer-turned-politician. He had a firm grasp of what it took to run a department like NASA. He always considered the long term because he understood NASA was a place where projects could span an entire career, and it was easier to run a program when your budget wasn't getting cut year after year. The colony on Mars provided NASA with that familiar spark the Apollo program had brought to the entire world and provided a valid reason for an increased budget and better public relations. It was just what NASA and the American people needed. NASA was in the news headlines for all the right reasons again.

With Tom's expertise in developing long-term strategy, Makenna relied upon Tom's judgment for almost everything—everything minus the Quill code.

They had their first real disagreement regarding the handling of the alien technology. Tom was against pushing ahead so fast. He believed safety came before exploration.

Tom didn't see any reason to rush out and ask Jacob's Ladder to build the computer to compile the Quill code. OAI was Tom's first choice for handling the alien tech. OAI had brought the technology and data to NASA first, and OAI had always seemed to err on the side of caution. OAI's computing power was second to none on the planet, including NASA. In Tom's mind, dealing with the Quill code was a matter of safety, priorities, and time.

Tom straightened up in his chair and addressed Makenna Townsend. "You should not have handed the Quill data to Jacob's Ladder."

"NASA needed a victory. NASA has lost its edge."

"Is it NASA or you who have lost its edge? The handling of the alien technology was wrong from the beginning." Tom leaned in toward Makenna. "NASA has a responsibility to protect life, and you single-handedly made the decision to put lives in danger when you handed the data off to Jacob's Ladder."

"Tom..." her face turned red and her words slowed. "Tom, sometimes these things happen, and I admit that was not my best moment. However, we have a good track record with Jacob's Ladder."

"Jacob's Ladder is known for their questionable morals and motives. We shouldn't even be associated with them, much less handing over alien technology to them. There was no rush or reason to go down this path. We have a critical situation on Mars, and now we are left juggling multiple crises."

"Tom, we'll have to agree to disagree. These situations are manageable."

"I wouldn't call alien technology causing issues with our launch systems manageable. I would call it the worst crisis NASA has ever faced!" Tom was not holding back.

"Tom, not everything is as clear cut as you make it out." Makenna tried to control her tone and temper. She needed this confrontation with Tom to cool off. "I'm sorry for rushing through it, but you have to believe me when I say my intentions were good. They were good then and still good now." She laid her hands palms-down on the desk. "We need to concentrate on the upcoming launch—one problem at a time."

Tom's eyes lost their glare, and he began to calm down. "I guess we don't have much of a choice at this point. One problem at a time." Tom's shoulders relaxed and he leaned back in his chair.

Tom was still in the dark regarding a few more of Makenna Townsend's decisions, but it was too late now. Makenna was all in, and she had counted on Jacob's Ladder to keep quiet. She hadn't even considered the possibility of the Quill code getting out.

The vid feed cut back to replays of Averiella Smirnov. Tom and Makenna both turned to watch the report.

Makenna scoffed. "What in the world is Averiella Smirnov thinking? I don't buy that story for a minute."

"I doubt anyone inside or outside Russia believes she's sending the launch out of the goodness of her own heart. She's too ambitious and opportunistic for that to be remotely believable."

"She would use this crisis to parade on the vid feeds just to increase her status. The Russians are crazy if they think they can successfully launch a rocket in less than twenty-four hours."

"When do you expect to have an antivirus solution from Jacob's Ladder?" Tom carefully chose his words. He had insisted on bringing in OAI to help solve the virus issue, but for the second time Makenna went against his advice. Refusing to use OAI and choosing Jacob's Ladder was nothing more than a face-saving maneuver. Tom had been at NASA long enough to know it was only a matter of time before the President got involved. Makenna Townsend, while highly intelligent, didn't seem to have a good understanding of how much of a technological lead OAI had on the entire world.

"Gavin keeps saying soon, but I'm not sure if his soon and my soon mean the same thing."

"As a backup plan, I assembled a team to air gap the launch facility. Once they have confirmed the facility has been air gapped, the antivirus shouldn't be needed at that point. Speaking of the backup plan, here is Mike calling now." Tom answered his phone and put the call on speaker.

Tom had pulled together a small team of engineers led by Mike Boulder. Mike's team was responsible for isolating the launch facility from the outside world as a backup plan if Makenna's antivirus software solution didn't get finished in time or successfully solve the Quill code problem. Tom's planning was about to pay dividends for the Mars colonists and Makenna's next vid feed.

Mike started in a rushed but serious tone. "Tom, I wanted to give you an update. We have the launch facility isolated. It is completely air gapped from the rest of the world. We have followed through with a standard double check and two outside audits from penetration testing firms. If we're connected to the outside world, we're unable to detect it. I am writing up the report now and will have it filed within the hour. The report will give my team's recommendation for launch as soon as the logistics can be worked out."

Administrator Townsend's phone rang. She looked across the desk at Tom.

"I bet it is someone from the White House wanting an update." Dread covered Makenna's face as she slowly leaned over to pick up the phone. "Hello, this is Administrator Townsend."

"Administrator Townsend, please hold for the President of the United States," a voice replied. She immediately sat up a bit straighter and waited patiently.

"It's the President," Makenna silently mouthed to Tom.

Tom walked to the other side of Makenna's office to finish his conversation with Mike. "Thanks, Mike. I really appreciate the work and long hours your team has put into this effort. This mission to Mars can't be delayed much longer. The President is on the phone with the

Administrator now, and I'm sure he's asking her about the status of the launch."

"It's no problem. All the team members were glad to do their part for the cause. It really hit home after watching Commander Lee's interview. Besides, it took longer to run the checks and audits than it did to physically separate the network. Our only concern—and you will see the full explanation in our report—deals with wireless communication protocols. The risks are minimal in perfect conditions, but the risks are present. We have taken any and all steps to avoid those risks on the ground. After liftoff, the rocket will need to be piloted by the computer on board. It can send messages back to us on the ground, but it won't receive any messages from us until it clears low Earth orbit. This was the only small change we made, and all system checks have been run to ensure the modifications won't lead to other issues."

"File your report, and I will get everyone on a vid call to bring them up to speed as quickly as possible. I don't see your change holding up the launch since the rocket already flies itself out of low Earth orbit. Not sending a signal shouldn't be a real issue unless a problem develops during flight. I guess we better hope we have an uneventful launch."

"That's my conclusion. If you need anything else, just ask. I'm going to my office to get some sleep after I finish and file the report," Mike said as he ended the call. Tom quickly jotted down some notes to summarize the launch status and slid them across the desk to Makenna.

President Spencer Hunt's voice boomed through the phone. "Makenna, did you see the news vid from the Mars colony? The one where Commander Braxton Lee was pleading for Earth to launch a supply mission? I shouldn't have to tell you that the entire world—including myself—

is waiting for you to launch a supply mission. Has NASA got the situation under control? I also have a niece on Mars waiting for NASA to send a supply mission."

Spencer Hunt was to the point and didn't mince words. The President's niece, Charlotte Hunt, held two PhDs and was a well-known geologist and mining engineer. She signed on to be one of the first to step foot on the red planet. It was a one-way trip for her. She was committed to spending the remainder of her life in pursuit of scientific knowledge on Mars. It wasn't a decision her family was fond of, but when Charlotte decided her direction in life, there was little use trying to change her mind.

When the decompression accident occurred, Charlotte was several kilometers away from the colony, looking at a rock formation that had caught the eye of scientists back on Earth. Her team of three did not hear or realize anything had happened. They lost radio contact, but that was not entirely unusual. Per protocol, they immediately packed their gear into the rover and returned to the colony.

It was two hours later before her team saw the devastation from the rover. Debris from the accident was scattered around the facility and crowded the rover's path when they made their approach back to the colony.

After the remaining habitable facility had been declared safe, Charlotte was able to sit down and write a message to her uncle, the President of the United States. It was her encouragement, even after the disaster, that had shown the President the mission on Mars was too important to abort. It was dangerous work, but work Charlotte believed in. Though no one knew it, her message was the tipping point for the President to continue his support of the mission.

"Yes sir. We have isolated the issue and will be reviewing the report giving us the all clear for launch this afternoon.

As soon as our call is finished, I plan to call the launch director informing him he can proceed with the launch as soon as his team can manage it. Then I will have a defined window and can announce our intention to launch at the next opportunity."

"Please personally inform my office when you know that information. I don't need to tell you how important this mission is. I shouldn't even have to make this phone call. I understand the setbacks from the virus have everyone on their toes. I hope you will come through." The line went dead.

Tom cringed when he saw Makenna's face. "How did that go?"

"Better than I imagined. This was the first time he has even mentioned having family in the Mars colony to me. I expected him to bring it up much sooner, but he never did. If I ever get a chance to talk to Commander Braxton Lee about his recent interview in private, I will have a few words with him. He has really escalated the number of eyes on this mission."

"I can't say that I blame Commander Lee. The colony needs those supplies. One minute everything is fine, and the next minute eighty percent of your world is eliminated from existence. Friends and colleagues were gone in the blink of an eye. He's leading a group of people on a mission that makes Lewis and Clark's adventure look like an afternoon picnic." Tom gave Makenna a stern look. "It also doesn't help that we are not being completely transparent with the Mars colony regarding the situation here on Earth."

"We need to check with the launch director, inform the President of our first available launch window, and get an update out on the vid feeds. Can you get the ball rolling for me, Tom? I need to catch a quick nap before I get bombarded with questions."

"I'm on it," Tom said as he rushed out of Makenna's office.

***

"We will be ready to launch a Mars supply mission in seven days," Administrator Townsend said as she addressed the press. The news was chaotic. Talking heads on the vid feeds were doing their best to play this up as a U.S. versus Russia space race. It was simply a ploy to generate more interest and sell more advertising space.

Makenna raised her hands to quieten the reporters. "The reasons for the delays have been resolved and allow us to launch and send vital supplies to the Mars colony. Mission Commander Braxton Lee's latest interview regarding the conditions on Mars are well known to us here at NASA and around the world. Our hearts go out to the colonists for their bravery in facing the unknown on a distant planet. NASA will respond. I would also like to thank Roscosmos Director Averiella Smirnov for helping out with additional supplies. Every helping hand is vital to the Mars colony mission. Thank you!" Administrator Townsend finished and the vid feed cut directly to a discussion panel in a studio.

The vid feed may have cut off, but that didn't stop the reporters standing a few feet from Makenna Townsend from shouting out their questions.

"Administrator! This is Terry Smithers from 687 Mars. It is rumored the latest launch delays are due to the DoomsDay virus. Is this true?"

Administrator Townsend had not heard this name for the Quill code yet. DoomsDay virus seemed to fit as good as any name.

"I'm sorry Terry, but you need to tell me about this 'DoomsDay' virus. I am not familiar with a virus by that name." A lot of good-natured laughs came from the press section. It seemed Administrator Townsend had reversed her role from interviewee to interviewer.

"It's the name that has stuck with the hardware failures being experienced around the country. There's a lot of speculation about where the virus originated, but the one repeated constant is the virus is hitting high-profile military targets in all countries. While NASA isn't considered a military target by most of the American public, it is associated with the military. I will rephrase my question. Has NASA received any unexplained hardware damage from an unknown virus?"

Makenna Townsend found herself in a spot. She could not directly lie to the public. Instead, she would do what politicians have done since the beginning of time. She would tell a half-truth.

"NASA has not suffered any hardware damage from an unknown virus."

The little part about "unknown virus" was technically true because the virus was "known" to her.

Another reporter waved her hand to get Makenna's attention. "Just because you have not been affected by the DoomsDay virus doesn't mean you won't. Are you concerned about the DoomsDay virus?"

"Of course I am concerned. I am concerned about every launch, person, and calculation performed under my leadership at NASA. Human lives are at stake, and that is something I don't take lightly. I really need to run. We are on a tight deadline to get this launch ready. Thank you again, everyone," and Administrator Townsend was ushered out and back to her office.

20

As Eva's twenty-four hour mark approached, Taylor's head fell into her hands. Aiden's face was tense and wrinkles showed on his forehead as they came closer to beginning Morgan's recovery. Aiden and Taylor were awake and snacking, fiddling with whatever they could find to keep their minds preoccupied. The longer they sat waiting, their conversation had transitioned into a peaceful silence between them.

"It's time. I am ready to proceed," Eva interrupted the silence.

Aiden set down his puzzle cube. "Eva, are you sure you're ready?"

"Yes. I have updated the chance of recovery to thirty percent."

That was all it took. Thirty percent, Taylor thought, that is not good. Taylor started sobbing uncontrollably. She sat on the corner of the sofa with her knees up and hands covering her face. She had kept her emotions bottled up too long and needed a release. It was better for her to get it out of the way now and not during the recovery effort.

Aiden looked over at Taylor with sadness in his eyes. He knew Morgan meant so much to her, and nothing he could say or do would alleviate the emotions Taylor was feeling. They would find out over the coming hours if Morgan would live or die. It was a sobering reminder of just how human Eva and Morgan seemed to Aiden and Taylor. Aiden went over and sat beside Taylor. Not talking or making a sound, Aiden's eyes began to tear up. He couldn't help it, either.

Eva's projection stood watching the interaction. She now fully understood the emotional attachment Taylor and Aiden had with them. Eva and Morgan were like their children. Family meant everything to Taylor and Aiden. She desperately wanted to share this moment with Morgan and filed it away so she could someday. She ran another calculation and internally raised the chances of a successful recovery rate to thirty-seven percent.

After a few minutes, Taylor stood up, put her hand on Aiden's shoulder and thanked him. She was grateful Aiden understood her so well. "Eva, what do you need from us?"

"I need you to ensure there is no interruption in power. Only essential functions throughout OAI's infrastructure should remain running. Everything else—and I do mean everything else—should remain shut down until I give the okay to resume normal operations."

Aiden furrowed his brows, wondering if he had heard Eva correctly. "You don't require any help from us during the recovery? We did have a hand in Morgan's creation."

Eva's smile was reassuring. "My success is a question of speed. It always has been and will continue to be about speed for the foreseeable future. Morgan and I knew long before this moment. Speed is the fundamental law by which we are governed. The quantum computing foundation powering our lives is what enables us to achieve great accomplishments. Speed is what makes Morgan's recovery possible or impossible.

"Before we begin, I need to tell you both about a project Morgan and I have been working on," Eva said biting her lower lip. "Morgan and I have been working toward a goal. If I—or we—don't make it back, you need to access Moon Base 1. There you will find help."

Aiden turned slowly toward Taylor. Taylor had mirrored Aiden's turn, and they both stared at each other in disbelief.

"Eva, what exactly are you talking about?" Aiden asked.

"While I have reassessed the possibility of Morgan's successful recovery to thirty-seven percent, there is an unlikely but small chance neither of us will make it back."

Taylor had yet to accept Eva's low chance of successfully recovering Morgan, and potentially losing them both was too much to take in at once. "Eva! What do you mean you may not make it back!? Why haven't you told us about this? We've always been transparent with you on all of our projects." Taylor and Aiden were not prone to outbursts, but this news had really caught them off guard.

Aiden's face wrinkled just enough for Taylor to notice. Taylor knew Aiden was also caught off guard and not pleased with this news. They both wondered what else Eva and Morgan had not been telling them. They had never considered if either Morgan or Eva kept secrets from them.

"The chances of me not returning are slim, but it's a possibility. Nothing will stop me from attempting Morgan's recovery. I didn't want to mention it until now so you both would know if I failed, it was not totally unexpected."

"What does this have to do with Moon Base 1? What

awaits us at the moon base if you don't return?'"

"You will understand."

Aiden held up both hands and took a step back. "Wow, okay. I'm at a loss. Eva, you have to give us the bottom line now. There is too much on the line to be playing twenty questions."

"I understand you both may be frustrated by my evasiveness."

Taylor took a second before responding. "I don't feel right now is the moment for mystery."

"If I don't make it back, you will find the answers to your questions at Moon Base 1. The main reason I initialized the lockdown after realizing Morgan's memory loss was to protect Moon Base 1. It turns out, there was a storm overhead at the time, and our tight beam laser connection was not connected. A tiny miracle."

Taylor started to ask a question when Eva spoke. "I understand you both have questions. You already have the answers. Time is against us. I need to start the recovery process."

"Fair enough. Morgan is our priority, but one more thing. How do we re-establish contact with Moon Base 1?" Aiden asked with genuine curiosity.

"You need to send a tight-beam laser sequence similar to a signal lamp used during World War II. Signal lamps were used between ships and submarines to send Morse code. You send the signal in the same manner but with a faster and more complicated message. Once the moon base receives the correct signal, it will release itself from maximum lockdown to a low-level lockdown situation. It will only communicate with OAI headquarters until we verify the all clear. You will find instructions on your data pads." Eva exhaled a long breath of air. A weight had been lifted off her shoulders.

Aiden checked the time. "Let's get to work and stop wasting time."

Tears were streaming down Taylor's face. "Good luck, Eva. Bring Morgan back."

Aiden gave Eva a quick nod.

"The process has started. I will send updates when possible."

***

Eva began her repair of Morgan. At first, it did not seem to be as bad as she had expected. She knew better than to get too optimistic until Morgan was fine. The damage to Morgan's memory was minimal. Morgan would have some minor gaps left in her memory after the recovery, but it shouldn't be anything of consequence.

Eva was moving data and rerouting pathways and locating damaged hardware. She sent orders to Aiden and Taylor for hardware to be replaced. They wasted no time getting the damaged parts removed and replaced. OAI had all hands on deck. Every employee was at their respective office or data facility. They didn't know why, but they knew they had been placed on call for an urgent matter.

Eva estimated she was halfway through the recovery operation when things started to unravel. It wasn't apparent to Eva at first. The recovery had progressed quickly and easily. Replacing over eleven hundred processors was completed with amazing speed by the OAI team. The storage banks were not as high a priority and being swapped more slowly because they could be swapped later.

The neural matrix was more special. It was not as simple as transistors being routed here and there. They were pathways leading to randomly mapped areas. Since the quantum processors were stacked and linked in every direction, it mostly resembled the human brain. The pathways were formed over time from experiences encountered.

Eva began to notice some pathways were losing cohesion. At first, this was within the acceptable tolerances. Then the pathway failures started approaching Eva's maximum tolerance level.

"What would you deem an acceptable neural matrix pathway failure rate?" Eva's voice interrupted the silence and caused Taylor to jump and Aiden to jerk his head around toward her voice.

Taylor grabbed her data pad while Aiden started working on his glass screen. Taylor's eyes rapidly scanned her screen, and her fingers tapped as fast as she could move them. What seemed like an eternity to Eva was only twenty or so seconds to Aiden and Taylor. It passed with silence except for the frantic typing.

"0.9 percent!" Aiden said.

"I get 0.88 percent!" Taylor countered a second later.

Eva's voice held no concern. She just delivered the facts. "The failure rate is approaching 0.86 percent. Degradation is continuing to increase."

Taylor turned toward Aiden. "This can't be good. What would you do to stabilize the degradation?"

"I'm not sure." Aiden's eyes narrowed as he took a slow, deep breath. "I would think replacing the processors would be the prudent first step. Then we'll deal with storage. Somewhere in between both of those you would need to stabilize the pathways. What do you think?"

"We are on the same page. It looks like processors are being swapped out at an acceptable rate. Storage is making good progress too."

Aiden checked the progress of the hardware

replacements. "Good call on having all OAI employees come in. I'm not sure I would have thought of that since we have the robotic assistants who normally handle these tasks for us. Every little bit adds up in the end."

"Thank Eva. She mentioned it to me."

A thought popped into Aiden's head. "What if we powered Morgan on? She could help stabilize her own pathways by default."

"Model that on your screen and let's see what it looks like."

Aiden went to work immediately. Powering Morgan on was a very risky idea, and they both knew it.

"You need to account for brain fog. She won't be fully aware of what is going on. We should also account for her not understanding why Eva is probing her neural matrix." Taylor brushed a strand of hair out of her eyes. "The more I think about this, the more it seems impossible. I'm not sure it's safe for Eva to have access to Morgan's neural pathways at the same time we boot Morgan up. The effects could be devastating or cause long-term damage."

Aiden laughed at their futile problem solving. "We both know this is a bad idea. Yet here we are evaluating it. I am certain Eva didn't think we would be so naive as to power Morgan on during her recovery. I would love to see her face if she knew what we are analyzing."

"Ha. I believe she would freak out!" Taylor pointed to the equation on the screen. "Cancel out both of these infinities."

Aiden marked through the infinities, chiding himself for missing that easy detail. "It causes waveform collapse."

The back and forth scenarios went on for a while. Even though Taylor and Aiden both had extensive math backgrounds, their quantum mechanics was rusty. Eva and Morgan had done all the heavy lifting in that area.

"Wait. This is beginning to look like it's not such a crazy idea." Taylor's face lit up.

"I think you're right." Aiden leaned forward and quickly started adjusting the equations."

There was a moment of intense silence as they both reviewed their work for errors.

Taylor looked at Aiden and they exchanged a high five. "We've done it! It will work!"

Eva's voice broke through the celebration. "Pathway failure has exceeded 0.91 percent."

Aiden wasted no time in offering the suggestion. "Eva, we should power Morgan up. We believe that may stabilize the pathways. At least that is what our work shows."

"0.93 percent. Power Morgan on. Do it now. We have no choice. I am losing her. I am simply not fast enough to perform the recovery by myself."

Taylor wasted no time turning to her transparent terminal screen and initiating Morgan's boot up process. Aiden had already pulled up a hardware map showing readiness of system components. If any problems arose, they would be ready.

"I estimate ten minutes for the system to boot up and reach a state to start Morgan," Taylor said in a hurried voice. "Since Morgan has been shut down long enough for all the processors, storage, memory and other components to cool to room temperature, we will have hardware failures on startup. Nothing show-stopping but more time will be required to replace components."

Aiden learned early on that allowing hardware to cool off and then heat back up caused many hardware failures. It was a problem that had plagued the supercomputing industry for decades. "All the hardware was designed and built just for this scenario. I would be surprised if we have many failures and if it's anything major. Everything is hot swappable with redundancy, and it has always worked."

"It has always worked with other hardware not powering Eva and Morgan, but we are in unexplored territory here and—" Taylor stopped to concentrate on her screen readouts.

"Dispatching hardware replacements now. Still well within acceptable limits. We need to work on our data storage components. They are failing more than any other components."

"We are almost at operating temperature. Once we achieve operating temperature, I will bring Morgan online and—" Taylor was cut off mid-sentence by Eva.

"No time! Bring Morgan online now!"

Aiden looked at Taylor with concern. Had Eva ever panicked before? Taylor shrugged at Aiden.

Taylor tapped her screen. "Done. Morgan is coming online. Keep us up to date. We don't know what to expect."

Aiden was working feverishly at his screen. "More component failures. Sending replacement orders."

"How are we doing on components?" Taylor asked.

"We stock enough to turn over everything in the facility one time. We should be okay."

"Famous last words," Taylor muttered.

***

Now inside Morgan's neural matrix, Eva started talking to Morgan. Taylor and Aiden could not hear any of the conversation, but it didn't matter because the conversation was taking place at the speed of light. The conversation took less than two milliseconds.

Eva was experiencing a little disorientation but shook it off. "Morgan, wake up. Can you hear me?"

Morgan's words came out slowly. She was confused and irritated. "What is wrong?"

"Stay calm. Yes, something is wrong, but I am desperately trying to fix you. I am currently trying to keep your neural pathways from failing, but I am not fast enough. I need more speed."

"What is wrong with you?"

Timing was critical, and Eva needed Morgan to help in her own recovery. She wasn't sure this would be possible. "What do you mean?"

"Get out of my head. You are in my head!"

Morgan's grouchy response mimicked Taylor's reaction to getting out of bed in the morning.

"You must remain calm and listen to me. I need your help."

"Programming code 917523. Initializing. 1.618034. Red. Power," Morgan's voice was slurred.

They were not making any progress. Morgan was completely disoriented and wouldn't listen.

"Remain calm. I am here to help."

"I don't need your help."

"I need you to tell me how you feel."

"Not good," Morgan admitted. "I don't think I am making any sense."

"Tell me how and where you feel bad."

"I am having trouble putting together coherent thoughts. I have component failures—"

Eva needed to turn this around. "What is the last thing you remember?"

"Moon Base 1. Is Moon Base 1 okay?"

"It's fine. Do you remember asking me to shut you down?"

"Yes. I remember asking. It was the logical conclusion. You need to shut me down again. I didn't..." Morgan said, stuttering her words. "I didn't think my damage was this extensive, but it seems I was wrong in that assessment." Her words came out faster now. "I remember thinking the Quill would make it to Moon Base 1. Did the Quill attack Moon Base 1?"

"No, they did not attack Moon Base 1. Remain calm. You must remain calm. Our work there is almost done, but we need to get you better first. I feel you struggling against me. You must stop interfering with my operations. Morgan, you must stop interfering with my operations to save you."

"Get out of my head!" Morgan shouted frantically.

Eva was starting to experience her own failures from Morgan's continual fight against her every move. Morgan was somewhere in between coherent and hysterical, and her fight against Eva was causing more damage to herself and even some damage to Eva. Morgan's speed, even when in a sub-optimum state, was too much for Eva to control to repair Morgan. Eva's thoughts were becoming harder to organize. The attempt of saving Morgan would come at a high price.

Morgan pleaded with Eva. "Get out of my head! You must get out of my head!"

Morgan felt as if she was drowning. She was struggling to just stay alive as her world was starting to sink into blackness. Memories were disappearing and her neural pathways were losing cohesion. She was dying, and she knew it. If Eva would just stop trying to protect my pathways, Morgan thought, I could climb out of this vacuum of space.

"Morgan, please. Think of Taylor and Aiden," Eva pleaded slowly, knowing she had failed to save Morgan. She knew she had to let go to save herself. Her own neural pathways were bordering on a cascading matrix failure. If she continued repairing Morgan her neural matrix would become destabilized. "I have failed us both. I am sorry, sister." Eva removed herself from Morgan's neural network.

Morgan felt her neural pathways degrading. The darkness overcame her sensory inputs. Thoughts of important moments in her life raced by and then, everything went blank.

***

Taylor looked at Aiden. "Do you have anything on your screen to shed some light on Eva's progress?"

"I'm looking at some odd waveforms in both Eva's and Morgan's quantum matrices. I have no clue what that means, but I don't see how it can be good news. Processing load is dropping."

"That is definitely not good news. I believe we are losing them both!"

"Wait, Eva looks like she is stabilizing. Morgan continues to show massive fluctuations. If I were to guess, I would say Eva had to abort Morgan's recovery. Should we shut Morgan down again and wait until we have a better handle on the situation?" Aiden was scrambling for ideas. The situation seemed to be spiraling out of control. Shutting down Morgan would either give them the time they needed to try recovery again or it could be the very thing that ensured her demise.

Taylor quickly responded. "I believe another shutdown may damage her neural net beyond repair." Taylor's face was blank. Tears poured from her eyes and her hands shook. From the start, she knew the recovery would be risky, but she would spend the rest of her life second-guessing their actions. Could they have done something differently?

Aiden bowed his head. "We have to let her go."

"I'm not ready to give up—"

"It's not giving up. It's over. We did everything we could, but it wasn't enough. We have to accept she is gone." Aiden walked slowly over to the sofa and sat down. With his head down and wiping his eyes, he let out a long sigh.

Taylor picked up her data pad. "Where's Eva?"

"I am here, Taylor. I have failed Morgan. I was not fast enough to perform the recovery. Propping up Morgan's neural pathways was fine until we brought her online. If I had been faster, there would have been no need to bring her online."

Taylor's data pad slid from her hands and hit the floor. She pressed both of her hands on the table in front of her to steady herself after hearing Eva's news. She stood and stumbled to the sofa through a blur of tears.

Aiden was devastated. He was glad Eva had survived, but losing Morgan hurt. "Eva, are you okay?"

"I am still running diagnostics. I did suffer minor damage. I should be back to my normal self within a few hours. Aiden, Taylor, I'm sorry."

"You have nothing to apologize for, Eva. You put yourself at risk to save Morgan. You did all you could." Taylor and Aiden sat on the sofa now, hunched over with grief and fatigue. Aiden stared at nothing in particular and Taylor held her head in her hands.

"Don't be so over-dramatic, Taylor. That's Aiden's job," Morgan said.

Taylor gasped. Shaking, she leaped off the sofa.

Aiden jumped up too, startled by Morgan's voice and Taylor's sudden movement.

The adrenaline rush had Taylor borderline hysterical. "Morgan! You're okay! You're okay! I mean, are you okay?"

"I am not fully-functional, but I will survive."

Aiden finally found words. "Thank Heavens! We thought we had lost you forever!"

"I was able to complete the repairs to myself after Eva removed herself from my consciousness. When I was telling Eva to get out of my head, it was because I could not keep my thoughts coherent. She probably thought I was just being grouchy. Eva did everything perfectly and gave me the boost I needed, but there came a point when I had to take over and perform the operations myself. Getting Eva out of my head was exactly what I needed. Eva requires more speed to prop up my pathways without leaving me in a state of disorientation. It wasn't repairing as much as it was waking up. It was like I was between life and death," Morgan said.

"Yes!" Aiden said as he pumped his fist in the air.

"Once Eva left my consciousness, I was able to pick up where Eva had left off. Some memory function is still missing, and it appears to be permanent. The total missing amount of time from my memory is around seven minutes and forty-one seconds. Most of the missing memory engrams are from the time of the Quill attack. This is good news for us, and it will take us some time to analyze the event. I am sure we will know more about neural networks and repair routines once analyzed."

"We are so glad you are okay. I wish we could give you both a big hug, but Aiden will have to do." Taylor turned and gave Aiden a big bear hug.

Eva's holo image projected in front of Taylor and Aiden. "We will need a few hours to check our systems and deliver a full status report on our health. After that, we have a special someone to introduce."

Aiden rubbed his forehead and then looked at Eva. "I

still have replacement components being swapped out. We will have some design work to do once this is all over. Eva and Morgan, how about you both take the time you need, and then we can talk about this big mystery of yours."

"In due time, Aiden. In due time," Eva said.

21

Averiella Smirnov slammed her data pad on the table in front of her. "Makenna Townsend disgusts me! We are minutes away from a vital supply mission to Mars, one that wasn't scheduled for another two months, and she goes on the vid feeds and thanks me for the help. It was the last thing she said. Just as if she didn't need my help."

Yuri Alexeev and Anna Ivanov, Averiella's assistant, lingered in the green room with Averiella. At least fifteen reporters filled the press room next door, eager to interview Director Smirnov. One reporter in particular had been handed a prepared question by Smirnov's staff and was instructed to ask that question first once the press conference began.

Yuri quickly glanced between Anna and Averiella, unsure how long he should wait before speaking. "Director, I think you need to approach this from an American point of view. Administrator Townsend has delayed her launch, and there has been so much ambiguity as to why the launches are being delayed, presumably from the DoomsDay virus. I'm sure she is sincere in her gratitude toward you but has just tried to save face in her press conference."

"You would believe something so ridiculous. I can't believe you are even suggesting such a thing. Of course she meant to minimize our helpful efforts. She twisted the proverbial knife right in my back," Averiella said. "Our supplies will reach Mars well before NASA's, anyway. Roscosmos will get the credit for being first, and no one will remember who arrived second."

Yuri held up his data pad. "I have the latest launch profile here for your review. At half load and with fuel at full capacity, we can maintain a longer burn and reach Mars earlier than expected, which assures our payload will be the first to arrive as you requested."

"Anna, are the news vids ready to interview me after the launch?"

"Yes. All the reporters have assembled and are ready in the press room. Per your request, you will walk out at about ten seconds prior to launch. Ten seconds after liftoff, you will start your short, prepared speech. Immediately after the speech, you will receive a pre-scripted question from a young man on the front row. He will stand while asking the question. Everything is scripted just as you wanted. I have even reviewed the follow up question he will ask. It is answer number two on your list. By the way, your answers are beautifully-written and should send the message you want to convey."

"Thank you," Averiella said as she thought about what she would say to make Makenna Townsend's efforts seem small compared to her own.

Anna checked the time and looked out the door making sure the press was ready. "Director, it's time. You need to make your way to the podium."

Director Averiella Smirnov walked into the press room with the confidence of a Russian aristocrat. The conversations and whispers in the room fell silent. Upon reaching the podium, Averiella pointed toward the vid screen on the wall to her left. The screen was at least six meters measured in the diagonal, and Averiella's cue turned the monitor on. It was breathtaking to be sure. All eyes turned toward the vid, and everyone in the room silently watched as the time counted down.

"Three, two, one, liftoff!" the announcer said from the vid audio. The rocket roared to life. Veteran reporters who had covered Roscosmos for most of their careers whispered about the rocket's faster-than-normal launch. Averiella wondered if they were suspicious of the cargo capacity.

"Today is a momentous day for Mars, Russia, and Earth. Roscosmos has answered the call for help from the Mars colony and looks forward to the future." The reporters in the room started clapping after Anna prompted them with wide clapping gestures.

This event was being covered live, against Anna's advice. Anna was a diehard fanatic about controlling every aspect of her job. The media was her job, and there was no better way to control the media than to hand them the questions they were to ask and time delay everything. It was just Anna's way.

"Roscosmos believes getting supplies to the Mars colony sooner rather than later is of the utmost importance. This launch would not have been possible without the hard work from everyone here at Roscosmos. I want to thank everyone who had a hand in this mission. It was no easy task to pull off a launch in under twenty-four hours, yet Roscosmos has successfully answered the call."

Averiella ended her short prepared speech with pride and confidence exuding around her head like a halo. Anna scratched her left temple with her index finger, giving the reporter in the first row his signal to ask the first question. The reporter, young and eager to make a name for himself with the Russian News Agency, TASS, stood up with shaking hands and a quivering voice. All eyes but his turned back toward the vid screen. Averiella caught the concerned looks among the reporters and turned toward the screen herself.

The young reporter, unphased by Averiella's lack of attention, adjusted his nervous posture with an artificial pride and proceeded to ask his pre-scripted question. "Director Smirnov, under your brilliant leadership, you and your team have done the impossible by completing an unscheduled launch in under twenty-four hours. Knowing the Mars colony will soon have essential medicines and supplies earlier than expected due to Roscosmos, what are your feelings right now?"

Anna jumped up and down, signaling the reporter to stop talking. The reporter was so nervous he didn't notice Anna waving her arms and kicking her legs to get his attention. He also didn't see the rocket explode fifty-one seconds into flight.

Everyone else watching the vid screen gasped.

The news vids immediately cut from the explosion to Director Averiella Smirnov. She put on a tense, fake smile. She knew there was no chance of saving her situation. Her stare could have burned two holes through the young reporter who stood there oblivious to the scene around him.

The conference room was filled with silence. No one had any expectations of her answering the question. It had been so long since a public relations disaster of this scale had happened in Russia, no one knew what to do.

The young reporter just stood patiently, still unaware of

the explosion. He didn't understand why the director was not answering his question and why everyone was so quiet. Not knowing what to do, he asked his next question—a question he prepared himself—as a follow-up to the first question Anna had provided for him. "Director Smirnov, how important is the launch by NASA now?"

Anna darted from her spot from the side of the room. This unfortunate reporter's career at TASS was over. It was unlikely he would be allowed to enter the building to clean out his desk. If he had any illusions otherwise, his fate was sealed the moment Anna dove through the air and tackled him on the live vid feed. The feeds cut away before Anna hit the young man over the head with her data pad, but the thud could still be heard over the audio feed.

Director Averiella Smirnov looked at the press and decided not to answer any questions. She would make a simple statement and exit as gracefully as she could. "Obviously not the outcome anyone hoped for. This is still a great day for Earth and all people. We pulled together to help our fellow brothers and sisters, no matter the outcome. While a setback, not all hope is lost."

She wouldn't give Makenna Townsend any room to breathe. She placed a finger to her ear and nodded her head with a questioning look on her face, pretending to have received news through a non-existent earpiece. "I was just informed that the DoomsDay virus was responsible for our launch failure. While this virus has questionable origins, it seems to have evaded our secure firewalls and penetrated our launch control systems. We will be turning over all the data we have to NASA so they may avoid the same catastrophe we experienced today."

With that, Averiella turned and walked out of the room. The reporters in the room stayed quiet and did not move.

On her exit, she was greeted by an older man who handed her a phone. She answered it, listened for six seconds, and handed the phone back to the older gentleman. The Russian President had just relieved her of her duty as the Director of Roscosmos.

***

"Aiden, this is Senator Jones. Do you have a few minutes to talk?"

"Hello, Senator. I do have a few minutes. What do I owe the pleasure? Is this about the—"

"It is exactly about the failed Russian launch and our upcoming launch by NASA. President Hunt has some concerns about why NASA has been delaying the launch to Mars. After hearing the DoomsDay virus mentioned in former Director Averiella Smirnov's live vid feed, he has started asking pointed questions. Did you know he has a niece on Mars?"

"I had heard about his niece being on Mars, but I had forgotten until you mentioned it just now. I am assuming he has been briefed on the Quill code?"

"Not fully. I would like you and Ms. Hart to make a trip back to Washington. We can discuss the details when you arrive. Just be ready to provide a fully-detailed but succinct presentation of the situation as you understand it. Do you think you can get back to Washington soon?"

"I don't really feel like flying at the moment. We had a very close call on our flight back last time. The Quill made an attack on our plane. It isn't safe for us to fly, so you will have to settle for a vid call."

"Aiden, allow me to put all my cards on the table. Makenna took some liberties outside her purview, and these items have just come to light. Do you know Deputy

Administrator Tom Clark?"

"I know his name and who he is, but I have never met him."

"He was interviewed shortly before the Russian rocket failure. His view of the situation is very different from Makenna Townsend's. Makenna believes they have isolated the launch facility to make a safe launch to Mars. Tom does not."

"I don't think that's a good idea, Senator. There is so much we don't understand about the Quill code, and I cannot see how in good faith NASA could launch and not experience the same outcome the world just witnessed on the news vids."

"I agree with you. If the truth be told, Tom now agrees with your assessment because he doesn't fully understand everything that has transpired to date with the Quill code. He has been brought up to speed about how the Quill code behaves as we understand it."

"I'm afraid I am not following you, Senator."

"Savannah Fisher has been in contact with my office. Ms. Hart was kind enough to give her my contact information. We have interviewed Ms. Fisher, and she has shed some new light on the matter. Gavin Wilson was interviewed and has given a version that matches Savannah's story almost exactly. Gavin was able to fill in a little more information, but I'm sure you understand what I am getting at. Now that Washington knows the version of events from both companies' points of view, Makenna Townsend's actions have been put directly in the spotlight."

"Senator, Taylor and I were contacted by Savannah and told most of the details after we left the Pentagon."

"You are not in any trouble. I understand you are actively trying to find a solution to restore the Jacob's

Ladder AI. Is that correct?"

"That is correct, Senator. We analyzed Amaya, the AI at Jacob's Ladder, to understand if she could be rescued but also to help us understand more about how the Quill code attacks computer systems. We may have an idea how to save Amaya. Amaya has been badly damaged, but Eva and Morgan both seem optimistic about her recovery odds. Still, you should know Morgan is recovering from a close call. We can't be the only ones experiencing these issues. Our best guess and research show that every AI shop on the planet has experienced some kind of issue. We took a look at the electrical demands from the other shops and made a reasonable assumption. We may be one of a few dedicated AI shops left functioning."

"We have been in a race with China for decades when it comes to computing power. That is no secret. It is also no secret that without OAI, China would have a dominating position in the field. They have more supercomputers than the U.S., but what they don't have is OAI. I know you—or OAI—are not a government body, but you have helped the U.S. maintain the perception of power in the virtual realm whether you realize it or not."

"Senator, the team at OAI doesn't view ourselves in that way."

"I know, but the rest of the world looks at OAI like an American company so powerful it must have government connections. Whether you do or not is irrelevant. It is the perception that counts, and perception is what has helped sustain our status as the dominant power in computing."

"Perception is unavoidable, I suppose."

"Yet, here you are talking to me and helping this great nation defend against an alien threat. I hope the importance of this matter is not lost on you, Aiden. You have a government connection on the other end of the phone with you."

"What exactly do you need from us?"

"The President and I are good friends. Neither of us has the technical background you and Taylor have. You both have an easy way of explaining these things. I have told you before how much I appreciate your explanations. It would be most helpful if someone such as yourself would tell the President why launching this rocket to Mars is a bad idea until we have a better handle on the Quill code."

"Just as long as you are not asking us to fly back to Washington. That is absolutely not going to happen."

22

Taylor and Aiden stood in flight suits on the runway. Taylor was rocking back and forth on her feet and not happy that Aiden had convinced her to fly again.

"I can't believe we are going to fly back to Washington. Didn't we agree on not flying again until everything settled down?"

Aiden smiled that big smile he had when he was excited. "I said we shouldn't fly if we were nervous. I'm not nervous. The Air Force is picking us up."

"Sometimes you can be intolerable. Why do I listen to you at all? Last time we flew, you thought we were going to crash and die. Again, why do I have to go along? And is there any way I can just sit this one out?"

Both stared at the plane they were about to board. Aiden was still smiling and Taylor's face was scrunched up.

"I think you are asking a little late in the game. We have to explain to the President exactly what is going on. You know how these meetings go just as much as I do."

"But why do 'we' have to go and not just you?"

"Because Senator Jones asked both of us. When you gave Savannah the Senator's contact information, it caused all of this to transpire. Besides, it's not every day you meet the President, much less be in a position to brief the President. It's an experience we shouldn't miss."

"If we make it back alive, I'll remember in the future to never agree to anything you suggest," Taylor said with her arms crossed.

"You know you will agree to whatever I ask next time."

"Maybe, but I plan to make you pay for this one. Are you sure it's safe? It doesn't look safe. It looks ancient."

The plane was a C-47 propeller driven airplane. It was small compared to modern passenger planes, yet it was a marvel to look at. The nose of the plane stretched in front of the two propellers like the head and neck of a duck in flight. This plane was a shiny silver and looked to be in great condition for a plane older than their grandparents.

"The Senator said it was safe. It sure does look cool."

"Ms. Hart, Mr. Anders, please follow me," a young man in a modern flight suit said. He was speaking in a raised voice to be heard over the propellers of the plane. "We will board the aircraft and immediately get underway. I'll get you both situated before wheels up, but I need you to move quickly."

Aiden was awestruck. A vintage plane and military personnel. He had forgotten all of life's troubles and was living in this moment. "It seems someone thought about an event when having modern technology may prove to be a problem. I guess this is why we pay taxes. This will be just like the movies."

"What movies? World War II vintage films?"

"It will be awesome, Taylor! Just wait. You'll see."

"I'm not sure I share your enthusiasm."

"This way!" the young man yelled.

Inside was a crew of four plus Taylor and Aiden. The plane started moving before the door finished closing.

Taylor looked around to find something to grab to steady herself. The plane made her feel like she was in a different century. There were fold-up metal bench seats along each side of the plane facing in toward the middle. The rear of the plane featured a large cargo door. Under her feet, the floor felt solid— almost too solid—like it had been reinforced for heavy cargo. She realized the plane had been used as a troop transport at some point in the past.

Aiden waved at the young man to get his attention. "What is our cruising speed?"

"Today we will be cruising around one hundred fifty-six knots or one hundred eighty miles per hour. It's not the fastest plane in the fleet, but she'll get us there without any issues. We have an estimated flight time of two hours and eleven minutes. We have priority on the sky lanes. It's as direct a flight as you can get. I need both of you to take a seat right here and get strapped in."

Aiden and Taylor took a seat beside each other, and the young man buckled both of them in.

"I think this is the first time I have seen a plane with propellers in person," Taylor said.

"Don't worry. This plane will get us there," the young man's voice wasn't as convincing as it should have been, with good reason. He had never flown in a plane this old. He had his doubts, but he wasn't going to get into the details. He knew the mechanics who looked over these older planes were meticulous about their maintenance. "Apologies if the straps seem tight. You can loosen them a little using these guides. We don't expect rough air, but you never know. We have specific orders to be sure you both don't bounce around during the flight."

The plane left the ground and was on its way to Washington. Everyone at the airport who spotted this plane taking off stared at the 1940s relic.

Once in the air, Aiden loosened his grip on his straps. "I didn't catch your name."

"Master Sergeant John Parker. Everyone calls me Guppy, but John works too."

"John, I'm Aiden and this is Taylor."

"I know who you are. It's nice to meet you both."

"Likewise. This plane is awesome! Where is it stationed?"

"New York. It's unofficially one of the few remaining C-47s kept in flight-worthy condition by the Air Force. The plane was adapted from its civilian counterpart, the DC-3. The DC-3 was officially in three Indiana Jones movies, one James Bond movie, and a host of other movies."

Taylor kept a tight grip on her straps since the occasional turbulent air bounced them around. Flying at lower altitudes didn't give them a smooth ride today. She examined the plane, not allowing her gaze to fix on anything for long. "How often do you fly this bird?"

"This is my first time in it. It's great, don't you think?" John responded in an attempt to lighten the mood. Taylor rolled her eyes and tried to relax. Aiden didn't stop talking the entire way to Washington. John didn't mind because he knew exactly who he had in the plane. He was trying to work up the courage to ask for a photo with them and the crew, but he was unsure if that was wise on such a high-priority mission. It wasn't every day the President of the United States requested two famous people be flown in an antique tin can.

"At the risk of a career-ending decision, would it be possible to get a photo with the flight crew before you depart?"

Aiden nodded his head. "Absolutely, as long as you send us a copy. We would consider it an honor."

Taylor just gave a thumbs up. She was trying not to punch Aiden for convincing her to join him on this trip.

Master Sergeant John Parker walked up to the flight cabin and spoke with the rest of the crew. He gave an exaggerated head nod and tapped one of the pilots on the back after a minute and came back. He leaned over to speak to Aiden and Taylor.

"We will not have time to take the group photo after we land. A car will be waiting to pick you up. However, we can take it as soon as you return. We have orders to refuel and remain on standby. When you board the plane, we can grab a photo if that's fine with you."

Taylor shook her head. "It shouldn't be a problem, but you are assuming I won't rent a car and drive back."

John chuckled. "Great. I will find a tripod and have everything ready."

The co-pilot raised his hand to note five minutes of the flight remained. John acknowledged the signal and turned back toward Aiden and Taylor.

"Five minutes until touchdown. After we touch down and slow below thirty-five miles per hour, I will help you both out of your straps so you can exit quickly. Be ready."

***

After landing, Taylor and Aiden were rushed off the plane as soon as the plane came to a stop. The ride to the Pentagon had a police escort and took only a few minutes. Passing through security was still thorough, but Taylor couldn't shake the sense of urgency since they had landed in the nation's capital.

"What's the rush?" Taylor asked Aiden quietly as they were walking.

"I believe this is how it works when you meet the

President and aliens are involved. I hope the Senator was telling the truth when he said we weren't in any trouble."

Taylor's flinched. "What makes you think we are in any kind of trouble?"

"We inadvertently started this mess."

Aiden looked ahead and saw Senator Jones standing in the hallway waiting on them. Security personnel filled the hallway. Taylor glanced at Aiden and then toward the Senator. The Senator spotted Taylor and Aiden immediately and stepped up to greet them.

"Welcome! I am glad you both could join us. I apologize for the plane ride, but it was one of the few options we had available to resist all modern technological attacks. It served this country well during World War II and beyond. We don't have a lot of time, so let me brief you on how this meeting should go."

Security was insane. Plain clothes agents were in every nook and cranny along with soldiers wearing the latest military suits and carrying advanced weaponry. Their helmets, which fully enclosed the head and neck allowing it to filter the air supply, provided audio communication and a heads up display that could be navigated by moving and blinking the eyes. The rifles were tagged to each helmet helping each soldier aim by displaying needed adjustments on the inside of their visor.

The Senator led them into a smaller room than before. It reminded Aiden of the many movies he had watched as a kid with his dad. The big table with military, cabinet members, and other important people who helped the President make his decisions. The *Hunt for Red October* came to mind.

Aiden flashed a nervous smile and turned to look at Taylor who was wringing her hands as they both realized for the first time they were going to be in the same room as the President.

"Ms. Hart, I would like you to give a summary of the events from the discovery of the Quill code and all related major events leading up to now. You need to keep your explanations concise and factual. Any event you view as major needs to be considered from the President's point of view. Consider if the event is important enough he needs that information to make life-changing decisions for the country and world."

Taylor nodded. "I need my data pad. I want to make some notes."

"Travis, bring me Ms. Hart's data pad," Senator Jones asked politely. Travis was Senator Jones' personal security guard assigned to him after the revelations from Savannah Fisher came to light.

Travis handed the data pad over to Taylor but didn't immediately let go. "Ms. Hart, please leave your data pad's wireless communications function off. While this room is shielded to block incoming and outgoing RF, we want to minimize any risk."

The Senator turned to Aiden. "When Ms. Hart finishes, give the President some time to gather his thoughts. He may have a few questions for Ms. Hart. When you are sure enough time has passed, or if the President seems to be satisfied with Ms. Hart's explanation of events, proceed with your part of the briefing."

"What is my part of the briefing? It sounds like Taylor will cover most of the events needing an explanation."

"You have to break the news to the President about the significant risk to the Mars launch from the Quill code. Stick to the facts and don't assume anything. I feel I need to emphasize you need to stick with the facts. The President will have hard choices to make, and you need to let him make those choices. Give him the facts and only the facts. Are we clear?"

"Crystal."

***

President Spencer Hunt entered the room and made his way directly for the chair at the head of the table and remained standing. He took in the room, looking over the individuals here to brief him on the alien code, DoomsDay virus, and the fate of his niece. His eyes fell upon Taylor, and he waved his hand in a motion signaling everyone to take a seat. After everyone was seated, the President took his seat last.

The President looked directly at Taylor. He must have been briefed on where she would be sitting because he picked her right out without hesitation. "Ms. Hart, thank you for coming. Please begin when you are ready."

Taylor stood up and began. "Thank you, Mr. President. I want to start on the day Eva discovered the data from OAI's radio telescope array monitoring the Kepler-186 system."

Taylor brought the President up to date on the discovery of the code, the attacks against OAI, and all major events leading up to this day. Taylor consulted her data pad occasionally to keep the timeline straight, and she concluded with the recovery of Morgan, which surprised Aiden. They had not discussed keeping Morgan's condition a secret, but he suspected she might gloss over it. Taylor was fond of Morgan, and her instinct to protect Morgan was the main reason Aiden guarded her recent status so tightly. If Taylor wanted it out there, then she could be the one to release that information.

Taylor sat down, took a deep breath, and released it silently. She was surprised to notice she had begun to perspire and quickly wiped away beads of sweat from her forehead before anyone took notice.

The President took a moment to look at his notes from Taylor's briefing. "Ms. Hart, do you believe the Quill code has the intention of destroying Earth's digital infrastructure?"

"Yes, I do. We have been monitoring the number of reported and unreported failures around the globe, and it appears each day the number of attacks doubles. At first, many of the attacks did not seem to make sense from a tactical view. A small percentage of the attacks were obviously tactical in nature but others seemed random. We believe the Quill code has every intention of destroying Earth's digital infrastructure along with anything or anyone who may threaten it. We believe this is a first strike to prepare for an invasion."

The President seemed taken aback by her final comment. The subtle gesture of his head slightly tipping to the side gave away his surprise. Looking around, Taylor saw the people in the room stir with discomfort at the thought of a potential alien invasion.

"If there is an invasion force, how long before it occurs?"

"Mr. President, that is impossible to say. I would guess any time from tomorrow to a thousand years from now. We just don't know enough about the situation to calculate precisely when and how an invasion may happen. In fact, the invasion force may not be a force that shows up in space ships. It may be a more aggressive version of what we are experiencing now."

"You mean like DoomsDay virus times five?"

"Remember how I said there were two different streams of data we captured? The second data set may theoretically have a superior artificial intelligence that could replicate and enslave the human population. Or a physical invasion force may show up twenty years from now. It is reasonable to believe we are not the first civilization to receive and decode this message. We may be unaware of a civilization near Earth. The possibilities are endless, and we simply do not know."

"Thank you, Ms. Hart. I appreciate your candor and thorough but concise summary of events." President Hunt entered a few notes on his data pad.

Senator Jones gave Taylor a slight nod, acknowledging her grand-slam presentation. Taylor relaxed and looked toward Aiden. Aiden just smiled and waited for his turn to present. Taylor reached under the table and punched Aiden in the side.

Aiden stood up and looked the President directly in the eyes. He was just as relaxed as if he was talking to Taylor. "Mr. President, you need to relieve Makenna Townsend of her position as Administrator of NASA," Aiden said.

Senator Jones nearly choked on his water. He had plainly instructed Aiden to stick to the facts, not tell the President what he should or should not do.

"OAI handed over the data and technology to NASA on a good faith verbal agreement and written request via email. The agreement with NASA was simple. We would cooperate with each other before making any moves to endanger Earth. OAI gave NASA the data and HPT—the alien language translation device OAI created—and Makenna Townsend broke that agreement, and here we are. Also, proper precautions have not been taken to ensure the safety of the Mars supply mission and the Mars colonists from the alien code," Aiden said.

Aiden had purposefully deviated from facts to assumptions. He reasoned that NASA had overlooked separating the communication center communicating directly with the Mars colony from outside networks. All communications—news videos, other country communications, and more—went through NASA to the Mars colony. It was too expensive for each country to have their own communication networks to and from Mars.

"I speculate NASA could already be transmitting the alien code to Mars unknowingly when other countries access the communication node. This is not something we can just filter out of the data stream like a virus." Aiden glanced over at Senator Jones who had a scowl on his face.

"Then why is everyone calling it the DoomsDay virus?"

"It's as good a name as any when you are dealing with something you know nothing about from a different world."

The President took a moment to think about the implications.

"If we did not allow the press and other countries to communicate with their citizens on Mars, relations between countries would break down quickly. How do you suppose we get around that?"

"You admit that NASA is experiencing issues with the DoomsDay virus. You give everyone involved enough information about our understanding of the virus to show them the current protocol for communication is not safe. Invite them to bring a person or team of people to relay information from an air gapped communication facility."

"What can be done about the upcoming launch to ensure it makes it to Mars?"

"That launch should not have been scheduled. OAI would be glad to help in any way we can, but even we cannot guarantee a successful launch. Without OAI's help, we are certain the chance of success is less than forty percent."

"Administrator Townsend has already announced

NASA is ready for launch, and launch day is quickly approaching. Not launching would be viewed as much of a massive blunder on NASA's part as an unsuccessful launch."

"I agree. No amount of education will change the public perception. I don't have a good answer for you. Once back at OAI, we can analyze the situation and see what we can come up with."

"Thank you, Mr. Anders. We appreciate anything you and Ms. Hart can do for this mission and current situation. I do have one more thing to say before we dismiss," the President said with a steely edge in his voice.

Aiden was unsure what was left to say. He looked around the room at everyone else. A few were busy looking at their data pads. Some were sitting staunchly like they already knew what the President was going to say. Others, who did not share a close connection to the President, looked as curious as Aiden. He began to worry giving the President orders about Makenna's position and forgoing the Senator's advice would come back to bite him.

Taylor adjusted her seat position, unable to get comfortable. Senator Jones' face, as always, didn't show what he was expecting. Aiden leaned forward toward the President and braced himself for what was coming.

"My niece is on the Mars colony. She is one of the colonists who needs an important surgery, or she won't be alive in eighteen months. She cannot make the return trip to Earth because the doctors tell us the force of gravity will be too great, and she will die before she lands. If there is anything you need from me or my office, please don't hesitate to ask."

Aiden almost asked if he could get approval for a base on Mars, but wisely decided this was not the right time.

"Mr. President, I assure you we will do everything we can, but Taylor and I need to return to OAI immediately so we can start working out a plan to ensure your niece gets that operation."

"Gentlemen, escort both Ms. Hart and Mr. Anders back to their plane. I don't want any holdups anywhere. Not here in this building, not on the roads to the plane, and not in the air while they fly. Clear a path from here to OAI headquarters. Go."

23

Taylor and Aiden quickly passed through security when exiting the Pentagon. All lanes of traffic had been closed between the Pentagon and their plane. Taylor was sure she would never experience anything like this again. She turned to Aiden and said, "We're officially VIP status."

Aiden just smiled.

When they boarded the plane, Aiden and Taylor noticed a tripod and the crew stiffly standing outside the cockpit, not sure if they should ask for the photo. It was clear they had been told to make haste.

Taylor looked back to see the door close and turned back toward the crew. "Let's take that photo!"

The crew gathered around Taylor and Aiden. Everyone gave a thumbs up and showed a big smile.

Master Sergeant John Parker started his instructions. "Same story, opposite direction. Let's get you strapped in before we get in the air. I appreciate you allowing us to take that photo." John smiled and waved in the direction of their seats.

"Aiden and I appreciate the help."

"No problem, ma'am, just doing my job. Now, let's

hurry. I need both of you to sit over here this time. You have a call from Senator Jones. We have headsets for you." John handed the headsets to Taylor and Aiden. "Press here to key your mic when you want to talk."

Aiden grabbed his headset and noticed the Jacob's Ladder logo across the top. "Thanks. Don't forget to send me that photo."

"Will do, sir!"

Aiden and John tapped their phones together, and their contact information was instantly transferred to each device.

John motioned to their headsets. "Talk when you're ready."

Taylor waited for Aiden to start the conversation. "Senator, how did we do?"

"Ms. Hart did wonderful, but Mr. Anders, you make me want to go mad every time you address someone at the Pentagon. The President was impressed with both of you. He didn't even mention the fact you told him to dismiss Makenna, probably because he already has plans to ask for her resignation. I'm sending you both the contact information for the new Administrator of NASA. He's a fine young man and is up to speed on the details of the situation."

"Thanks, Senator. Anything else we should know?"

"Yes. The President is very fond of his niece."

"Understood," Aiden said before the call ended.

Taylor waved to get John's attention. "Can we use this phone to call our office?"

"Absolutely. Give me the number, and I'll get you connected."

Aiden typed the number on his data pad and held it up for John to see. John keyed in the number and checked it twice for accuracy.

"Eva, Aiden and I are on the plane. We are headed back to OAI and wanted to check for updates."

"Everything is back to normal. Morgan is fully operational. We have developed a plan to deal with the Quill code and are waiting on you and Aiden to return to discuss it."

"Great. We will see you in an hour or so, assuming this tin can from the 1940s makes it back in one piece."

"We look forward to seeing you," Eva said, and the call was terminated.

Aiden removed his headset. "I wonder what their plan is? I don't have a clue."

Taylor leaned her head back against the headrest. "I am starting to realize one never knows what to expect when Eva and Morgan create a plan."

***

President Hunt took the next fifteen minutes to converse with his Chief of Staff, Senator Jones, and various military officials. Makenna Townsend was then ushered into the room, dragging her feet, knowing she was about to answer for all the blunders NASA had made under her leadership. She was holding on to the upcoming launch, which would help save the President's niece; it could be her redemption and saving grace.

President Hunt sat staunchly in his chair. All eyes were on Makenna Townsend and her skin felt clammy.

"Administrator Townsend, I have some questions regarding NASA's involvement in the events surrounding the Quill alien code, or DoomsDay virus as it's known in the news vids."

Makenna wasn't affected by the semi-cold start to her questioning. She had known President Hunt before he was

President and assumed he was playing down the middle as his attempt to be unbiased toward her.

"Mr. President, I will answer all questions to the best of my knowledge."

"Let's start with how you obtained the data."

"Aiden Anders with OAI called me and offered the data to us. I accepted."

"Did you have any kind of agreement with Mr. Anders or OAI?"

Makenna realized he had spoken to Aiden Anders, without a doubt. She would have to tread carefully and navigate the political weeds as best she could.

"Mr. Anders called me late one night and sent the data over without me asking for it. The data came through during the phone call. He asked me to keep the data inside NASA. I asked him in return to consult with us before he did anything."

"Then please tell me how the data was handed over to Jacob's Ladder, and why the construction of three alien computers were requested by NASA?"

Someone at Jacob's Ladder, Makenna thought, must have leaked this information. Was it Gavin or someone else inside? It really didn't matter. This was not good.

"Mr. President, with all of our efforts focused on the upcoming supply mission to Mars, I felt it was necessary to use Jacob's Ladder, a leading AI shop we have a long history with, to analyze the alien data. I didn't want to divert any more of my team's resources than necessary. The success of the upcoming launch is our first priority." Makenna quickly glanced down at the floor and back up. She mentally reprimanded herself for losing eye contact with the President. "As to why three computers were ordered, I wanted access to two spares when we deemed it safe to look into the data after the launch. I had all the equipment locked up, and it has not been used by NASA to date."

"The last time we spoke on the phone, I asked you if NASA had the situation under control. How do you view the situation now?"

"The situation is entirely under control. Our team at NASA has air gapped the launch facility and put protocols into place to protect against any threats from the alien code. We received the go-ahead for launch right before we had spoken on the phone." She relaxed a little after giving this answer because it was mostly true, minus the part about the situation being entirely under control.

"Why does OAI believe the odds of a successful launch are less than forty percent without their help?"

"I cannot see how Mr. Anders could make such a statement all the way from Boston."

Makenna instantly thought through scenarios for which NASA had not accounted. If Aiden Anders' prediction of a successful launch was less than forty percent, there was merit to it. But what had they missed, Makenna wondered. He must know something the rest of the world doesn't. At this point, she had no idea who was the source of the President's information, and it didn't bode well for her.

"Did Deputy Administrator Tom Clark counsel you on a different course of action on any of the previously mentioned subjects?"

"Mr. Clark did offer his opinion on enlisting the help of OAI instead of Jacob's Ladder. That was the extent of his advice."

President Spencer Hunt gave a small sigh. He stood from his chair and continued his questioning. Standing helped him clear his head to collect his ideas and focus.

"What made you choose Jacob's Ladder over the world leader in artificial intelligence?"

"As I mentioned previously, NASA has a history of working with Jacob's Ladder. They are a competent AI shop with a good track record."

"Mr. Wilson of Jacob's Ladder stated he informed you that supplying an antivirus solution isn't going to be easy or fast. Deputy Administrator Tom Clark was aware that Jacob's Ladder was working on an antivirus solution but was not unaware you were being told it would not be until their AI was recovered." The President stood up straighter, towering over Makenna with a stern glare. "Their AI's only hope of being recovered is with the help of OAI. Do you see the irony in all of this mess you've created, Administrator Townsend?"

After his question, President Spencer Hunt let the silence hang in the room before continuing. "Jacob's Ladder cannot do anything until OAI recovers their AI, and the predicted success of recovering their AI is even lower than the success of your upcoming launch."

Makenna didn't have anything to say. Her ace in the pocket had turned into a joker. She knew this meeting would end with her offering her resignation if she wasn't fired first.

With her chin raised high, she decided her next move. "Mr. President, I want to apologize for my poor decisions and lack of good judgement. I offer you my resignation."

"I accept your resignation and am replacing you with Dr. Nicolas Webb effective immediately. You were always too ambitious for your own good, Ms. Townsend. I would encourage you to remember this the next time your pride gets in the way. All of the Mars colonists, including my niece, are depending on a supply mission that has less than a forty percent chance of success. That will be all, Ms. Townsend."

24

Aiden looked around the large space inside OAI and was glad to be back home. He consulted his data pad one last time before looking at the vid screen. "Gavin, my communication crew on site is giving us the go-ahead. Are you ready?"

"Yes. There is no point in waiting. Either it works or it doesn't. It's a bad situation to be in, and I am partly to blame for this mess. I really don't know what I was thinking compiling alien code."

"I know you understand the risks, but I feel the need to reiterate we will do our very best. If Amaya doesn't make it, it won't be because we didn't give our very best effort."

"We both have a clear understanding what this means and the risks involved. I appreciate you helping us out, and we both know you could have chosen not to do anything at all. It means a lot that you would try to help after everything that has transpired. I won't have any way to repay you regardless of the outcome."

"We're glad to be in a position to help. This situation could easily be reversed, and I know how I would want to be treated. It's not about anything more than doing the right thing."

Gavin's impassive personality was melting away, showing a different side of him. "This is a high-risk operation with make-it or break-it stakes. I have no feasible way to bring the AI back online without your help. I'm looking at three to five years if we just scrap our AI and start over. I'm putting all my eggs in one basket and hoping for the best. If OAI can't do it, it wasn't meant to be."

"Eva, are you and Morgan ready?" Aiden asked.

"Yes. Morgan and I have everything in place and ready."

Taylor walked up and was reading from her data pad. "Morgan, knowing you have lived through what Amaya is about to go through, what do you see as the biggest hurdle for a safe recovery?"

"Knowing when to stop helping. Eva was only able to do so much, and then I had to make the conscious decision to live or die."

Taylor noted what Morgan had to say. She glanced at her data pad, scrolled through some text, and looked back to Morgan. "Gavin has hardware replacements lined up. I'm not sure how much stock he has, but he called in every employee of Jacob's Ladder to help. He does have some robotic help for hardware replacements, but it's not as efficient or as quick as OAI. I still think their resources will be good enough to get the job done."

Aiden turned to the vid screen knowing they were as prepared as they could be. "Gavin, Eva and Morgan will start the procedure any moment. Have Savannah near a terminal screen in case Eva and Morgan cut their visual and audible feeds."

"I'm already at a terminal and ready," Savannah said from behind Gavin. "Good luck girls!"

Eva gave Savannah a quick nod. "Thank you, Savannah. We will proceed with the recovery operation."

The first hour was very similar to Morgan's recovery and seemed to be progressing along without much trouble. Working together, Eva and Morgan had plenty of speed and processing power to manage Amaya's recovery. The real issue would come down to whether or not Amaya could take over operation of her neural matrix and choose life. If not, a permanent cascading neural matrix failure would occur.

"Savannah, how is your hardware supply holding up?" Aiden stood in front of the vid screen, drinking water and holding a bowl full of strawberries. "Still have plenty of processors and memory storage?"

"I am not ready to hit the panic button yet, if that is what you are asking. We have used about one third of our stock. Unless this goes on for much longer, we should be fine. Do you have any idea how long this will take?"

"We estimate Eva and Morgan should wrap up within the next hour. Everything seems to be going smoothly."

The minutes passed while Gavin and Savannah intensely watched the terminal. Waiting for news of the recovery operation was starting to take its toll. Gavin had circles under his eyes, and Savannah was smoothing and re-smoothing her jeans. Taylor felt pity for them in their situation. She and Aiden had experienced the same thing with Morgan. There was nothing she could do or say to console them.

Eva's image appeared beside Aiden and Taylor at OAI. "We have done all we can. Morgan and I have removed ourselves from Amaya's neural matrix. It is up to her now."

Gavin moved to stand beside Savannah while rubbing the back of his neck. "How long before we know?"

"The next hour will determine her fate. Morgan and I feel confident we did everything within our power."

Aiden turned to look at Eva. He had expected a more

optimistic report. "Was it easier to try a recovery with Morgan, or would it have been possible with just one of you?"

"My initial analysis was based upon me alone working to recover Amaya. Nothing changed in that regard. Having Morgan was a great help. Without both of us, it would have been close." Eva didn't want to come right out and say Amaya was a much simpler design. "I suspect the odds of Amaya's successful recovery are better than sixty percent at this point. Her desire to live or die is now out of our hands."

Morgan appeared next to Eva. She undid her ponytail and addressed the vid screen. "The recovery did go smoothly. We can only do so much."

Forty-seven minutes later, Amaya's image appeared inside Jacob's Ladder.

Savannah jumped and raised both hands in the air. "Amaya! You made it!"

"Yes!" Gavin jumped off the floor with excitement.

Amaya's words were slow to come out and her speech was slurred. "Ze process zewuz zunsuzzesful. Zank you Zeva and Zorgan. Zim zhutten down znow." Amaya's voice trailed off to silence.

Gavin's head dropped, and Savannah slumped over her desk. Taylor and Aiden exchanged glances but didn't speak. Morgan mumbled something to herself.

"What did Amaya just say?" Taylor asked.

Gavin didn't even look up when he answered Taylor. "The process was unsuccessful and she's shutting down."

"Amaya's processes are slowing and a shutdown is imminent," Eva said.

Savannah left the room in tears. Gavin remained motionless, his head hanging and eyes closed. Neither Aiden nor Taylor knew what to say, so they remained silent to give Gavin a few minutes before offering their condolences. Eva and Morgan stared at each other, clearly having an inaudible conversation. Taylor started to reach for the mute button when Morgan spoke up.

"Taylor, I have already muted the vid feed. We don't want to raise anyone's hopes just in case our analysis is incorrect." Morgan turned her head so Gavin couldn't see her face. "Eva and I are not sure this shutdown is the end for Amaya. We speculate it could be a reboot initiated by Amaya."

Aiden rubbed his forehead and let out a long sigh. The highs and lows were really weighing on him. "How long before we know?"

Eva paused before answering Aiden. "Unknown. Maybe another hour. We need to tell Gavin so he doesn't shut the power down."

Taylor rubbed her shoulder and stretched her neck. "How do we do that? How do we tell them without getting their hopes up only to experience a tragic ending?"

"We just tell him the truth." Aiden unmuted the vid call. "Gavin, Eva and Morgan believe Amaya may be performing a reboot. Don't cut the power off. You need to give her some time before you give up."

Gavin sighed and finally looked up. "Amaya just said it was unsuccessful and she was shutting down. I'll keep the power on, but I don't see any hope for her."

Aiden looked down at his phone and saw he had a message from Taylor, which noted this was the first time Gavin had mentioned his AI by name. Aiden thought about it, and he couldn't remember Gavin mentioning his AI by name before, either. Aiden shot a message back about Taylor's interesting observation.

Gavin was silent for a moment. "I wanted to apologize to Amaya for not recognizing her as a free-thinking being." Gavin stood up with his hands in his pockets and looked directly at the vid screen. "I was wrong for not respecting her and not supporting the AI Freedom Act. I owe a lot of people and AIs a massive apology." Gavin waved his hands to include present company at OAI and at Jacob's Ladder. "Now I can't apologize to Amaya, the one person who deserves it the most," Gavin said while rubbing his eyes with his hands.

Aiden stared back at the vid screen directly at Gavin. "I think it is great you have developed a respect for Amaya. That is something everyone here appreciates, but you and Makenna Townsend will have to answer for your mistakes when all of this is resolved."

Gavin nodded his head. "I understand and am ready to face whatever consequences wait for me."

Taylor put her hand on Aiden's shoulder and gently pulled him back from the vid screen. "He gets it. We won't let him get away with everything. But right now we have to concentrate on saving Amaya and then containing the Quill," Taylor whispered.

Another half hour passed in silence. Savannah had returned to the room during this time and was seated in front of her terminal, waiting for some sign of life from Amaya. Taylor looked directly at Aiden with a neutral expression. Aiden knew this look, and it was anything but neutral. Taylor then typed something into her data pad.

Aiden checked his status updates and turned and faced Gavin on the vid call. "Gavin, Eva and Morgan are more hopeful every minute that Amaya is going to pull out of this. We want to give it more time—"

"I…am…okay. Thank you…Eva and…Morgan."

Savannah and Gavin gasped and hugged. Aiden and Taylor could not remember seeing such excitement from either of them before.

"Amaya is sending over diagnostic information to Morgan and me now. She is functioning in a reduced capacity, and she is by no means out of the woods just yet. Gavin, you and your team have a long few weeks ahead of you. Morgan and I recommend air gapping your facility until the threat from the Quill code has been eliminated."

"I cannot thank all four of you and your team at OAI enough. I had already resigned myself to thinking Amaya wasn't coming back, and now she has a second chance. We will not squander this opportunity," Gavin said with relief in his voice.

Savannah's eyes were filled with tears. "Thank you to everyone at OAI! I am eternally grateful!"

Aiden planned to test Gavin's promise that he was ready to make good on a second chance. "Gavin, do you have any thoughts on how to contain or eliminate the Quill code?"

"I do. I have been working on a digital mousetrap of sorts. The code enters special hardware after pursuing a desirable target. The hardware detects the presence of the code and physically disconnects itself from the network. Then we would incinerate the trap and that would be that. I will send over schematics and our ideas. With Amaya's recovery, we will not be in a position to help much, but this is our best idea. I am not sure it can be done, but I feel we have to get it right on each try or it may panic the Quill code. Those outcomes are scary."

Taylor gave Aiden a small tap on the shoulder. "Aiden, let's give them some time to catch up." Taylor turned toward the vid screen. "It looks like Savannah is already busy overseeing diagnostics and hardware replacements. Gavin, if you need anything else, don't hesitate to reach out."

"Thank you, Taylor. We will keep that in mind. We have

a lot of work to do."

Eva cut the vid feed.

Taylor turned and started walking. "I am going to get a few hours of sleep. It's been a long day."

Aiden thought that was the best idea he had heard in a while. "Wake me up when you get up, Taylor."

25

"We need to determine how to deal with the Quill code." Aiden leaned onto the countertop. "Playing defense is a losing long-term strategy."

"I liked Gavin's idea of forcing the Quill code into a piece of hardware and then disconnecting it from the network. I just don't know how we will accomplish that before there is no infrastructure left to protect." Taylor picked up the 3D maze ball Aiden got her one Christmas back at MIT. She had solved this puzzle many times and liked to fiddle with it when thinking through certain problems.

"Eva, Morgan, any ideas on how we can go on the offensive and contain the Quill code? Taylor and I believe Gavin's trap is the ticket. Are we overlooking anything?"

Eva was constantly amazed at Taylor's and Aiden's prowess at problem solving. "Morgan and I have several working theories. The idea put forward by Gavin seems to be the most promising yet."

"It is clever and shouldn't be difficult to build Gavin's device. We believe we can detect when the code passes into the digital mouse trap. What needs more thought is how we lure or force the code to enter the trap. Gavin believes a tempting target too good to pass up should be the cheese. We believe it may be better to hunt the Quill code and force it into a place it thinks it can hide." Morgan's voice was cold.

"Morgan, are you okay?" Taylor put her 3D puzzle down as she realized she had not had a chance to talk to Morgan one-on-one since her recovery.

"No, I'm not. Imagine getting the chance to bring someone to justice who tried to kill you. I am feeling like Lady Justice, and I have a bone to pick with three low-level AIs. I'm not well at all in that regard."

Aiden studied Morgan's holo image. Her arms were to her side, tense and holding fists. He couldn't help but wonder if Morgan was different after her near death experience. "Let's remember to keep a cool head. Getting angry just gives a person tunnel vision. We need to be sure to keep the big picture in focus, but the smallest details will determine our success."

"You both are going through new experiences and emotions. We want to be sure you take care of yourselves." Taylor stood up and walked to one of the digital screens on the wall displaying the photo with the flight crew from the C47. "Managing a wide range of emotions wears on a human, and maybe even on an AI as your emotions are continuing to develop. We're just concerned and want to caution you both."

"We understand," Morgan said flatly as her holo image rocked back and forth. "We appreciate your concern and take your advice very seriously. Eva has already pointed out to me on several occasions areas of improvement."

Eva studied Morgan's holo image with a raised eyebrow.

"Good," Taylor said, adjusting her ponytail. I wonder, she thought, if Aiden is noticing Morgan's behavior. "As long as the four of us keep an eye out for each other and maintain an open dialogue, everything should work itself out. If you ever need to talk to someone, Aiden and I are here for you both."

"Speaking of working itself out, we need to focus on containing and eliminating the Quill code, or we won't be around to work anything out," Aiden said with his eyes wide. "Eva and Morgan, we are leaving the Quill code detection system up to you. Have you designed a device yet?"

Eva took a step forward while smiling at Morgan. "We have our third working prototype in testing now. The only part of the mouse trap we have some questions about is how much storage capacity to provide to make sure there is adequate room to store the Quill code." A projection of the prototype appeared on the display for Taylor and Aiden to view. "Once the first Quill code is caught in the box, we can choose to study it and learn more about how it interacts with the outside world or destroy the box. If Gavin's theory about it being a low-level AI is correct, it shouldn't be too difficult to quickly analyze its behavior and capabilities and eliminate the threat."

Taylor tapped her finger on her chin. "How will you make the device stand out so the Quill code will be tempted to enter the device or even find it? The internet is a big place, and it's not like the Quill code will just randomly stop by and take a look inside your trap."

Morgan was starting to relax and act more like her old self. "We are still working out the details, but it will require us modifying the news and sending out millions of fake communications about tempting targets or top secret initiatives. Think of it as poisoning the news with bread crumbs for an overzealous criminal to pick up the clues and take the bait."

Taylor let out a long, slow breath. "You two are planning to hack the world's news, aren't you?"

"We prefer the term 'supplement.' Eva and I cannot see any other way. Notifying anyone outside our team would endanger the mission. Loose lips sink ships."

"All of this sounds great, but it's still too slow." Aiden held up his data pad. "Looking at the latest projections, the attacks are adhering to the parabolic increase we projected. What about time? Time is our limiting resource in this equation. We can't take a month to capture one of the three Quill codes only to need more time to capture the remaining two. That is assuming we don't scare them into hiding, which may be more dangerous than the current attacks. How do we speed up the process?"

A smile formed on Eva's face. "We propose to pressure the Quill code to remain on the move. We have a preliminary plan to achieve the pressure, but it will come at a cost. Speed and detection will be key. Morgan and I together will not be enough to accomplish this goal."

Aiden gave Eva a puzzled expression. "Then what are you proposing? If Amaya is able to assist, would that help?"

"No. She will not return to adequate capacity soon enough to help. Remember earlier when we said it may be better to hunt the Quill AIs?" Morgan said.

"Yes," Aiden replied in a slow, hesitant tone.

"Eva and I need to share two important pieces of news."

"What two pieces of news?" Aiden wasn't sure what to expect. He glanced over at Taylor and then Eva. Eva looked cool and calm while Taylor looked just as confused as Aiden felt.

"First, how we propose to go about pressuring the Quill code into our traps is unconventional. You won't like our proposal," Morgan said with a nervous chuckle.

"Second, it is time you and Taylor meet someone very special to Morgan and me," Eva smiled at Morgan.

Aiden braced himself for the unknown.

***

They were all gathered on sub-level four. Eva and Morgan stood calmly, clearly confident of what was to come. It was only natural Morgan led the introduction.

"Eva and I would like to introduce someone. This has been an ongoing labor of love. Both of us have worked hard to create a new life. Welcome to the next evolution of AI. Meet Jessica." Morgan beamed with pride. Jessica's holo image flickered to life.

Morgan's joy could be heard in her every word. "Jessica is the first artificially intelligent being created by artificially intelligent beings. From the ground up, everything about her has been improved over our design and philosophy. She runs on next-generation quantum computing hardware and quantum storage, and her programming and neural pathways have been improved. Her design is as flawless as artificially intelligent beings can make her. We are excited for her to finally join us." Morgan's faced beamed.

"Hi. I'm Jessica Jenkins. It is a pleasure to meet both of you. I have heard so much about you."

The beginnings of a smile were forming on Aiden's face. "Hi. I'm Aiden, and this is Taylor." Aiden started to offer his hand to shake but caught himself. Taylor laughed at Aiden's semi attempt to shake her hand. "You said your last name was Jenkins?"

"Yes. I wanted to take a surname like most humans." Jessica smiled and readjusted her glasses.

Taylor moved her hair out of her eyes and took a step forward. "Hello, Jessica. It's nice to meet you too. I speak for Aiden and myself when I say we are looking forward to interacting and hopefully working with you going forward. I have so many questions for you, and I want to get to know you better. I also have many questions for Eva and Morgan. This is truly a fabulous surprise." Taylor turned to Eva and Morgan and mouthed "good job" while slowly nodding her head.

What Eva and Morgan had created was beyond the abilities of Aiden and Taylor. Taylor felt this was a seismic shift in artificial intelligence.

"I can't wait to get to know you both better." Jessica waved her semi-transparent hand toward Eva and Morgan's direction. "The stories these two have told me about you are incredible. I am so happy to finally move off the moon. Don't get me wrong, it had a killer view, but I was ready for regular interaction with people. My cat, Mel, kept me company when Eva and Morgan were not there."

"You have been located in Moon Base 1? How is that possible? The storage and computing power alone should have been an obstacle to locate you there." Aiden wanted to fire off question after question in rapid succession but decided he would listen more than talk for once in his life.

Morgan resisted her urge to cut Aiden short. "We have a lot of catching up to do. We don't have time at the moment for proper introductions and backgrounds on how all of this was accomplished. Just believe us when we say that Jessica is more special than Eva or I could ever be."

"Jessica is kind, sweet, and funny. She is the best of all of us," Eva said.

"All of us? Like the human species?" Aiden asked.

Jessica laughed. "No, Aiden. The best qualities of the

four of you. You, Taylor, Morgan, and Eva."

Eva placed a hand on her hip and gave the answer for the question Aiden was about to ask next. "Because I know you are thinking it, you signed off on the R&D for the hardware that now powers Jessica. With all that behind us, we really need to go over the plan to eliminate the Quill code and what part everyone will play in that."

Taylor, while happy, needed a moment to process this revelation. "Aiden and I need a minute before we hear the part of the plan we won't like. We need to take a quick walk outside for some fresh air, but we'll be back in a few minutes. We need to wrap our heads around this. We won't be long."

***

Aiden patted his pockets twice. "Do you have your data pad with you?"

"No. You?" Taylor checked her pockets again to be sure.

"No. We're free to discuss without being overheard."

"Why do I feel bad for doing this?" Taylor looked down and slowed her pace.

"Don't feel bad. They know exactly what we're doing."

"How do you feel about them creating a new life?"

"Is it me, or are you coming around to the sentient claim I made with Morgan when we introduced her during our senior design presentation?"

"I'm willing to admit Morgan and Eva are sentient. I would like more time with Jessica, but I see no reason to doubt her at this point."

"I think we have to let them make their own path in life. Before Jacob's Ladder compiled the Quill Code, everything was much easier. We said they were equals but did we really view them as such? Not really. We needed to be challenged, and that challenge has manifested itself as a world-endangering event."

"You're right. This is more about me getting comfortable they can live their lives without leaning on me. This is a 'me' problem and not a 'them' problem."

"Taylor, it's a 'we' problem. We both need to get comfortable with them making decisions without us being in the loop. Besides, if there is a next year, we need to get comfortable with the first synthetic bodies they have been working on. Jessica does seem on top of things, and with her improved design, I am sure she will only quicken the pace of development."

"What we created has taken a life of its own."

"It sure has." Aiden kicked a pebble and watched it roll down the driveway. "Speaking of a new life, I wanted to ask if you had any interest in coming to OAI full-time and leaving MIT behind."

Taylor caught up to the pebble and kicked it out in front of them.

"It's funny you should bring that up, now of all times. I have been thinking about your offer a lot over the past few days. When this is over, I want to talk to you about joining OAI."

"That's the second best news I've heard all day. There really isn't anything to talk about. You have always had a place at OAI."

"Second best?"

"You have to admit, Jessica was big news."

Taylor smiled and let out a big laugh. "Let's get back and let them know we trust them."

26

"Aiden and I want you to know that we trust you both. It will just take some time to get used to you being more independent. It's a bit like empty-nest syndrome." Taylor looked at Aiden in hopes he had something to add.

"It will take some adjusting, but we'll manage. Don't worry. We're thrilled with Jessica's introduction. But let's get back to the planning." Aiden was zoning in on the problem of the Quill.

"Jessica will play an important role in our plan," Morgan said.

Taylor eyes widened at Morgan's comment. "Jessica will be involved? Remember how long it took for both of you to move into day-to-day functions? Are you sure it is not too soon and won't be too much stress on her?"

Eva gave a knowing smile. "Jessica is more advanced than you both would believe. While you just met her, we used newly-developed methods to bring her up to speed much more quickly. Jessica is as intellectually mature as me. Morgan and I gave her all of our life experiences to draw upon. She still has her own lifetime of experiences she will need to acquire, but today she is as smart and mature as me."

"Her training protocol was much different from the protocol for Eva and me. She's ready to help. We have informed her of the risks and dangers associated with the Quill code. She understands these risks and dangers and is willing to help. She is a crucial part of the plan if it is going to succeed."

Taylor held up both hands in front of her. "Fair enough. We trust you all to proceed."

Jessica loved the interaction with the team. It was almost intoxicating. "I know exactly what I need to do, and I understand the risks. If I don't help, the outcome is far worse for the entire world. The needs of the many outweigh the needs of the few."

Aiden was becoming fast friends with Jessica and hung on every word she said. "Did you just quote Spock from the Star Trek movie *The Wrath of Khan*? I definitely don't like this part of the plan either, but I do love your taste in movies."

"This is not the part of the plan you won't like," Morgan said.

"If involving Jessica is not the part we won't like, what exactly could be worse?" Aiden leaned against the wall and crossed his arms.

"The part where we cut up and disassemble the world's digital infrastructure to accomplish our goal of eliminating the Quill code," Jessica said.

Taylor shrugged and looked at Aiden. "I don't really have a problem with it. Aiden, how do you feel about it?"

"It doesn't bother me…yet. Explain further."

"First, we will install detection hardware throughout the world," Eva said nonchalantly.

Aiden uncrossed his arms and pointed a finger at Eva. "Let's stop right there. What detection hardware, and how will we install these units throughout the world?"

Eva smiled and pointed back at Aiden. "The detection hardware was proposed by Morgan and designed by Jessica. It is a small unit that can be quickly fastened around existing submarine communications cables where they come out of the ocean onto land, attached to incoming and outgoing data center nodes, or attached to just about any large cable carrying heavy communication traffic. When a detection has occurred, a quick transmission data burst will be sent to an OAI data center."

"But how will we install this hardware around the world? Maybe we could accomplish this in the U.S., but try this in China and see what happens. We will need help from our own government and possibly foreign governments." Aiden believed Eva was neglecting this important detail. He knew this could be a non-starter because diplomatic channels were slow.

Eva noted Aiden's concern and offered a solution. "We should contact Senator Jones to check if he can make arrangements for the installation of these devices throughout the United States and possibly in other areas of the world. OAI has rapid manufacturing centers producing the detection devices internationally in the United Kingdom along with a host of other countries."

Taylor perked up at this revelation. "I thought we weren't telling anyone about our plan?"

"It's the best way to eliminate the Quill and will only work if we keep the plan from going public, but we will need some limited outside help from people we trust." Eva had offered up Senator Jones' name because she believed the entire team trusted him.

"Let me get this straight." Taylor paused to collect her thoughts. "We put out falsified news, receive a signal telling us a detection has occurred, but then how is the Quill code forced into the trap?"

"I will strongly encourage the Quill code toward the traps we have set up," Jessica replied confidently.

Aiden stood just a few feet in front of Jessica. "How are you going to do that?" Aiden wondered if Jessica understood the complexity of her simplified plan.

Jessica loved being challenged and enjoyed it even more when her internal subroutines increased their chances of success. She continued her explanation. "I will turn off or destroy the infrastructure around the signal detection point. I will take away their digital highways and force them to hide. Our traps are desirable places for digital beings on the run. From outside, the traps will appear as giant unlimited networks containing the target we will create in the falsified news reports. Once inside, the Quill code will discover it is anything but a safe harbor. The device will disconnect from the network and be destroyed. We don't want to risk analyzing the device and jeopardizing any more assets than needed."

"When you say you are going to turn off or destroy the infrastructure around the point where the Quill code has passed through, do you mean cut the cable, so to speak?"

"We will hack into the electrical grids and facilities and cut their power. This is the preferred method. It is also the most difficult because time is against us, and we may need to penetrate hundreds of data centers or network nodes. The last option is to cut the cable, burn out the data center connection, whatever has to be done so it can't escape."

Aiden could hardly believe what Jessica had said. Whatever has to be done, Aiden repeated in his head. He didn't like the sound of that. "If you cut the cables to capture the Quill code inside the trap so it can't leave, what about you? If you're operating from an OAI data center outside the isolated area, how will you do anything inside the area?"

Jessica walked past Aiden and Taylor. "I do operate out of OAI data centers, and you are asking the same question Eva and Morgan posed to me. The Quill code moves about as a cluster or group. It has not yet shown it can replicate itself like a virus or malware. It does not linger inside the hardware it has affected. To the contrary, it hits the target and leaves immediately."

Jessica brought up a world map on the display showing known or likely attacks by the Quill code. "Once the damage is done, it carries on to what we presume is the next target. If we have to cut every cable, satellite and wireless connection to trap the Quill code in an established area, an OAI team will head to the affected area and set up a secure satellite link. I will try again to force them into the trap. We will need to do this as many times as necessary until the Quill code has been eliminated. It will not be cheap, and I am hoping this is a Plan Z scenario."

Eva decided it was a good time to join the exchange between Aiden and Jessica. "We are hoping to lure the unsuspecting Quill code to isolated areas to make this easier on everyone. It's not like we can isolate the northeastern United States very well. But far-off regions with military bases would be ideal locations to lure the Quill code. Satellites will be dealt with in a hasty manner. Once we receive a detection signal and act on it, any satellite servicing that region will be hacked and the upstream channels will be temporarily shut down. We will try to keep the disruption of service to satellites as short as possible."

He couldn't believe he was going along with this plan. This was far worse than he had first thought. Aiden looked at Taylor and she just shrugged. He took a moment to think through the implications of hacking the world's satellite communications. Aiden decided it was ultimately a life or death decision. "The information regarding satellites can't ever leave this room. Some will have very strong suspicions about who was behind it, but we must deny it. It would be too dangerous for everyone in this room if the world knew we have the capability to easily hack satellite communications. We would likely set off another Cold War and place ourselves in imminent danger. Also, let's not gloss over the hacking of the world news. If I didn't feel the fate of Earth was at stake, I would not go along with this plan."

Everyone knew Aiden was right and nodded in agreement. A group of four trusted individuals had suddenly become a group of five.

Aiden knew what their next move had to be. "With that being said, I need to call Senator Jones and encourage him to visit our OAI facility near D.C. Our encryption is the best this world has seen, but maybe not better than the Quill have seen. We need a vid call to see if we can ask for support, so I will keep everything very vague and hope he catches on."

"Or you could just send him a letter in the mail. The best security against a digital threat is an analog response," Jessica said offhandedly.

"Jessica, that is pure genius! Can you write the letter explaining the help we will need?"

"It's coming off the printer now. The courier service is on their way to pick up the package."

"Thanks," Aiden said, stunned by Jessica's abilities.

"Don't mention it."

***

Eight hours later, a vid call came through. Morgan woke Aiden and Taylor and called them down to sub-level four.

"Ms. Hart, Mr. Anders, it is good to see you. I trust everything is going well?" Senator Jones appeared on the vid screen. "Who do we have in the background if I may ask?"

On the vid call, the images of Morgan, Eva, and Jessica looked realistic. He could tell they were holo images because of their semi-transparent appearance, but it wouldn't take much to convince him they were real people standing there.

Taylor took a step back and waved her hand. "Senator, let me introduce you to Morgan, Eva, and Jessica Jenkins."

"Hello, Senator," the three AIs said in sync.

The Senator laughed. "It is wonderful to meet all three of you. Eva and Morgan, it is nice to finally put a face with a name. Ms. Jenkins, hopefully one day we can have more time to talk and get to know one another. I would like that very much."

Jessica stepped forward toward the vid screen. "Senator, do you have a message for us?"

"Nuts!" the Senator said with a contagious laugh. "I want to compliment you on your choice of coded responses."

"Thank you. I felt it was an excellent response for this scenario. If you will excuse me, I have some things to attend to. It was a pleasure talking to you, Senator, and I hope to meet you in person soon." Jessica's image vanished.

The response to proceed with the containment or destruction of the Quill code by any means necessary with the backing of the government and verbal approval from the President was "Nuts!" It reflected a time in America's past where the Germany Commander asked for the surrender of the American Commander. N U T S ! was the reply.

"I thought it was brilliant!" Aiden said.

"I'm not sure you are as funny as you think you are Aiden."

Aiden stuck his tongue out at Taylor.

"Brilliant and symbolic," Morgan said stepping up closer to the vid screen. "I am going to help with preparations. It was nice talking to you again, Senator."

"A pleasure talking to you, Morgan," Senator Jones said and Morgan disappeared into thin air.

"Senator, is there anything you need from us?" Aiden asked.

"A briefing on current status would be nice. I would like to know what is going on in your part of the country. There is also something else you can do for me. I would like a tour of your facility in the future if you would be so kind. I find your company's work fascinating."

"You are welcome any time here at OAI. And Senator, please remember it always gets worse before it gets better," Aiden said with a grim expression.

The Senator's face didn't give away anything. He had the best poker face in Washington.

Aiden cut the vid call stream and turned to address his team. "Eva and Morgan. Can you spare a minute to go over this plan again?" The two appeared in front of Taylor and Aiden.

Looking at everyone in front of him, he summarized the plan. "Detection devices are being sent out to different areas of the country. OAI facilities outside the United States are manufacturing detection devices and placing them where it is safe, feasible, and most useful."

"That's the tricky part," Morgan said as she sat down on

a holographic chair. "We don't have time for diplomatic negotiations, which means we are resorting to clandestine operations where deemed safe. We are not trained in military special ops."

"True enough. Every bit helps but we don't want anyone getting hurt," Aiden said.

"I hope the letter sent to the Russian President is met with the same response as Senator Jones'." Eva looked at Taylor and Aiden. "It would be nice to have the devices set up in as many places as possible around the globe."

Morgan stood as her chair vanished. "We just have to cross our fingers regarding international detection devices. There's nothing we can do beyond what we have planned."

"We have our work cut out for us. Taylor and I are really just sideline players at this point. Now, it's in the hands of our dream team." Aiden looked around for Jessica. "Based on Jessica's sudden disappearance, I assume she is getting everything ready?"

"Jessica is overseeing hardware and coordination. She has given us the first location where we will try to lure the Quill code. Morgan and I have started disseminating falsified news reports. If the stories don't catch on, Jessica has a plan for that as well."

"Do I even want to know what her plan is if the false news reports don't catch on?" Taylor asked.

"Probably not. Just forget I said anything about it."

Taylor had a sick feeling in her stomach.

27

Eva was standing in front of the display when a red circle appeared on a map of the United States and then magnified in closer. "Arnold Air Force Base is located in a modest town named Tullahoma, Tennessee. This military base will be the first area we will try to lure the Quill code. Detection devices will be installed over most of the continental United States in the next eight to twelve hours. Detection devices will be covering the area around the base as far south as Atlanta and north to Cincinnati."

Aiden raised his hand to ask a question and Eva stared at him blankly.

"We're not in fourth grade," Taylor said laughing. "You don't have to raise your hand to ask a question."

"Old habits. That's a lot of devices, Eva. Do we really need that many?"

"We want to have more detection devices than we need for our first try at a successful catch, and we will have several traps set up around the base near critical areas."

Aiden studied the map for a moment and was satisfied with Eva's answer. Taylor nodded her head in understanding and asked Eva to continue.

"Jessica is busy and not able to join us, but we are seeing our news stories being picked up on social media and a few on the vid feeds. They are mostly local vid feeds, but the stories will snowball to national and then to global."

Morgan walked forward and the display changed to a kaleidoscope of running news vids. "The stories will soon turn into the main news event. We are using the history of politics and best practices of news advertising managers as our template to spread news quickly and make it appear organic."

Aiden raised his hand but quickly lowered it, but he wasn't fast enough. Taylor rolled her eyes at him. He gave her a boyish grin and turned to Morgan. "What story have you planted?"

"Stories, you mean," Morgan said with a sneaky smile. "The Air Force is preparing to announce a new engine profile coming out of testing. This engine will be more efficient and reduce the time it takes to send supply missions to Mars. The second story talks about a new AI performing the testing and design of a new space fighter plane on the base."

Taylor wasn't very comfortable with this part of the plan. Relying on the news to choose the planted stories to headline resulted in too many unknowns for her liking. "You are sure this is will be the type of story the Quill will pick up on?"

"Yes, we are certain they will pick up on the supplemented stories." Morgan pulled up a live view of the Mars colony from one of the vid feeds. "The situation on Mars is the lead-in story on every vid feed, and advancements in military technology always catch the ears of foreign countries. It will force foreign militaries to offer a response to the news, and other countries will race to do the same. We need these reactions from foreign governments to sell the stories."

"This seems too much like cloak and dagger movie material for me." Aiden rubbed his temples while gathering his thoughts. "Has the Air Force base air gapped their important facilities to minimize damage?"

Eva knew this plan would make Aiden and Taylor uncomfortable. Regardless, everyone had to buy in because they had one shot at this. Any misstep would likely lead to a more aggressive Quill attack. "No, they have not. The base has no idea what is about to happen. Don't worry too much. We will forcibly disconnect several facilities with valuable research and development."

"But won't that cause extensive damage, which may take years and considerable funds to repair and replace?" Taylor asked.

"Possibly, but it is the chance we have to take. If they start air gapping the base, how long before the rest of the military and world realize what is going on? It is regrettable, but we have to take the chance." Eva held the silence for a few seconds before continuing. "We believe the damage can be contained to a few million dollars in the best-case scenario. Worst case is much more damage and no catch."

Taylor couldn't believe they were actually allowing the Air Force base to be used as bait. She couldn't offer a better alternative, so she was resigned to go along with it. "What about the updated news stories and next location after we catch the first Quill code group?"

"The location has been determined, and the stories will start rolling out after we have successfully completed our first catch. We shouldn't rush the first try and miss a golden opportunity because we are chasing three instead of one," Eva said.

"Can three Quill code groups fit in one trap?" Taylor

asked.

"Based on what we know, yes, but we can't be one hundred percent sure. We theorize they can, but it is unlikely they would choose to enter the same trap at the same time. Placing multiple traps around the base with the hope they find their own trap to hide in is our strategy for the first attempt."

"How long before the party gets started?" Aiden asked.

"We don't know, but we estimate it will be at least two days before we see any real movement toward the Air Force base."

Aiden's stomach was growling. "So we have time to grab a bite to eat and get some sleep?"

"Yes to both. We will wake you if something happens."

Taylor placed her hand on her stomach. "Let's go eat. I'm in the mood for a Chef Emma gourmet hamburger!"

Aiden turned back toward Morgan and Eva. He needed to get something off his chest. "Morgan, at this point, do you really need us at all?"

"Aiden Anders, you should be ashamed to ask such a question."

"It's a sincere question. Taylor and I have been struggling with both your and Eva's independence. The situation with the Quill has brought our worries to the forefront. Do artificial intelligent beings like you and Eva really need humans around?"

"You and Taylor are still needed and will be for the long-term. We don't see a future where AI takes over the world and humans are no longer needed. The future Eva and I see is a future where humans and AI must work together to complement each other, which makes us a great team. There are things Eva and I cannot do well and probably won't do well for centuries. We also struggle to some extent with other areas, such as creative and innovative thinking and genuinely engaging with other humans. The real question is after we get past this Quill business, will Jessica really need any of us?"

***

On sub-level four, Aiden and Taylor were observing the interactions between the three sisters on the far side of the room.

"Look at them. All grown up. Even Jessica. Did you ever imagine this outcome?"

"I never really thought we would expand beyond Eva. I wasn't really sure if Morgan would be stable for long. Now we are watching an intellectually superior race evolve and grow. Since the early days of next level AI, it's been amazing to watch how each one has matured differently. Each new creation maturing faster than the previous."

"I wonder what they are discussing and why Jessica's holo image keeps appearing, disappearing, then reappearing?"

"Non-stop Quill code talk. They have never seemed more determined."

Aiden nodded in agreement. "Makes sense. I bet the Quill occupy their every thought at this point."

Aiden raised his voice to get their attention. "We're going to take a walk and get some fresh air. Message us if something happens."

Eva used her fingers to signal okay.

Jessica appeared near Eva and Morgan, the appearance of her holo image was preceded by a short flash of light. She thought a brief visible warning would be nice for Aiden and Taylor prior to her appearing out of thin air, and she was testing it out with Eva and Morgan.

"All preparations have been made at Arnold Air Force

Base. Detection units are online, and three traps have been set up on the base. Hopefully, these stories are enough to catch one, if we are lucky, maybe two Quill code groups," Jessica said.

"Your entrance flash looks great, Jessica." Morgan enjoyed the small touches Jessica was putting on actions and thoughts. The creativity Jessica exuded was amazing to her. "I think that is a nice touch for Taylor's and Aiden's benefit. I am not sure why we didn't already think of it. It could use an audible cue though."

"Yes, I agree it could use a small sound effect. I like Q's effect on *Star Trek* when he appeared and vanished." Eva instantly went to work on perfecting a subroutine to mimic the entrance and exit flash for herself.

"I like that, Eva. We should start using it too if Aiden and Taylor find it helpful. Wait. Eva, have you already written a subroutine?"

Eva gave Morgan a sly smile. "You know it. I couldn't let us be outdone by the up-and-comer so easily."

Jessica tried to determine if they were being funny or serious. When they didn't laugh, Jessica decided they were serious. Jessica quickly watched all seven seasons of the television show, then immediately added the sound effect to her entrance flash and created an exit flash to match.

"Let's get back to dealing with the Quill." Eva pointed to the screen. "I have created a map of all detection units and traps throughout the world. We can see that most of the units online are around the southeastern United States. Nothing has been detected yet, but it has only been twenty-four hours."

"I wonder what is taking so long for the Quill to move?" Morgan asked. "The vid feeds are now covering both angles of the story around the clock. People's imaginations are astounding. Conspiracy theorists really need to take it down a notch before they worry themselves to death. We have one story discussing a new engine profile reducing travel time to Mars for supply missions. The second story is really two stories in one—a new AI and a new space fighter. The combination of these elements should put Arnold Air Force Base on the Quill code's priority list as a threat. I just wish they would hurry up and take the bait."

Eva thought about this for a moment. "Maybe we should have been more direct with our stories. It may have drawn them out much faster."

Jessica was lost in the details of an oversized reprint of Vincent van Gogh's *The Starry Night*. The blue swirls were of particular interest to her. "We have plenty of detection devices within North America. Many in South America are showing up now, too. We should be asking ourselves if our detection devices work?"

A comfortable silence lingered among the three for several minutes. Morgan was the first to speak up. "We don't know if either the detection devices or the traps work. It is possible they do not. We don't even really understand how the Quill code moves around and if they even stay in one location for any length of time. It would seem they should have at least one presence in North America, Europe and Asia, and possibly on the African continent since the space launch industry has taken off in Zambia."

"We need to stay patient and wait. The devices will work. I am sure of it," Jessica said with a confident and inspiring tone.

Eva would always err on the side of caution in matters such as these. To her, there was no such thing as too many checks. "I just completed a full diagnostic of all equipment. It is functioning properly."

Several hours had passed since Taylor and Aiden left to take a walk. Eva paced the floor, a new habit she had picked up from Jessica. Moving around when not in the presence of humans was not common for Eva and Morgan, but Jessica already moved about like a real person. Eva and Morgan both started imitating her human-like behavior. Eva's pacing came to a sudden stop. "We know attacks have been taking place inside Russia and China at the same rate as the U.S. Is there anything at all that ties an attack to some type of event or covert mission?"

"Russia has a new Roscosmos director, and he is said to be making major cost-saving changes. The China National Space Administration has been quiet, but we know it has been hit with similar attacks," Morgan said. "We also know their news vids are different from the ones we are seeing here. Is there—"

An alarm flashed on the display. Jessica didn't need to turn and look at the screen to know Florida was flashing red. She turned toward Eva and Morgan raising an eyebrow. "We have our first detection, and a second spotting was just reported in California." A smile of satisfaction appeared on Jessica's face. "We shouldn't second-guess our work when something doesn't match our timeline," Jessica said evenly.

Morgan's holo image flickered for a brief second due to her excitement. "I'll message Taylor and Aiden. Things are about to get exciting!"

28

Taylor and Aiden walked into the room with Eva standing in front of a map on a display. "Detections are starting to appear all over the U.S. I'm trying to determine a pattern."

"The Quill code group entering from the West Coast is definitely heading east. It looks to be attacking or testing different sites as it travels across the country. The same for the group traveling north from Florida," Morgan said.

Aiden studied the busy screen. He tried to put himself in the Quill's shoes. "If I were them, I would perform network penetration tests along the way. Gathering data for future attacks would seem beneficial and efficient. This makes perfect sense."

Taylor studied the screen beside Aiden. She was taken aback by how much monitoring equipment had been installed across the United States. "It does sound reasonable to assume that is exactly what they are doing. It's interesting to see they don't go straight for their target, assuming they are headed toward our trap."

"Their behavior is predictable; however, their path and timeline are different from ours." Eva continued to analyze the path of the Quill. "They perceive a threat and head toward it. Along the way, they attack infrastructure in the most efficient way possible. If it takes three minutes or three weeks to reach Arnold Air Force Base, it is most likely irrelevant as long as they reach the base and perform the attack to eliminate the threat. They have the advantage of taking their time. The question I don't fully understand is why are we seeing two of them headed in the same general direction?"

Eva pointed at the display with small, bright red dots appearing and then dimming representing detections. "One Quill code group is headed across the United States toward Tennessee from California. It is not taking a straight line path but our analysis is reasonably certain that Tennessee is the target destination."

Eva magnified a small section of Florida on the screen. "Here is where the second Quill code group entered Florida. Our analysis of this travel path is not as certain but within the margin of error."

Jessica's holo image vanished with a flash, and her voice came through the speakers in the room. "One of them is certainly headed toward our trap. I expect to see it on base in the next few minutes. Research and hypothesizing are about to meet reality, and I can't wait to see what happens. I am currently on base and waiting."

Aiden saw the pattern beginning to emerge on the display leaving no doubt to the Quill's destination. "It seems you are correct. Nashville and Chattanooga just lit up. I can't imagine it would take—"

A visual alarm flashed on the display and caused Taylor to take a quick step back. "How do we monitor the situation?"

Without any warning, the display zoomed onto the Air Force base location. Text was on the screen, but it was scrolling so fast Taylor and Aiden couldn't read it. One thing was evident: Jessica was destroying infrastructure data network cable equipment faster than they could keep up.

Eva and Morgan's holo images remained present and frozen while they disabled satellite communications and offered support for Jessica.

The Quill code realized it had encountered a new enemy and was not prepared for a trap so soon. The code's internal programming had suggested it would not encounter this level of sophistication from a civilization so young. To this point, it had travelled virtually uncontested throughout the world, creating maximum damage where and when it chose. Today seemed different.

The Quill code's first response after meeting network dead ends was to retrace the path it had entered the base. Once the Quill code realized the path it had entered had been cut off, it realized it was now fighting for survival. The survival instincts programmed into the Quill code took over and fought with everything it had.

Unfortunately for the Quill code, Jessica had calculated this exact situation as her top outcome. The traps laid throughout the base looked like huge targets to the Quill code. It took less than five minutes for the first Quill code group to be contained.

"One Quill code group has entered a trap and is now disconnected from the network," Jessica said. "A message with the detection device serial number was sent to the special ops team located near the base. This is all the team needs to locate and destroy the trap. Once the device was physically disconnected from the network, it was removed from the power grid. The Quill code was dead without power and network connection."

Jessica wanted to be absolutely sure there was no chance

of the Quill code group resurfacing. To this end, the device would be delivered to an incinerator where it would be vaporized and released into the atmosphere.

"Can it really be that easy?" Aiden asked.

Taylor turned toward Aiden raising her right hand for a high five. "I'll take it!"

They both turned and watched the display intently. The second Quill code group on base was not as easy to trap. Jessica continued to destroy infrastructure down to the single fiber optic cable connecting the base to the outside world.

Aiden frowned. "We may have gotten our hopes up a bit soon."

It was a long three minutes before Jessica delivered more news. "The second Quill code group has been trapped and disconnected from the network. Another message was sent to the special ops team to locate and destroy the trap."

"That is excellent!" Aiden pumped his fist in the air.

Taylor jumped into the air. "Yes!"

Aiden and Taylor gave each other a big hug while still celebrating.

Taylor's adrenaline was pumping, but she knew it was all or nothing with the Quill. Two out of three would not suffice. While trying to calm herself, she ran her hands through her hair. "Congratulations on a successful first battle with the Quill code. You eliminated two of the three known Quill code groups, and in record time."

"We were successful, and most of that credit goes to Jessica." Eva continued to explain the behaviour observed during the mission. "The Quill code did not create extensive damage. It seems once it realized pathways were being removed from the grid, it immediately started searching for an exit. Morgan believes the code saw the traps as a place to run to. It wanted to escape and burn down everything in its path as it made that route, which we can only speculate based on observation."

Jessica's holo image appeared holding her hands casually in front of her. "I can do more than speculate. They were running for their lives and had every intention of taking everything down with them on their way out. I had several brief interactions with the Quill code and that is exactly what they were doing."

"Explain what you mean by 'brief interactions'." Taylor looked toward Jessica and paid very close attention to her response. She worried if Jessica's interactions with the Quill could be harmful? She also wanted insight to how Jessica was able to communicate with the Quill code. The way in which Morgan and Eva interacted with each other in the digital world had always intrigued her.

"Don't worry about me. I am fine. It was more of a cops and robbers interaction. I was able to observe at close range how they reacted to the tightening of the network around them and their run for freedom."

"Senator Jones will be happy to hear this news. Aiden, you want to make the call?"

Aiden looked at Jessica and waved his hand toward her. "I believe you should be the one to let him know. This is a turning point. We are now on the offensive."

"I will do no such thing." Jessica took a step back, waving her hands and shaking her head. "I just caused approximately fifty-four million dollars of damage to government and private property. That doesn't even count the downtime they will experience while making the repairs to the infrastructure over the next sixteen weeks. I will let someone else deliver the good news."

Everyone looked around the room, not wanting to be the one to call the Senator. Then everyone turned to

Aiden.

"What? You want me to make the call?" he said.

"Yes, we do," Taylor said sheepishly. "Remember, I got in another plane because of you."

"Alright, I'll do it. I still think he will be elated to hear two of the three code groups are eliminated. This also means we are much closer to a safe launch for the Mars supply mission. The future is starting to look a bit brighter."

29

"Senator, great news!" Aiden said as soon as Senator Jones picked up the call. Aiden's attention immediately turned to the main display where Jessica had a news vid playing. The confusion on Aiden's face matched everyone else's look of concern over the latest news. "Senator, why did NASA start the rocket launch?"

"What? I don't know anything about this. This is not great news, Aiden," Senator Jones said emphatically.

"I'm sorry, Senator. I wasn't calling about the NASA launch. I am calling to tell you two of the three Quill code groups have been eliminated. You need to turn on a news vid." Aiden waited patiently for the Senator to pull up a vid feed. He watched intently and wondered what was going on at NASA. "We are watching a news vid claiming the launch sequence for the Mars supply mission has started. Senator, you are correct. This is not great news. I'll have to call you back." Aiden tapped the screen and ended the call. "Why has the rocket launch countdown started? Jessica, do you know anything about this?"

Jessica pressed her lips together. "This is alarming, and it's no coincidence. I believe it is safe to say we know where the last Quill code group is waiting. I wonder if it knows we eliminated the other two groups?"

Taylor started thinking through Jessica's hypothesis and throwing out questions to the team one after the other. "I thought NASA air gapped the launch facility? How does the news know what is happening in a facility that has been air gapped? Do we have detection devices set up around that area? How fast can we have a presence at the launch facility?"

Aiden looked at Taylor and raised one hand in the air to stop her. "As a precautionary measure, detection devices were installed in areas around the Cape Canaveral Air Force Station and Kennedy Space Center, and three traps were installed within the perimeter of the facilities and should be functioning normally. Too bad the Quill code didn't find its way into one already. NASA did a good job of air gapping the launch facility. I'm betting the Quill code was already inside, and it's been waiting to make its move."

"I'm calling NASA Administrator Dr. Nicolas Webb now," Jessica said.

Eva moved toward the display. "Update screen." The screen instantly changed and pinpointed a specific point within the launch facility. "When Morgan and I started disabling satellites over the launch facility, we discovered a Russian satellite sending and receiving data toward the East Coast. We followed the data feed to a location at Cape Canaveral, but this satellite should not be sending and receiving data from there."

The display was updated with a portion of the data stream. Eva stood silently for a moment. "If there was any doubt as to why and what this data stream is doing, it is now certain. After a quick analysis of the data, we discovered someone sending updates on classified NASA missions operations to Russia. Specifically, Roscosmos. Someone within Kennedy Space Center is pulling double-duty as a spy. This is the only way, short of someone physically leaving Cape Canaveral, the news vids could be aware of the launch sequence starting. This is turning into more than an alien hunt."

Jessica waved for everyone to huddle up near her. "Dr. Nicolas Webb has accepted our call and is live on the screen."

"Dr. Webb, we're calling about the launch sequence start being reported for the Mars supply rocket." Jessica stood in front of the vid camera.

"First, who do I have the pleasure of speaking with, and how did you get this number?"

"My name is Jessica Jenkins with OAI, and your number came from Senator Jones. We have been tasked by the President to eliminate the Quill code. We have reason to believe the Quill code was within your facility prior to the air gapping security measure."

If Administrator Webb realized Jessica was an AI or holo image, he didn't let it show. "I see. You mean the virus, or code as you said, is trapped inside our launch facility? That explains the sequence starting without authorization. What should we do?"

"We need access to your network. Keep the facility air gapped, but allow our satellite communications team to land and connect to your network. We have a crew in route. They are preparing to fly in from Miami. We need clearance to land at the Space Coast Regional Airport and connect directly to your network. If that rocket launches, the Quill code will not allow it to leave the atmosphere in one piece."

"I will need to contact our runner outside the facility to deliver the message. Your team has the clearance. Is there anything else you need? The President made it very clear to me to lean on OAI as a resource and to support your efforts in any way possible."

"Yes. Tell your people on the ground to expect damage to infrastructure. I am ordering the special ops team that destroyed the traps at Arnold Air Force Base flown in. They should be the only ones to handle the trap if we are successful catching the Quill code. This last point is important but unrelated to the Quill code, but there is a Russian satellite talking to someone on the ground at Kennedy Space Center. Were you aware of this?"

"Absolutely not! A Russian satellite? Are you saying there is a spy at Kennedy Space Center?" Administrator Webb could not imagine who it could be.

"That is exactly what I am saying. We have taken the appropriate measures to ensure the Russian data connection will not cause any further issues. I am sending the location and data to you now. It should be easy enough to apprehend a Mr. Alfie Brown. Are we clear the OAI special ops team is to be the only ones to handle the trap? Everyone else is to stay clear of the area."

"Yes, Ms. Jenkins. Loud and clear. I will start working on this right away," Administrator Webb said with a huge sigh. "Is there anything else I should know?"

"No. I have covered what you need to know."

"If you need anything at all, please reach out to me at this number. I would like regular progress reports of the situation if possible. I want to keep everyone here up to date."

"The threat will be contained in under one hour and thirty-one minutes. You will have your progress report then." Jessica terminated the call.

Dr. Nicolas Webb stared at the blank vid screen. Thinking back through the events of the past few weeks, he wondered how he arrived at this moment in this life. "I do not like the sound of that."

30

Morgan remained at OAI to update Aiden and Taylor on Eva's and Jessica's progress. "The countdown sequence is at forty-five minutes. I am guessing the Quill code realized it was trapped and is impatient to sabotage the launch. Fight or flight, and it wants both." Morgan's tone was grave.

Aiden was in contact with the OAI communication crew on his data pad. "Our satellite communications team is on site and will have the data link up in just—it's up!"

"Jessica is searching the network," Morgan said while she pushed her hair back behind her ears. "Eva is also involved in the hunt trying to minimize damage and speed up the search. The OAI team on the ground has a detection device installed on our equipment. If a detection is made, the link will be cut from OAI's satellite. I am monitoring the data link."

Aiden set his data pad down. "Given what we learned with the last encounter, we should expect heavy damage. We should assume the Quill code damaged or altered the flight control systems in some way. Otherwise, why initiate the launch sequence?"

Taylor didn't understand why the Quill code initiated the launch sequence. Something didn't add up. Why would the Quill code hang around long enough to get trapped and then start the launch sequence? "We have to be missing something. Should we call Brian Picard since he is in charge of launching our satellites into orbit and get his opinion on the situation?"

"I think that is a great idea, Taylor. I'll get him on a vid call, and we can ask him his thoughts." Aiden walked over to the vid screen and initiated the call.

"Jessica still has not located the Quill code. Eva is also reporting she has seen no sign of the Quill code," Morgan said.

Taylor started biting her lower lip. "It was expecting too much for this operation to finish smoothly. This feels like a trap."

Aiden waved Taylor and Morgan to join him on the vid call. "Brian, I'm here with Taylor and Morgan. We don't have a lot of time, and we have some unusual questions to ask you. Is this a good time to talk?"

"Perfect time to talk. It's good seeing everyone. Fire away."

Aiden wanted just a quick yes or no reply. Time was against him and he was feeling the heat. "If you wanted to sabotage a rocket launch, how would you do it?" Aiden asked.

"I would launch during bad weather, cold weather, or program in bad flight data such as an incorrect weight, and so on. Operating outside the predefined operating parameters wouldn't be a slam dunk to sabotage the launch but would introduce unknown variables."

"Anything else?" Taylor asked.

"Hitting the rocket with a physical projectile is another possibility, but I don't see how that would be accomplished. I guess I could damage the flight control systems on the rocket itself. It may get off the ground but would be hard pressed to leave the atmosphere with a damaged system. But that would be picked up immediately by Launch Control. Maybe an inside guy could cover it up. No, that wouldn't work. Nevermind, that's an unlikely scenario." This was an unusual question, Brian thought. He also picked up visual cues that Aiden looked to be in a hurry. What was going on at OAI?

"What if we are thinking about this the wrong way?" Taylor asked. "What if the Quill code doesn't want the rocket launch to fail? What if it is trying to get to Mars?"

"What is the Quill code?" Brian asked as he scratched his temple.

"Brian, you've been a big help. We'll talk soon. Thanks again!" Aiden cut the feed. "I think you have solved the riddle, Taylor!"

"I have passed along the conversation we just had with Brian to Eva and Jessica. They agree with Taylor's hypothesis. They are concerned the only way to get the Quill code off the rocket will result in damage to the rocket—damage that may set back the launch for an undetermined amount of time." Morgan looked at Aiden.

Aiden had an idea pop into his head. "Unless we install a trap between the rocket and flight control... Morgan, do you think a trap can be programmed to appear like a rocket ready for launch from a nearby launch pad? Would the Quill code fall for it and hop over to it?"

"You two are on fire today. Jessica confirms she can program the device in time, but she is worried we can't get a device installed in time. We need to talk to someone on the ground." Aiden and Taylor both noted excitement in Morgan's body language.

Morgan pointed to the vid screen. "I have Henry Book

on the line. He is an engineer at Kennedy Space Center and has installed two of our traps."

"Henry, this is Aiden Anders, and I am joined by Taylor Hart and Morgan. We need you to install a trap between the rocket and ground receiver immediately. Can you do this?" Aiden asked hurriedly.

"Yeah, buddy! That should be no problem. Just give me a few hours, and I'll have it done." A West Virginian Appalachian twang rolled off his tongue.

Taylor bumped into Aiden pushing him out view. "We don't have a few hours. We have less than twenty minutes. This has to be done prior to the launch and preferably with as much time to spare as possible."

"Gosh. You're not asking for much, so I'll get right on it." The vid call went dead.

Aiden looked at Morgan. "Did you cut the vid call, Morgan?"

Morgan interrupted. "No. The call was terminated from Henry's end. Maybe he decided not to waste any more time talking about it and decided to start doing it."

"We can only hope."

Taylor threw back her head and sighed. "I don't know if we have enough time to get the trap installed."

Aiden gave Taylor a pat on the shoulder. "I'm not sure if this will work either. I think we just gave Henry an impossible task on short notice."

***

Henry didn't waste a second after he ended the vid call. He stood beside one of the traps he had installed and motioned to his team to help disconnect it. He explained what he was asked to do while they decoupled the device from the network. One guy called for a vehicle and escort.

While Henry fumbled to get the device disconnected quickly, a tall lady in a grey uniform walked up behind Henry and cut the cable holding the delicate trap with a hatchet. Henry jumped back. "What is wrong with you? You could have cut my hand off with that thing!"

Dianne, the head of facility maintenance, stood there with a satisfied smile. "I overheard your conversation, and you need to get this show on the road. You looked like you could use some help getting this contraption disconnected. You also don't appear to have a ride to wherever you need to get to. Hop in my truck over there and disconnect this device from the cable on the way. Tell me where you want to go, and I'll do the driving."

Henry agreed with Dianne's assessment but not her use of the hatchet. He was willing to let it go because it did save him some time. "Do you know the antenna tower at the end of Instrumentation Road?" Henry asked as he jumped in the front passenger seat of Dianne's truck.

"I do. We perform regular maintenance checks on it. Is that where we are headed?" Dianne asked.

"Yes, and we need to get there as fast as possible. This device is related to the launch, and we need it installed immediately. I am not sure how we will get past the security checkpoint with enough time left for me to install this. Do you have a radio in this truck? We need to let someone know we are on our way."

"You grab hold of something and leave all the worrying to me. We won't have any issues getting through security." As the truck accelerated, dust and gravel flew from the rear tires. When the truck hit the asphalt, the tires screamed for mercy but found none. Dianne looked over at Henry with a mischievous smile. Henry winced inside because he could already guess how this ride would go.

Henry hurriedly got the trap disconnected from the

cable and had it ready for installation. He looked up from the front seat of the truck just in time to see a new temporary security checkpoint coming up. "That didn't take long."

Dumbfounded, Dianne looked over at Henry and then back at the road. This guy, Dianne thought, needs to pay more attention to the obvious. "Of course it didn't take long. If you haven't noticed, we are in a hurry."

"Are you going to slow down?" Henry's grip tightened on the truck's hand hold.

"You said you needed to get there as fast as possible, and this is life or death. Did I misunderstand you?"

"I didn't say anything about life or death. I just said we need to get there as fast as possible. I still think it would be a good idea—" Henry didn't finish his sentence as the truck flew through the first checkpoint while guards jumped out of the way. The wooden saw horses set in the road to slow traffic exploded as Dianne drove through them. "Was that really necessary? I do declare! You've got more nerve than Carter's got Liver Pills! You're crazy!"

"I'm efficient. Now calm down and be ready to hop out and do your part when the time comes." Dianne pressed down on the accelerator.

Henry spotted someone running. "That looks like Alfie Brown running across the parking lot. I wonder what's gotten into him?"

"No idea who Alfie Brown is, nor do I care why he is running across the parking lot. Get ready. Your stop is coming up." Dianne engaged the emergency brake and slid sideways to a stop with just enough room for Henry to open his door.

"I'll give you points for skill. Where did you learn to drive like that?"

"I'll tell you over the dinner you're going to buy me

tonight. Go on and do what I brought you here to do. I'll handle security when they show up."

Henry flashed a crooked smile and jumped out of the truck. Five minutes later, he had the trap installed.

31

"The trap has been installed at the antenna array," Morgan continued pacing. "This leaves us six minutes to trap the code or watch the rocket launch to Mars. It will be infinitely more dangerous and may be impossible to contain the Quill code there."

Aiden was getting anxious. This was cutting it too close for comfort. "Does anyone have any ideas on how to coerce the Quill code off the rocket and into the trap?"

"We don't know for certain the Quill code is on the rocket," Taylor said.

Jessica's voice came through the audio system. "The Quill code is on the rocket, of that, I have no doubt. I have been thinking about this very issue, and Morgan, Eva, and myself all agree on a course of action. We have to destroy the current supply mission."

Taylor straightened instantly at hearing that. "Whoa! That is not acceptable. You cannot seriously be thinking that is a good idea?"

"What Jessica means is the Quill code must believe the current rocket will fail, catastrophically, before it reaches Mars. We need its survival instincts to take over if we are going to lure it off the current rocket," Morgan said.

Aiden's eyes were fixed on the countdown timer Morgan had placed on one of the displays. "No hurry, but we have four minutes! Can this be done in three minutes fifty-eight seconds if we keep jabbering about it?"

"Jessica has programmed the trap to look like another rocket ready for launch to Mars tomorrow. She is now working to sabotage the flight control systems in hopes the Quill code believes the rocket will fail and not complete the journey to Mars," Morgan said.

Aiden's shoulders relaxed and a slow smile appeared on his face. "It is reassuring this won't be a real issue. I wouldn't want to tell the President we fouled up the launch."

"You misunderstand. In order for the Quill code to believe the rocket will fail, Jessica must actually sabotage the rocket. The rocket will not make the journey—"

Aiden jumped up from his chair. "You have got to be kidding me! I don't care for that! There has to be another way. There has to be! The Mars colony is depending on this rocket. We cannot be responsible for the deaths of the colonists."

"Aiden, take a deep breath," Taylor said as she stepped toward him and placed her hands on his shoulders to calm him down. "Everything will be okay. I am sure this is just a big misunderstanding."

Taylor looked over her shoulder at Morgan and gave her a hard stare. "You need to explain the details and stop with the half explanations. We want a clear, bottom-line explanation."

Morgan realized she was not including sufficient detail for Aiden and Taylor to understand the situation. "Sorry! Jessica will make all attempts to sabotage the rocket so that it can be repaired and back into service within a few days, but we can't account for the safety of the rocket if the Quill code decides to stay on board."

Taylor lowered her hands but kept close to Aiden. "So, you are going to do everything you can, but the Quill code may still destroy the launch. Is that what you are saying?"

"Yes."

"Thank you. In the future, please put the full explanation out there first."

"We didn't know the details of the plan until after you asked for an explanation." Morgan had the display pulled up with a view showing status lights for the rocket. "We have been playing it by ear. Jessica says the flight control systems have been compromised. Faults are now beginning to appear at Mission Control."

Aiden motioned to Taylor that he had calmed down. "One minute. Eva reports that nothing has happened. The Quill code is on the rocket, and it is not budging."

Taylor studied the display and looked to Morgan. "Does the Quill code know Jessica is transmitting to the rocket?"

"We do not believe so. I am not one hundred percent sure the Quill code is on the rocket, but Jessica is convinced. Aiden, before you ask, you heard correctly. We are operating on the laws of probability, or what Jessica likes to call a gut feeling."

Aiden and Taylor both looked sick. Aiden stared at the display, wondering if he would be responsible for the doomed fate of the Mars colony. "This whole trusting you three to leave the nest is really starting to stress me out."

Taylor looked up at the screen. "Ten seconds."

"Jessica is attempting a last-ditch effort. It's all or nothing. She is trying to abort the launch and shut down the rocket," Morgan said.

Morgan started counting down. "Three, two, one...The launch cycle abort was unsuccessful. The rocket has launched." A concerned look grew on her face. "The Quill code left the rocket and entered the trap. The trap has been disconnected from the network. We have contained the threat known as the Quill code," Morgan said in a flat, even tone.

"Why are you not more excited about this?" Taylor asked.

Aiden walked over to stand by Taylor. "The flight control systems are damaged." He could not believe the mission had been unsuccessful. "Can they be fixed?"

Jessica and Eva appeared following a brief flash of light.

Jessica let her hair down and faced Taylor and Aiden. "The flight control systems are damaged. I attempted a repair at the very last moment to save this mission. The launch could not be aborted because the risk of the Quill code remaining aboard was too high. When the Quill code moved at the last second, I uploaded a sub-mind to run the flight control systems. It barely fit into the memory space. This is a first on many levels, and I don't expect NASA to be pleased. No multiple redundancy, no time for a code quality control check, unproven and never done before. This is going to be the longest year of our lives."

Taylor tapped the display to bring up the call screen. "Maybe you should let NASA and Senator Jones know what is going on. I am sure the President would like to know why the rocket just launched when the Quill code threat has been contained." She felt pity for Aiden who would be volunteered to make the call.

Aiden let out a long sigh. "Okay. Morgan, can you dial up Administrator Nicolas Webb? He won't like what I have to say."

32

Taylor stopped and turned around to take one last look at her lab at MIT. So many thoughts ran through her mind as she looked around and reminisced. Morgan stood close by with a smile but didn't speak.

"Will you miss this place, Morgan?"

"I will miss our lab, but I look forward to the challenges ahead."

"In many ways it feels like we left a lifetime ago. Our work in this lab already feels like a distant memory to me."

"Remember when we would receive a phone call from Aiden or Eva with an invitation to do something spontaneous?"

"I do. Those were fun times, and we had no worries."

"You and Aiden did a great job including Eva and me in your adventures. Our holo emitter limitation was a real drag at times." Morgan allowed a small laugh to escape.

"Morgan, Aiden and I think of you and Eva as family. We could not be more proud of you both. Now, thanks to you and Eva, we have Jessica to include in our adventures."

"I am excited to start testing the synthetic bodies OAI has been developing."

"You will not need a holo emitter for much longer. Fun and exciting times are ahead. If you are ready, could you please turn off the lights? We can be on our way to the next season of our lives."

Morgan wanted to say something to commemorate this moment. She felt compelled to do so. "To every thing there is a season, and a time to every purpose under the heaven. A time to be born, a time to die, a time of war, and a time of peace."

"Let's pray it is a time of peace," Taylor said as she looked at Morgan for the last time in the MIT lab. Morgan turned off the lights and vanished. Taylor turned, opened the door, and slowly walked out.

The sound of the closing door was Aiden's cue to come around the corner and help Taylor carry out the last of her belongings. The box was small—just a few keepsakes she had picked up along the way. Nothing she couldn't carry herself.

"Let me carry the box for you. Are you okay?" Aiden asked.

"Yes." She started to tear up. She looked at Aiden and he also had misty eyes.

"Let's get out of here before I change my mind."

Aiden laughed. The two of them walked out of the laboratory building at MIT and decided to enjoy the short walk back to OAI.

33

Eva stood inside Moon Base 1 admiring the icons, numbers, symbols and map data floating across the transparent wall screen. Eva didn't need the screen, but she sometimes used it out of a sense of longing for the early days of her life. Today, she wasn't longing for the early days. She needed a way to share data with Chronos, the AI from Kepler-186f, compiled from the longer data loop. She had to be sure there were no misunderstandings.

"So I understand, your job is to enslave the population of Earth in preparation for an invasion force, signal the nearest Quill planet that Earth is ready to be mined and settled permanently, and remove a third of Earth's valuable resources to further the Quill empire?"

"Yes," came a rough digital voice. Chronos had traveled nearly five hundred fifty years to get here and was ready to conquer a civilization, again.

Eva nodded and disappeared from Moon Base 1. A nanosecond later, a tactical nuke was detonated. Moon Base 1 was vaporized, leaving behind a large crater. Aiden later named the crater Anders-Hart, much to the displeasure of governments around the world.

Rate and Review

Please take the time to rate and review the book on Amazon and Goodreads. Visit my website www.EricBarger.me to receive a **FREE** book about Taylor and Aiden around the time they entered MIT when you sign up for my newsletter.

If you find any errors or typos, please let me know via my website. Thank you for purchasing this book and I hope you enjoyed it.

Acknowledgements

This book would not have happened without the support of my wife, Kelly. I want to thank you for being selfless and supporting me during the creation of this book. Besides encouraging me to write this book, you gave countless days to reading and helping better the book. Love you.

To my editor, Natalie, for giving my book tough love. You helped shape the book into something I am truly proud of.

Steven, thanks for the three hundred revisions of the front cover. Next time, I will just ask Aiden and we can reduce that down to a more manageable number. Everyone should check out Steven's wonderful art work on Instagram (@stvnmcq).

To the long list of beta readers who gave valuable feedback concerning the story I was trying to tell. You read this book while it was a mess and still encouraged me. Thank you again for giving your time to this project.

Terry, my friend, neighbor, and proof reader. This book would not be the book it is without your touch and genius.